What people are saying about …

DESIRED

"Everyone who likes historical fiction will enjoy *Desired.* Vivid and compelling—I loved it!"

India Edghill, author of *Wisdom's Daughter* and *Delilah: A Novel*

"To be a woman in the ancient world was a fearsome thing. In this sweeping story of the clash of pagan and God-fearing cultures, Garrett takes us into the lives and hearts of three women who loved Samson, and in the process, she shows us the longing for freedom and purpose in our own hearts as well."

T. L. Higley, author of *Pompeii: City on Fire*

"In *Desired,* novelist Ginger Garrett takes readers on a journey of Samson's life as seen through the eyes of the women who loved him, giving a fresh look at this often confusing hero of Scripture. You will never see Samson quite the same way again.

Jill Eileen Smith, best-selling author of The Wives of King David series

Praise for …

CHOSEN

"An exciting novel from a talented new author."

Karen Kingsbury, best-selling author of the Redemption series

"A story that is sure to be a classic! Exciting, dramatic, and filled with truth. A great read from the first page!"

Brock and Bodie Thoene, best-selling authors of the Zion Covenant Series and the A. D. Chronicles

"This book defies normal boundaries … a truly astonishing first novel."

T. Davis Bunn, best-selling author of *Gold of Kings*

"*Chosen* is a richly detailed retelling of Queen Esther's story. A gem of a read."

Carol Umberger, author of the award-winning Scottish Crown Series

"Ginger sweeps the sands of time from this figure of ancient history, giving her voice once again—and what a compelling voice it is! To revisit this ancient story is to gain a vision for the contemporary world."

Siri Mitchell, author of *Kissing Adrien* and *Chateau of Echoes*

DESIRED

Lost Loves of the Bible
Book two

GINGER GARRETT

DESIRED
Published by David C Cook
4050 Lee Vance View
Colorado Springs, CO 80918 U.S.A.

David C Cook Distribution Canada
55 Woodslee Avenue, Paris, Ontario, Canada N3L 3E5

David C Cook U.K., Kingsway Communications
Eastbourne, East Sussex BN23 6NT, England

LCCN 2011934293
ISBN 978-1-4347-6800-1
eISBN 978-0-7814-0789-2

The author is represented by MacGregor Literary

The Team: Terry Behimer, Nicci Hubert, Amy Kiechlin, Caitlyn York, Karen Athen
Cover Design: DogEared Design, Kirk DouPonce
Cover Photo: iStockPhoto

Printed in the United States of America
First Edition 2011

1 2 3 4 5 6 7 8 9 10

073111

For Ashley

MOTHER

I am not going to tell you my name.

I stood face-to-face with an angel of God, and after that, I could not remember my own name for days. When I die, there will only be one name on my lips. It will not be my own.

I will tell you of Samson, my son. One last tale, to be my *mitzvah,* my righteous deed, a true tale in this false world. I will tell my story, and his. I will speak for the dead.

I will tell you of men and angels, of sons and sorrows. I will tell you of the courage required to wait upon a silent God. I will tell you of the strongest man to ever walk the earth, and of what proved mightier than his strength. For the strength of a man cannot save anyone, not even himself.

But come. The hour is later than you know, and even now, in death, I must share my son with others. Do not tarry with them long. Come to me as quickly as you can.

I will begin my story with a tale about breasts, where all good tales probably begin.

PART ONE

BRIDE OF FIRE

AMARA

Late spring in the Philistine city of Timnah,
near the Mediterranean Sea

Mother and Father sat in the doorway, drinking bowls of wine and greeting passersby. The entire Philistine city of Timnah was wandering about. No work had been done. We celebrated the first sight of the Pleiades stars in the heavens, marking the beginning of the wheat harvest season. Everyone in Timnah owned a field, whether it be large or small. Timnah was famous throughout the Valley of Sorek for our grapes, olives, and barley, but most especially our wheat. Our wheat proved so soft that when ground, little leavening was needed. We claimed that the wheat was so light, it lifted itself. Everything grown here in the valley was good. We loved the land and the land loved us, yielding herself up, giving us happy lives and full stomachs.

Many marriages had taken place today. Not proper marriages of property, like the ones my father would someday arrange for Astra and me. These were marriages of men to men, marriages that were said to be the ultimate test of manhood. I did not argue their reasoning—the belief that one man could be so virile, even another man would desire him. My people had always honored passion in whatever form it took. We understood that men married other men for prestige. Men married women for labor and children.

Some men, like my father, had no interest in proving their manhood. He contented himself with my mother. We still loved Father a great deal. He had to prove nothing to us. I didn't even feel sorry for my mother; that's how much he loved us. She must have envied other wives, whose husbands took men in marriage and earned respect at the city gates. But whatever envy or discontent she suffered, she kept it well hidden in her heart.

Father sat in the doorway, happy to watch the festivities from a distance, laughing at the drunk jugglers and leering at the temple dancers. He drank wine and popped fat, glossy olives into his mouth while Mother rubbed his shoulders. A male servant belonging to a neighbor rushed up to us, displaying his wedding ring, a virgin's blush on his face. Mother hugged him, warning him not to be late to the market tomorrow morning. He winked and pranced off. Father rolled his eyes and plunged his hand into the olive bowl, spearing an olive on the end of his index finger. He removed it and placed it on his ring finger, with an exaggerated sigh of wistfulness. Mother punched him on the shoulder as Astra and I giggled.

Dagon's temple, which was only a two-hour walk from here, would be busy later tonight. After all the children had been put to bed and the lamps extinguished, and the newlyweds had drawn the curtains around their beds, the long-married and the still-single men would all find themselves on the same road, with the same thought in their minds.

Dagon's temple offered beautiful temple prostitutes of many ages. Men would prostrate themselves at the feet of Dagon, that great god of the fields, and then prostitutes would descend the cold stone steps and become Dagon to those men. In Dagon's name, they would make love to the men and release them of all their fears and concerns. The Philistine men were quite devout; none of them ever wanted to miss a temple service.

Of course, I had never been allowed at the temple to see such sights. What little I knew came from Astra, who had ears that always heard the most delectable pieces of gossip and lore. She had a gift for secrets. Though two years younger than me, she knew much more. Her hair was longer than mine, and darker, and her face more alluring, with almond-shaped eyes and a full, pink mouth. She had many gifts I did not, I suppose. I was not unpleasant to look at, but I was ordinary.

I lifted my face to the moon and let her bathe my unremarkable face. A shiver of anticipation went through me. The night, illuminated by moon and fire, woke strange new desires.

While the men worshipped, the wives left at home would drink too much wine and eat all the raisins before collapsing into bed with stained tunics. Children would creep from their pallets and rush out into the streets to play until dawn. We loved the festivals, which were always dictated by the planting seasons. We celebrated when it was time to plant, and begged Dagon for a good harvest, and we celebrated when it was time to harvest, and begged Dagon for good prices at market.

My father stood to leave, and my mother kissed him good-bye before announcing she would go to bed early this evening. I begged permission, and received it, for Astra and me to flee to the rooftop and spend the evening there. We had pallets on the roof for just such nights, but we did not sleep. As soon as we settled in, I walked to stand near the edge of the roof, raising my arms to welcome the night.

Had my mother ever felt as I did right then, my breath roaring in my ears like a lion, my heart racing as I stood on our roof, surveying the city? The wind moved beneath my tunic, lifting the fabric to float out between my arms like the wings of a butterfly. I was weightless and soft. I could pretend to be beautiful, fresh, powerful. Someday, perhaps, a man would notice when I walked past; I would hear his sharp intake of breath, catch the furtive second glance. In his eyes, I would see that I had truly become beautiful, and my beauty would make him afraid. Astra already had this effect on men.

Astra had warned me about what awaited us both. There would be a wedding, and sheets hung from the roof, the honorable stain of blood on display, and someday, birth cries. She heard what wives talked about as they worked.

But in this last season of our youth, before men had claim on either of us, these nights were delicious and intoxicating. We dreamed. We stretched out on the roof, staring at the stars, giggling, calling out on the winds to our friends who watched the stars too. We were cradled this way, above our parents, above our lives, under the stars.

"The incense burned out. Do we have any more?"

Astra was sitting cross-legged on her pallet, looking at the night's stars. The incense pot was within her reach, but I returned from the roof's edge to lift the lid and check inside. I saw the shiny sludge inside and reached for the little spoon, scooping a fresh dollop of incense from the little stone pot, ladling it into the square dish over the fire. Gray smoke grew at the edges and curled up, spinning and spiraling into the air.

I sat down next to her and took in the rich scent, holding my long black hair back with my hands at my shoulders, leaning over the fire and inhaling. Mother bought her incense from the Egyptian chemist who frequented our city, which rested between the coastal plains of the sea and the Judean Hills. He created blends of musk and florals and spices, fragrances that bottled emotions we had no names for yet.

I sighed with pleasure and poured a fresh bowl of wine for myself. Astra glanced at her own bowl, which sat next to her, empty, but I shook my head no. Too much wine gave her nightmares. She would crawl into my bed and weep, and nothing I said was of any comfort.

"Milk, then?" she asked.

"I'll have to go below."

"No. Don't bother." She straightened her legs before lying down on her pallet and grinning at me. I often served her like a slave and didn't mind.

"What do you think of Father?"

"You should choose your words carefully, Astra. One would think you were being disrespectful." The idea that we were permitted to form an opinion of him was sacrilege.

"I'm not. I feel sorry for him."

I lowered my voice into a rasping whisper. Astra had to learn caution. "There is no reason on earth to pity him."

"You're wrong. He was born into a modest family of modest means, and he has done no better himself. Mother never gave him an heir. Even Mother, his one chance at prosperity, left him no better off than when she married him. He is doomed."

I was shocked by her boldness. "What an awful thing to say. We will be better for him than ten sons."

"How? Name one way he will benefit from us."

"Our bride price. We might fetch a high price."

"For a rug merchant's daughter? He buys his rugs from the trade caravans and then sells them at market. He owns neither the loom nor the slave who weaves. He is only as rich as his next trade, and we both know that is not speaking of much."

"There are the olives."

Besides the plot of wheat we owned, which barely gave enough wheat for our own stomachs, we had a small grove of olive trees. They, too, yielded enough for our family and no more. She huffed in disgust at my suggestion.

I turned my back to her, but I was not angry. I was convicted. It was just like Astra to reveal the truth without even trying. I was so miserably selfish. Ever since I had gotten my first monthly bleed seven months ago, I had become obsessed with my next stage of life.

"I do feel sorry that he has no heir," I offered. "But even if we're not rich and can offer no lands or wells or camels, we are good workers. Men like hardworking wives."

But all I could really think of, secretly, was the grief I must soon face. When I was given away, Father would lose a daughter, but I would lose my whole family, my constant comforts, the peace of the familiar. Who would comfort Astra in the middle of the night when I was gone? Who would shield her from the plainer girls with critical tongues? I would have a new mother, too, a new set of parents to win over. I would have to please my husband, and his mother, and his father, and perhaps too his siblings and business partners and neighbors. All my energy would go toward pleasing others. And if I did it well, my only reward would be their expectations that I continue. I served my family vigorously, but I loved them, so the burden was soft. I did not know what I would feel for my husband and his family. Plus, I wasn't beautiful. Men were always nicer to beautiful girls.

My monthly bleeding came at a price. Money would exchange hands to secure my marriage, but my debt would never be cancelled. I would be in a new home, with a new mother-in-law who would squeeze my breasts to see if milk had come in, who would know when I bled and watch what I ate. I would lie under a man I did not know and had not chosen, and tend to some rotting old woman while my own mother walked into her white years all alone.

Faced with these same fears, Astra thought only to be sorry for Father. She worried over him, while I worried over myself. I kept my back to her while I struggled to stop the shaming tears that began to well in my eyes.

"Amara! Come here!"

I sat up and took a deep breath. Astra was at the edge of the roof, peering into the streets. Restless as she was, she had finished with our conversation long before I had even begun to process it.

"Look!" she said, pointing to the street below. "It's that Hebrew we heard of!"

I peered around her, down the street, and saw an enormous beast lumbering down the lane, all alone. He was a strange enough sight as he was, but because he was alone, he looked even odder. No one came to the festival alone, not even the Hebrews, who always traveled in great noisy clumps. The Hebrews hated us because this land was ours. They hated us for our wealth, and our iron, and our power, because they wanted it all for themselves.

But he was alone, with no friends or companions. He seemed not to miss them, though, judging from the way he surveyed the city unfolding before him, stopping to buy a stick of roasted pigeon from a vendor.

Timnah only had one prostitute, an ugly old woman who sometimes picked up business from those too tired to walk all the way to the temple, and she made great efforts to stand up and address him.

"Are you new to our city? Care for a moment's comfort?"

He laughed and fetched the vendor, a young boy, giving him a coin. The boy returned with another stick of roasted meat, which the man handed to the hag. She sneered at his big, grinning face but flopped down on her haunches and ate with ferocity. He moved on, seemingly unaware of all the eyes upon him. To him, we were the spectacle, the evil Philistines who had not departed his sacred land.

Long ago, the legends say, the Hebrews had a god they took with them out of Egypt. This god "gifted" them our land. All the Hebrews had to do, the god said, was kill us all first.

It didn't happen, of course. We were the people of iron, the people who could forge spears and knives to fillet a Hebrew down the middle and cut through his shield, too. They had no hope of conquering us. Technology was not our god, but it did deliver us from their god. And we worshipped in better ways, embracing pleasure instead of shunning it, welcoming all gods and denying none.

Astra jumped back and ran over to the fire. I assumed she was frightened by the strange sight of this man, with his thick, braided hair pulled back into one huge mane and a red scarf wrapped around his head. His black beard was long too, hanging down to his stomach. Despite his loose tunic, I could see that he was as broad through the shoulders as an ox's yoke, with legs of granite. The sight made my stomach contract with a feeling like excitement. He was handsome, as much as any Hebrew could be, with dark, wide eyes and lips that were soft and red, turning up at the edges in a sly smile. His hair drew my attention again, though, that mass of black fur stunning me. He looked very much like a man-lion, a miraculous, wild beast.

We had heard of him before but had thought the stories were just more Hebrew mythology.

Timnah rested between two popular trading sites, so we often saw oddities pass through our village. Men charged a small fee and lifted a veil on a cage, and we got a glimpse of a turtle with two heads or a monkey that wore a tunic and drank wine from a bowl. We were savvy customers. But this man was a shock to the system, a shock I felt all the way down into my thighs. No sight compared to him.

I retreated from the roof's edge to check on Astra. I was too late.

Astra dashed past me, clutching a stick from the edge of the fire. She ran right to the roof's edge and launched it, pegging the giant in the forehead. She fell flat against the roof, holding her breath in absolute terror as I stood there, my mouth hanging open in outright horror.

"Astra! What did you do that for?"

She giggled. "He's a Hebrew. He doesn't belong here. They have their own festivals."

I peered down into the street, my heart as still and cold as stone. The man was looking straight up at my roof. He was going to kill us.

"I'm sorry, my lord. It was an accident," I said.

A strange shimmer passed over him and was gone. A trick of the moon, perhaps. But when I looked again at his face, he was smiling at me.

"What is your name?" His voice was calm and even. I saw a red bump beginning to show itself on his forehead. I glanced back at Astra, narrowing my eyes at her. If he didn't kill her, I would.

"I cannot answer that, my lord. I have apologized. May you have a good night."

I stepped back out of his line of sight, my hands trembling. "He asked for my name," I hissed at Astra, who had fled to crouch by the fire. We sat very still, our ears hoping to catch a noise from the street, wanting to know what he would do next.

Astra's eyes were wide. "But you did not give it, did you?"

I shook my head. "I should have given him yours."

We sat until our legs burned and cramped from holding one position so carefully. I decided I had been mistaken about his smile. It could have been an evil leer. Street torches cast unreliable shadows.

With great caution, we unfolded our legs and moved to rest on our pallets, our eyes still wide as we watched each other's faces and listened. We heard nothing for the remainder of the night but the sound of children playing and women singing drunkards' songs.

By the hour when dawn began to glow pink on the horizon, Astra had fallen asleep, her mouth wide open, her black eyelashes fluttering against her soft cheeks. I edged closer to her and stroked her hair, which fell from her smooth forehead. I shook my head though she could not see my rebuke. She was filled with terrible mischief, true enough, but she had the pure heart of a child. I prayed Dagon would be patient with her and bring her a gentle husband.

Knowing that Astra would not wake, I slipped down the stairs and crept through the house. Its wooden floor made small groans and creaks. Father had not yet returned from the temple, but that was of no concern. Mother snored loudly, sprawled across her straw pallet. I pulled the blanket up from her feet, where it had gotten tangled, and draped it over her before sneaking toward the front door.

I peeked in our large clay jar of oil near the door. It was almost empty. We would need money, and soon, if it were to be filled again.

Babies were just awakening, and adults were just beginning to sleep. The festival changed everyone's sleeping schedule, except for the infants. Infants were unmoved by our celebration of Dagon. Their god was still milk. I loved the morning music of our streets; the newborns with their cracking cries, the donkeys that snorted and kicked at their bedding, the lambs that bleated for breakfast at the first sound of footsteps outside their pen. There was the sound of carts being wheeled through the streets, of merchants going to market to set up, of groans and sighs and angry roosters.

I sneaked into the street, gathering my tunic in my hands, lifting it away from my feet as I bent over. I wanted to see the street, to see if I could find any trace of the man's footprints.

I found them at the edge of the path just under our roof, where he must have stood to peer up at me when he was deciding whether to kill us. His footsteps were huge. I slipped my own foot out of my sandal and rested it inside one of his footprints. His footprint was twice the size of mine.

I heard my father coming, whistling the same song to Dagon that he always sang in the morning. I erased the footprints of the man with my toes, turning to greet my father.

"Darling one," my father said, grabbing me for a little peck on the top of the head as I ran to him and fell into step beside him. "How was your night at home with Astra?"

"Fine."

I glanced up at his face, but he did not frown or doubt me. He had big bushy eyebrows like two feral dogs that arched and lunged at each other as he talked. Long dimples ran down each cheek, deepening when he grinned, which he did often. My mother said he was a handsome man. I could not judge him as such. He was simply my father.

Other girls' fathers treated them with strict order verging on contempt, but my father treated me with leniency, despite my gender. He did not worry or threaten as other fathers did, and he did not mind when I discussed matters such as temple politics or money. But even so, I was careful not to abuse my privilege.

"And your mother?"

"Sleeping inside. Shall I start your breakfast?"

"Let's wait for your mother. I'd like to talk to you." He stood in the doorway. I looked around to be sure there was no sign of more footprints.

I saw it then, and almost died of terror.

A long red scarf had been tied to the top of our doorpost. The Hebrew had marked our house. He wanted to remember where we lived.

"You know that I love you as much as any father can love a daughter."

I could not focus on what he was saying. I only saw red.

"If you had been a son, this conversation would be different. I can't protect you forever."

My heart lurched up. "Why do I need protection?"

He laughed. "Don't be so unreasonable. Any family can ask for you in marriage now. You will go and live in another house, with another father and mother, a husband to serve, children." He wiped a tear from his eye before continuing. "If the other fathers see me do this, I'll be ridiculed at the city gates for all time. They'll make me grind barley with the women."

He didn't know that I might not live long enough to be pledged away. How had he not seen that scarf? And what did that scarf mean? If I took it down, what would that signal? Acceptance of guilt?

I decided to leave it and wait.

He cleared his throat and looked at me with a stern expression. I did not think it was a sincere one. "So if I am to accept an offer, I should know what would please you most."

The day was only getting worse. "Nothing would please me. I don't want to marry."

He laughed again.

"I can just live here with you and Mother and Astra. I don't want to marry."

"But you will."

"You don't have to get rid of me. I can stay here and work. I'll pay for myself, you'll see."

"Would you feel more comfortable talking to your mother? You can tell her what you want."

"I am not being demure. I don't want to marry."

"The sun doesn't ask if we want it to rise. Wind doesn't ask if we want it to blow. Nothing in this world cares what we want. Do not live in the wasteland of thinking that what you want matters. Especially being a woman. Now, perhaps we'll have that breakfast."

He turned to go inside and saw the scarf. I froze, waiting for him to connect its presence with Astra and me and our terrible behavior last night. He would have questions. And I was a girl who lacked all charm, even the charm of quick little lies.

He laughed and tied it around his waist. "Festivals! Madness always reigns."

The Pleiades twinkled above us. My husband, Manoah, and I sat on our roof, escaping the heat that lingered even at this hour. I poured a fresh skin of water into the crock at his feet. He slipped off his sandals, sinking his feet into the water, groaning in happiness. At our age, harvesting the wheat cost us more in physical exhaustion than eating the wheat would ever return. We had loved each other since we were children, so I could speak boldly to him, without fear of his hand.

"We can afford more servants," I said.

"We can afford to buy our clothes," he countered.

"I like to weave."

"I like to harvest."

I settled in beside him once more. A little bird alighted on our roof, cocking its head at me. It visited me often. I reached into the sack at my feet, grabbed a fistful of the wheat heads, and tossed them in its direction.

Manoah frowned. "We have to sleep up here."

"I always sweep up after he eats."

"That wheat is worth good money!"

"You are handsome when you are angry."

He frowned, but I knew a smile was beneath it.

Samson appeared on the stairs.

I smiled, patting the seat next to me. "Come! Sit!"

Manoah folded his arms, looking away.

Samson leaped up, skipping the last two steps. I gave him a good smile, and he came over, kissing me on the forehead before sitting.

"Give me your hands," I instructed Samson as I lifted a little pot of oil from the bag that hung on my sash. A little olive oil at night on hands roughened from harvest made all the difference.

Samson looked at his father. His father pursed his lips, looking away.

"I did not harvest today," Samson confessed.

"Why not?" I asked.

"I went to Timnah."

Timnah. A Philistine pit of filth. And at the time of the marriage festival. I looked up at the heavens, beseeching God. Samson was still a boy in my eyes. But he had a destiny to fulfill. His name was meant to be great. His, and mine.

"And what was your decision? When will you speak to the elders of the tribe?"

Samson looked confused. He looked to his father, a look of helplessness.

"You did not tell her?"

Manoah glared at Samson in answer.

"Mother, I did not go to spy or make war on them. I went to their festival."

"I am your mother. You can tell me."

"No, I did. And I saw a girl. I want her."

"You went to their festival?"

"Father."

Manoah held up his hands, standing and walking to the roof's edge, away from us.

"The festival?" I boxed Samson on the ears. "What kind of Hebrew goes to a festival for Dagon? And you, of all Hebrews!"

"Father!"

"Leave him out of this! Do you want to kill him, too?" I stood up and clutched my heart, gasping for breath.

"I saw a girl there. I liked her."

The stars swirled together, faster and faster, spinning all around my head. I must have groaned in agony, because Samson jumped up, putting his arms around me. He helped me sit back down.

"Slap me," I begged him. "This is a dream. I want to wake up."

"Father. Please."

"I want nothing to do with this!" Manoah roared. "You said you wanted to study the enemy, not marry one!"

Both men stared at me when I burst out laughing.

"It's a joke, then. Samson! You could have killed me. Wait till I tell the women at the ovens tomorrow. Oh! Our great deliverer, hope of our people, pretending to love the people who have oppressed us for generations, stolen food from the mouths of our children, mocked us, and robbed us!" My voice grew shrill as I talked.

"Mother."

"You don't want a Canaanite girl! They're flat-chested. They have no breasts." He knew nothing about women. I could at least reason with him.

He grunted. "Stop that. I like lean girls."

"Lean girls? They can't give you children! Tomorrow I will walk with you through our village. I will show you the girls I like best for you." I gestured to my chest, a promise of the big-breasted girls he could have.

Manoah rolled his eyes at me. As if I was making this trouble. I narrowed my eyes at him, willing him to feel their searing heat. He knew as I did how wrong this was. We had spent our lives and our wealth, preparing Samson to be a great warrior, a mighty deliverer. I had long forgotten all the shame of barrenness.

Samson appealed to Manoah, who would not look him in the eye again. "Father. I can't explain it. But she is the one I want. Get her for me."

I clapped my hands. A reprimand. "You want a nice Hebrew girl with big breasts. That's it. No more foolish talk."

"I don't want a nice Hebrew girl! And I didn't ask to be anyone's deliverer!" He stomped down the stairs in disgust.

I brayed at him and turned to Manoah.

"You let him go to Timnah. Alone."

Manoah shrugged. As if helpless.

"Timnah. A Philistine rat hole."

"It was better than Ashkelon."

"He's been to Ashkelon?" I grabbed my tunic at the neck with both hands, threatening to rip it in blackest horror. "My son? Ashkelon?"

Manoah trotted across the roof like a little puppy, waving his hand at me, casting glances about as if the neighbors would hear.

"No, no, no! He asked to go there. I said no. He did not stop asking. So I said, 'Go to Timnah. Come right back.'"

"You let my only son, the son born to me in my old age, the son whose birth was prophesied by an angel, the son born to be the great deliverer of our people—you let this son go to a Philistine rat hole, alone. And of course he picked a wife there. Which would not have happened if you had told him no!"

"He is a man now."

I made a coughing noise. I had to rest both hands against my heart and force a little breath in.

Manoah rolled his eyes. He took me by the hand and led me to our chairs, where he helped me sit and poured me some milk.

I sniffed at the bowl and turned my face away. But I could not hide my tears, which were real.

Manoah sat too. "I do not understand it either."

"Liking a Philistine girl?"

"Eh. Some are good-looking."

I raised my hand to strike him, but he caught it first. And kissed it, sweetly, then held it in his lap, my cold, wrinkled hand warmed by his.

Manoah sighed. "He was born to crush the Philistines, and instead, he is fascinated by them, begging me to let him go to their cities. Then he asks to marry one! It's my fault."

"You should have said no."

"It would not have helped. No, I failed him long ago."

"Speak plainly. I am only a woman."

"When the angel appeared to our father Jacob, what did Jacob do? He fought. He wrestled. He demanded a great blessing, and he got one. And me? An angel appears, and I ask his name. That is all I wanted to know."

"He might have had a nice name. It would have made the story better." I did not have to elaborate that point. Our story had been mocked openly for some time. Other women sniffed at me when I reminded them of it. Their sons did not need my son to deliver them. Their sons rather liked the Philistine way of life—the gods, the sex, the festivals. Their sons scolded our generation, telling us we must embrace the Philistine ways. The sacred land, that gift from God, was a small price to pay for such pleasures, they said. They had forgotten their destiny, which was why I could not let my son forget his.

"I should have asked many other questions."

I shrugged. Who could know what they should do or say when an angel of God appears to them?

"We wanted a son." I leaned my head over to rest on his shoulder.

He kissed it and sighed.

I looked up at the stars, fixed in their cold, brilliant course. Just like Samson and me.

Early the next week, we left Zorah, heading for Timnah and this girl. Samson walked with urgency, stopping just once, to fill a skin with water at the banks of the stream at Sorek. His behavior worried me. I had delayed the trip as long as I could, but my efforts had only increased his desire to see her.

My back aching, I stretched in the early noon sun. Manoah was not far off. In front of me I could see the land of the Philistines. Beyond their cities stretched the sea. That is what the Philistines saw when they arose: a shapeless, formless world of water and mist. I saw these people as they were: arrogant overlords and squatters in our territory, sleeping under our stars. God had commanded us to cleanse the land of our enemies, but we had always been too weak. Until my son came along.

The sun had risen high and strong over the fields and vineyards. We would be in Timnah within the hour to meet his Philistine girl. I climbed up on a rock to see farther. The workers swung their scythes in golden fields of wheat, low voices singing the songs of harvest. Young girls cut lengths of rope and passed them, one to another, to the older men who tied the piles of wheat together. Bundles of wheat were building at the edges of all the fields, like a golden city rising before our eyes.

Samson lifted up a dripping clump of honeycomb, with a dark grin on his face. A peace offering, perhaps. I shook my head. I didn't even praise him for bravery, risking a bee sting for me.

"You can't stay mad at me forever."

"I am not mad. I am right. What you are doing is wrong, and you know it."

"Eat, Mother. You'll be nicer."

I needed the honeycomb. He knew that, my son. Nights of nothing but tears for my bread had weakened me. How could I have eaten from our own harvest when the son of our deliverance was throwing his destiny, and ours, away?

I took and ate as I watched the Philistine field hands. The men who swung the scythes worked with the speed that comes only from age and experience. Some paused when they noticed Samson. I watched their eyes dart to one another, the frowns on their faces. Another dumb Hebrew, but a big one, they must have thought.

Harvest time meant busy hands and sore backs, even in this land. I saw baskets of broken wheat heads loaded onto carts, and carts bumping down the dusty roads. Big brown dogs barked and played, happy to be out on such a fine day with their masters. Philistines loved their dogs. They treated dogs better than they treated us. I burned inside for the coming deliverance. I would make the war cry of my tribe, deep from within my dry, old body, and Samson would rise up.

I licked my fingers clean, turning my face away from them.

We moved on, closer now, so close I could smell the workers sweating. Samson stopped one man to buy broken wheat heads from his cart. Soon I saw the Philistine girls here. Some of them were as scrawny as I had hoped. But a few—oh! A few were lovely, with beautiful skin the color of almonds and black hair that sparkled in the sun. Their bodies were lean but strong. I could see muscles twitching in their calves and arms, their whole bodies as slight and scandalous as a wink at an altar. But they were flat-chested. Every one of them.

They pointed when they saw Samson. I waited for the twinge of pain he always had at these moments, when strangers first saw him and his hair. He blamed me, all these years, for that. But God made him live as a Nazarite, not me.

A group of girls returning from the fields screamed in terror, dropping their baskets as an unseen assailant startled them. Samson broke from the path, charging into the field to confront their attacker. My heart lurched up; could this be the beginning? Had God heard my cry?

My donkey snorted, stamping its feet. I saw it all happen, very slowly—an omen, I think now, of all that was to come. A black cobra slid across the path, crossing just in front of me, disappearing into the fields again. It moved with grace and speed, the most beautiful evil. My donkey screamed in fright and threw me. From my perch, I landed on my bottom, the breath knocked from me.

I had arrived at Timnah.

I was next in line, but I was not impatient. Everyone in Timnah shared ovens, usually five or six families to each one. Ovens were set in a clearing with the houses in a curve around them. It was convenient and reduced our work; someone was always baking bread in the morning before you awoke, so the oven was always hot. If you had to start a fire and place stones over it and wait for the stones to heat, you would have no bread for that day. Next to the oven was a fire pit with a roasting spit over the center. We all shared that, too, and we could roast an animal or heat water or milk over it. Sharing was not just a lesson in patience; division of labor was its own reward.

The sun was warm, and I wiped my forehead with the back of my hand. Fall was almost here, ending my constant labors of tending the olive trees, airing out the house, and repairing any earthenware that was damaged in storage over the winter. Already this morning I had swept our home and gone out to collect animal dung and wood for the next winter's fires. After I baked our bread for breakfast, I would need to go out to the fields and help with the harvest. We did not have much to do in our own little field, but Astra and I always managed to hire ourselves out to another family for a few hours. This pleased Mother and Father.

I allowed myself the luxury of a long stretch in the golden sun. All of spring, summer, and fall meant hard labor and browned faces. But fall brought the early rains and then winter, at last, that blessed end to our labor. I would have lazy mornings and afternoon naps, and my palms would slough these thick calluses.

"Amara!" Neo and Talos waved as they headed out to the fields, using the winding common road that ran between the clusters of homes.

I did not wave back. I turned my back and gritted my teeth. Talos and Neo were sweet friends when we were children, but none of us were children any longer. I did not want to be their friend now. They might become bold and ask for me in marriage. I wished I hadn't told them so many secrets when I was a girl. Now they thought they knew me. They might imagine that gave them an advantage, an early claim, a clear right to possess me.

I refused to dwell on the darker side of fall, those long, lazy hours when men's minds were free to wander. Most betrothals happened in the late fall, just in time to get a new laborer for the husband's harvest. I would not be waving to anyone. Father needed me more than I needed a husband.

And yet, even with this fearful cloud pressing down, I could rejoice that the biggest labors were almost behind us. Astra and I had worked long hours this season to bring in a good harvest. Last year, the crops were plentiful; so this year, we had to work harder for less return. That was nature's way: one year of plenty, one year of want.

"The earth reminds us not to forget her power," Father said. "Hungry people are humbled people."

I did not see the wisdom in that. Hunger makes people want to find a new god. Yet we worked on without grumbling. Labor, especially in the olive groves, was a delight. The olive trees of Timnah were four generations old or more; some had been planted nearly a thousand years ago. Our olive trees were like family elders—beautiful, gnarled, and wise. We groomed their branches in the morning, pulling each toward us, carefully plucking the olives and letting them fall gently onto the blanket spread beneath us. We groomed each tree as though she were a beautiful and frail grandmother, and we spoke to her, and each other, as we worked. I remembered an outrageous lie that Astra had repeated to me.

"The Hebrew we saw?" Astra had ventured to me not long ago.

"Yes?"

"Do you know what Talos told me?"

"I do not." I inhaled the green scent of the olives and the crisp perfume of their leaves. Spying an olive with a crack, I plucked it and dropped it into a bucket around my neck. The broken olives would go to the goats.

"Talos said—and I am not making this up—that the Hebrews have a magical box they dance around and bring offerings to. It's the source of their god's power."

"Mmmm." Magic was commonplace. Charms and spells changed from tribe to tribe, but everyone had gods, and everyone had magic.

"And that is not all. When a male Hebrew baby is born, the parents must prove their devotion to their god."

"Do they sacrifice it?"

"Worse!" Astra lowered her voice to avoid being overhead, although the nearest woman was a good distance away in another grove. "They cut off his third hand!"

I stopped. "Astra. You shouldn't listen to lies like that. And Talos should not be speaking to you of such private matters." Astra was destined to be a wife, not a sacred prostitute. She had to observe proper morals.

"It's true. Talos has never lied to us."

"And how would Talos know? Has he ever seen a Hebrew naked?"

She frowned, considering that.

I laughed as I remembered her expression on that day. Sirena grabbed the flat wooden bread tool, resting it on what little was left of her lap. She scattered a handful of crushed barley across the surface and then pulled her dough from the crock at her feet, moving more from memory than sight, I guessed. Her belly was so big with child that I don't think she could see anything below it.

Using one hand to push herself off the stone she sat on, and another to clutch the bread tool, Sirena stood to take her turn at the oven. Leaning forward, she slid the wood trowel into the oven and gave the handle a hard tug, dislodging the bread and causing it to roll onto the hot stone at the bottom of the oven. With great effort she carried herself back to her stone seat, and after she had lowered herself back down, she closed her eyes and sighed.

I smiled to myself, watching her. She was beautiful, especially now that she had filled out. Looking out at the horizon behind her, I let myself relax for a moment too. Morning's white mist still clung to the gentle hills in the distance to the east, with only the green treetops visible. Breeze blew through the tall grasses in the fields around the houses, carrying whispers of crisp evergreens and the sharp tang of limestone. We heard donkeys snorting and oxen lowing as men harnessed them for work, driving them into the mist. A few pregnant animals stayed behind, growing fat, probably content to rest from the labors of the field. Everyone always tried to keep the male animals separate from the females to prevent the loss of a good working animal during this season, but nothing could prevent a female going into heat. Keeping the males separate was no guarantee of abstinence. More than once I had spied a wild-eyed male goat climbing a fence in the middle of the night.

Sirena's bread smelled divine. I peeked in to see if it was done. Perhaps I could remove it for her and let her nap for a few more minutes. The crust was just turning gold at the edges, so I knew to wait. The only thing worse than no bread was half-baked bread that went bad within the day, leaving no leftovers for the night's meal.

I could learn how other wives did their bread, what spices they added, how they got a crackling brown crust and still retained a soft dough center. Ovens were also where the younger girls like me learned to be wives. First they learned how to bake bread, which would keep their husbands alive. Then the wives told them of the art of keeping him alive for other reasons. I made a point to skip those conversations.

One wife, with a broad face and puffy eyes and hair that held absolutely no allure—all of her just plain and dark and lifeless—sighed as she took her cooling loaf from the resting stone and wrapped it in a cloth. She was tired, explaining to the other wives her morning. "He comes home, telling his master he must leave to take his meal. I'm telling you, he doesn't want a meal."

The other wives giggled. Last year I would not have understood. This year I do but wish I didn't. Why did men think this way?

Her husband seemed very dirty to me. He was not a noble man, thinking of that in the middle of the day when he should have been working. Why she laughed, I did not know. I would not be a wife like her, and I would not marry a man like that. If my father heard conversations like this one, he would understand I had made a noble choice.

Astra's cry brought me out of my thoughts with a start. She ran to me, her face pale and her eyes wide. I caught her in my arms, but she was breathless and doubled over with the effort of catching a good breath.

"Breathe, Astra!" I rubbed her back. "It's all right. Whatever it is, you're safe now."

I scanned the path she had come from, the winding dirt road that led past other homes and out into the fields. Though nothing seemed to be following her, I saw the other women reaching for their butchering knives. Men working in the fields displaced plenty of vipers, which took revenge on our ankles when they could. And with no wall around our village, sometimes even a hungry lion or fox wandered into our houses. Mothers had to be very careful not to leave babies in baskets unattended. Their cries attracted attention from more than just other women. During harvest, Mother always insisted Astra and I carry knives with us.

Astra righted herself and swallowed hard before grabbing me by the arms.

"The Hebrew has returned."

"What?"

"He has returned, and he brought two others with him. He was wandering through the houses, looking."

She didn't have to finish that thought. My hand flew to my mouth as the women shrugged and began putting their knives away. They decided there was no danger in a curious Hebrew wandering around our village.

If only they had known.

I pulled Astra away from the oven, off to the side. The women resumed their baking and gossip. Astra and I were still young enough that our own intrigues were of no interest to them. They assumed us to still be children since we were unmarried, and children were capable of nothing interesting, nothing that could cause any great calamity in their own lives.

"What are we going to do?" I asked. Astra always had a better idea of what should be done. She could see a problem from all sides, whereas I only saw it from mine.

"He is looking for something, but I couldn't tell what it was."

I had never told her about the scarf. Father still wore it as a sash around his tunic, and by now, it was nothing to me but a sash. I offered a suggestion.

"We could run into the fields. Come back at dusk."

"No. The men will ask too many questions if we don't have jobs. Besides, if we don't know why he is here, we don't know where he will go. I think we should hide inside the house. He would never enter our house."

"We can't get out of our work."

"Do you trust me?"

I nodded.

"Come with me."

"But wait—do you think he is still angry? About being hit in the head? He might demand money." Both Philistine law and Hebrew law required payment for bodily injuries. Father could lose what little he had. Then he would have to accept the first offer of a bride price, not the best. What had we done that night? I chastised myself. We might have just arranged to sell ourselves to the lowest bidders.

Astra shook her head. "He didn't look angry. He looked like"—she twisted her mouth as she sought the right word—"he looked like he was searching for something."

We had no real market, not like Ashkelon or his own cities in the Judean Hills, but sometimes we did have unique treasures. Perhaps he was here for a treasure.

"We will hope that is all it is," I said, grabbing her hand. I turned to the wives. "My little sister is not feeling well. If one of you will bake my bread for me today, I will bake yours tomorrow. Or you can wait and save the favor until you need to claim it." Sirena opened her eyes and agreed at once. I was offering her the chance to stay in bed tomorrow morning.

"Thank you, and may Dagon bless your child," I said with a grateful nod.

Astra led me from the clearing to behind the houses. On the far end, there was a spot of privacy where we could create mischief without being seen from any other house. That did not mean we were able to create mischief for long, though. Someone was always coming in from the fields or carrying food and drink back out to the fields.

Pulling me closer, Astra took out her knife and, in a blink, stabbed me in the finger. I squealed, but she grabbed my finger and squeezed without mercy, making the blood bubble up. Opening her palm, she squeezed the drops into a red pool in the center of her hand. I jerked my hand back and stuck my finger in my mouth, glaring at her. She didn't pay me any attention as she lifted her tunic and smeared the blood on her thighs.

"I'll tell Mother my cycles have started. She'll let me stay inside today."

Of course she would. No one wanted a menstruating girl in the fields during harvest. The wheat might be ruined. Astra was safe, but I wasn't.

"What about me?"

"I need you, of course. Your cycles have already begun. I'll say you will show me what to do. Mother can continue her work. She'll be pleased to have you stay with me."

I wondered what Astra would do next month and instinctively took a step away from her. She wouldn't get any more fingers from me for this.

As if reading my mind, she poked me in the stomach and laughed. "Don't look so grim. It's the best plan we have."

Astra grabbed me by my other hand, and we ran toward our house, my heart beating wildly. Thankfully, our house was close. I did not have the fortitude to run far with my heart racing ahead like this. We jumped inside and shut the door, and then collapsed into giggles. We were little girls again, playing tricks on the other children or taking part in some silly prank. But uneasiness sneaked in with us. This Hebrew was no child, and hiding from him was not a childish trick. We didn't know what he wanted, but he did have a claim against us. If he had not forgotten or forgiven his injury, he had a right to Father's money.

Mother came down the steps at the back of the house, returning from the roof. She carried our heavy wool blankets, taking them below to hang them out for a beating. Astra ran toward her at once and scooped the blankets from her arms. Of course she would do that, I grimaced, before the idea had even entered my head that Mother needed help. And yet, wasn't it Astra's quick thinking that was responsible for us hiding like criminals at the moment?

"Thank you, Astra," Mother said, gesturing to the front door. "Set them there. I'll take them outside later in the afternoon and hang them up for a beating." She turned her attention to me next, taking me in, then frowning. "Where is the bread?"

My cheeks burned from shame.

"Sirena is baking it for us today."

Mother raised an eyebrow. "Should I ask why a woman, so heavy with her first child, is baking bread for me, when I have two able-bodied girls standing right here?"

"My cycle started." Astra lifted her tunic and showed just the edge of the blood smear.

Mother stared at Astra, who gave her the biggest, widest, most innocent smile I had ever seen. Mother frowned, sensing mischief but unable to resist Astra's charm.

"I have to go to the fields. I can't stay with you."

"It's all right, Mother. Amara will stay with me. She'll show me what to do."

Mother looked between us, her eyes boring into our very souls. I squirmed under her intense gaze; Astra did not. I think she enjoyed it a little.

"Very well. Amara, show her how to bind herself with the linens. But I'll expect you both to work while you're home. Get the late meal prepared, ready our beds for tonight, and check the baskets to see if any need to be repaired. I don't want them to break while carrying the wheat. And make sure the crocks are clean, and carry them all to the roof. I don't want to lose any time once we bring the last of the olives home."

I was going to twist Astra's arm, hard, for this. Her ingenious plan had not completely saved us. We were still in for a day of back-breaking labor.

Mother wrapped her scarf over her head, careful not to obscure her face. She wanted protection from the sun, not a veil to announce she was a prostitute. We had to be careful with our scarves. A strong breeze could ruin a reputation. With her scarf tucked into place, framing her face but not obscuring it, Mother left.

I folded my arms and looked at Astra. "Get to work."

"What? By myself?"

"You got us into this. I'm going to take a well-deserved nap, and when I wake up, if Mother's chores are not finished, I'll tell Father and Mother everything you've done."

"You would not!"

"And how do you know that?"

"Because I know you, sister. You would take a secret to the grave."

She was right, and I knew it. But I kept my arms crossed, keeping my own secret this time, glaring at her until she set to work with a pitiful pout.

I woke, sweat beading down my neck into my tunic. The room was dark; Astra had let the oil lamps burn out. She slept soundly beside me, curled into a ball like a kitten.

Father's voice shook the reed walls as he approached the house. "Good news, girls!" He threw open the door and swept in, lighter on his feet than he had been all year. We were in the year of less, the year when we worked harder and ate little. He and Mother were never light or happy in these kinds of years. They aged terribly, each lean year making them two years older. I wished we had a way to make the fields produce more even harvests, especially the olive trees. We had no command over nature.

Mother was right behind him, lifting her tunic with one hand so she could keep pace. From her anxious face, I could tell he had waited to share this good news.

"Astra! Wake up!" I nudged her awake before jumping up, fumbling for a lamp. I stumbled toward the door, thankful for the soft light shining behind Father in the doorway.

"Let me light a lamp, Father. Wait for me!" I picked up a crock of oil, tucking it under my arm, and grabbed a small lamp before dashing into the courtyard to our community fire pit. I wanted to hurry, but this was not a task the wise girl rushed through. I filled the lamp with fresh olive oil and tested the length of the wick. I rubbed the top of the wick between my fingers, making sure it had not dried out. My fingers were slick and shiny, so I pulled a burning stick from the fire and lit the wick. The flame was flat and lifeless. The wick needed a trim to get that dancing effect I loved but there was no time, not if I wanted to hear Father's news.

I cupped one hand around the flame, walking back with care. Once inside, I set the lamp on the low table in the far corner, and set to work lighting the other two lamps in the house.

Father did not wait for me to finish. "I sold all my rugs."

"What?" My mother screeched. Astra ran to hug him. He pushed them back to show them his money bag, which always hung limp on his belt. The bag had grown so heavy since this morning, as if by magic, forcing him to hold it, supporting it from the bottom.

"Are we rich?" Astra squealed. "We're rich, aren't we?" Her eyes flashed the news to me. If we were rich, she hinted, my troubles were over. I would not have to be married right away, not even if the Hebrew demanded a payment for his injury. How much could he get for a bruise, anyway?

"We're richer than we were this morning," Father said, flicking his hands to set her back to her chores. He pulled Mother close and kissed her right on the mouth. We giggled to see such extravagance.

"Wait! You were in the fields today. I saw you!" Mother shook her head in confusion. "You weren't at the market at all."

"True, but a remarkable event happened. While I worked in the fields, a man the size of two oxen walked toward me. He had hair that cannot be described! It was longer than I have ever seen, hair all the way to the ground! And he was a huge man, a son of the gods, surely."

"This man, this son of the gods, bought your rugs?"

"Indeed he did."

I watched him for a hint of what was to come. Had the Hebrew revealed to him our crime? Dread sickened me, boiling around in my stomach.

"And what sort of man would he be, wandering around during the harvest?" my mother asked. "Has he no family of his own? Or perhaps his gods do not need to eat."

"I don't know. I didn't ask." Father sounded hurt, hearing her tear down his best customer. I worried that a fight was coming. They fought a lot in the lean years.

"What did the man say to you?" I asked.

"At first, he was interested in my sash. He was on the road leading out of Timnah and spied it from a distance. Turned right back and walked up to me, asking me where I had found it."

"What did you say?" My voice was thin and weak.

He shrugged. "I told him the truth, of course. You should always tell the truth, girls. Tell the truth, and you will escape many dangers."

He was so wrong! He had no idea what he had just done, what disaster his truth had just unleashed.

"So what did this man say about the sash?" I tried to sound interested, not panicked.

"The sash? Nothing. I assured him I was a merchant with many beautiful wares to offer. If he found the sash to be striking he should see my rugs. So he followed me to our stall at the market and bought them all."

Smart Astra moved to pick up the blankets, deciding to busy herself. If my face looked anything like hers, Father would see our guilt and confusion before we said even one more word. This Hebrew was a serpent setting a trap for us. I could already see Father had fallen into it and was besotted with him.

I needed a chore. I needed busy hands and a clear mind, so I looked around the room to find something to do. I could see all of our home from where I stood. Like most of the families in our village, we had one large downstairs room separated by support beams for the roof. In the far right corner were the pallets we slept on, preferring to sleep closer together during the winter. To my left, along the back wall, was a low table where we took our meals, sitting on our bottoms. My mother had another, smaller table just in front of me, where she often did chores such as stringing fruit to hang from the support beams to dry or sewing a patch onto a tunic. She had good light here from the door, which she liked to prop open whenever the weather held. Her friends knew that when the door was open, she was doing the sort of chore that was always better when good friends provided chatter.

I decided to tend to the meal table, which needed a good oiling after the drying heat of summer. Mother kept a small crock of olive oil on the table, so all I needed was a rag to rub it in. I rummaged around in the basket on the floor where Mother kept her rags, made from old clothes that were not worth repairing any longer. We never changed tunics, wearing the same one for every season and every chore, so our clothes did not last long. She was devout, however, in supplying us with new scarves quite often, especially before festival seasons.

I chose a small piece of knobbed linen with pitiful tears running through it. Pouring a thin green streak of olive oil across the tabletop, I knelt down beside the table and set my mind on my work. Astra came over, holding a blanket up for my inspection, as if I needed to see that yet another hole had torn the fabric.

"Why would he do that?" she whispered.

"I don't know. We owe him double now, though. You cracked his head, and Father sold him cheap rugs that won't last the winter."

A little spark of life passed between us, the familiar tweak that made us see the situation from a stranger's eyes. Astra giggled first. I shook my finger at her before I gave in to my own giggles. My ears heard my father speaking, but my mind was slow to bring his words into focus.

"We need a goat," Father told Mother. "And do we have any remaining cheese?"

I waved my hand at Astra's face to quiet her. We were having guests for dinner.

"None. The goats are pregnant." My mother's tone was thin and tense. This was the worst possible month to have guests for dinner. Pregnant goats gave no milk. We couldn't roast a pregnant goat, even if we were desperate, because it would mean giving up two goats. And the harvest was coming in, but it was hardly ready to serve guests. Olives had to be pitted and pickled and pressed; grapes had to be crushed and poured into wineskins; wheat had to be separated from the chaff, ground, and made into bread. All month, we ate raw heads of wheat, raw olives, and grapes. But you would not serve such a meal to strangers.

Father soothed Mother by stroking her shoulder and then reaching for her hand. He placed the fat bag into her palm and grinned at her.

"We have money now. Go and buy what you need. Go and buy *everything* you need. The other families will sell whatever you need. And fill the oil jar, to the top!"

I had never seen what money could do, and certainly never on my mother's face. She grew younger in the blink of an eye. She reached to me, wiping the tears away from my cheek. She thought I was crying in relief, and she was moved by my tears, which made her cry.

Father looked at me, and then back at Mother, with her own tears now, and threw his hands up in exasperation.

"You're all crying? I just made you wealthy, and you're crying." He groaned. "I'll be on the roof. Amara, bring me a bowl of grapes and call me when dinner is ready or our guests arrive."

He fled from us.

Mother ticked off her instructions to us, assigning chores and making her shopping list. Astra and I set to work as she left.

"Mother! Wait!"

She turned to me, a smile on her face. She delighted in me. Money in her palm made me more delightful too, I could tell.

"Which neighbors did Father invite for the celebration?"

I would have loved to have Sirena and her husband as our guests.

Her eyebrows rose and she gasped. "I didn't ask. Isn't that funny—money makes everything else unimportant!"

Astra and I danced as we worked, a lightness sweeping our feet along. Friends from the village were coming for dinner. We didn't even care who they were; we were blessed. Money meant joy in our hearts and freedom in our family and health to our bones. And money made us numb, so that we did not demand an explanation as to who our inopportune guests might be, or why a Hebrew beast would buy so many rugs, or even what else might happen that day.

One lie would catch up to us, but much later. Astra could now be given in marriage, too. After all, her monthly cycles had started.

Sirena brought our bread by while we worked, and Mother set to work kneading another loaf. The oven outside was free so Mother could get one more loaf in, and as long as the gods didn't spit on her plans, it'd be done by the time our guests arrived.

Astra and I worked until our tunics were stained with sweat. We finished polishing the tables, tidying the pallets and blankets, and removing old, dried herbs from their hanging hooks on the support beams. Mother had bought a new batch of herbs, and we worked bundling those together with ribbon and hanging them on the hooks for a fresh-smelling home. When there seemed to be nothing else remaining to do, Mother gave us a critical eye and a new list of chores, all of which involved our appearance. She thought we could use some attention ourselves.

The roof, with those breezes we loved in the summer, was turning too cold for a bath, so Mother heated water outside over the fire and brought a crock in for each of us to freshen up. She plaited our hair, securing them at the back of our heads with a sprig of rosemary for adornment. I suspected the rosemary was to help disguise any remaining scent of our hard labor.

Father came downstairs at last, keeping a wary eye out for more unexplained tears, and tightened the familiar red sash around his waist. As he did, a knock at our door echoed through the room. Astra clutched my hand in excitement. We hadn't had guests for months. I hoped it was Sirena. She might let me rest my hand on her stomach and feel the babe kick at it.

"I hope it's Talos!" Astra whispered. "He's more fun than Sirena."

I glared at her. For all her wisdom, she didn't see the danger in talking to boys.

Father opened the door, his back blocking our view as he offered solemn words of welcome. He stepped away, one arm sweeping back, gesturing for the guests to enter.

The Hebrew stood on our threshold with an elderly couple behind him.

Astra's grip on my hand turned ferocious. I knew I would have a bruise, but I felt no pain. I felt nothing, because nothing stirred in my body. My blood froze in my veins, my heart stopped, and I could not breathe. Only my eyes still worked, taking in this massive Hebrew man-beast, with that black mane cascading down to the ground, his dark eyes twinkling as if he found amusement in my shock and horror.

He lifted up his leg, which looked like the massive trunk of an oak tree, and crossed the threshold into my home and into my life. For that moment, as he moved through the doorway, he eclipsed all remaining light from the outside world, the torches, the stars, the oil lamps in windows. Everything went dark in his shadow. I shuddered.

He stood before my mother and nodded. "*Ahaziku.* Strength to you."

"And success to you," my mother replied in kind to the traditional greeting. She cut her eyes to my father, who was busy exchanging small pleasantries with the elderly man.

"I am Jocasta. Welcome to my home." Mother gestured to my father. "You have met my husband, Adon."

The man-beast nodded. "I am Samson. And this is my mother."

I gasped, just a little, as did Astra. I knew exactly what she was thinking. This woman was ancient. She could not have birthed this man—not unless she had given birth in her seventies. She was close to ninety. I would have bet my life on it. I shuddered again. The Hebrew was a strange man from strange people.

The elderly woman stood behind him in the soft light, nodding curtly. She had a soft, square face and must have been attractive in her day. Her lips were still shapely, and she had colored them red with a steady hand. Her eyes, though surrounded by deep folds of wrinkles, were clear and sparkling. But this is what puzzled me: Both she and her husband had neat, well-groomed hair. Her husband had a short, white beard and thinning white hair combed back away from his face. Her own hair was white as clouds and pulled into a single tidy braid, which was wound around the top of her head and secured with a jeweled pin. Their robes were clean, and the mother wore a single gold ring on her hand. These were not people who would raise a feral child.

My mother gestured to the low, long eating table. "Please be seated while my daughters prepare our dinner." They all moved to the table while Mother pulled Astra and me aside, presumably to give us instructions.

"Your father did not tell me they were Hebrews," she whispered. Astra and I stood mute, terrified to be implicated in this.

"They must be the ones who bought all his rugs!" Astra whispered. "That's why he invited them to eat with us. He thinks they will bring him more business."

Mother glanced back at the table. Father was helping the elderly couple lower their half-dead bodies to their seats on the floor. Samson was already seated. He looked like a giant of Gath with a child's play table in front of him.

"I hope you are right. I cannot imagine another reason why your father would invite them in," Mother said.

Astra reached out and took hold of our arms, pulling us closer in, a tribe of three conspirators.

"We can do anything for one night. We will be as pleasant as possible, just for one night." Astra declined to mention that we needed to be kind because she had smacked this giant in the head with a stick, and that he had cause—and means—to devour us all on the spot.

Mother rewarded her with a wide smile. "And they will return again with heavy purses? You think like your father."

"I am uneasy," I confessed. "The big one makes me nervous."

Astra's grip on my arm grew tight. "That is why we must be so pleasant, sister. We will disarm him with kindness. And then send him on his way."

I pursed my lips and let out a long silent stream of prayer. Dagon was miles away in his temple. I didn't know if he could hear me. Mother broke away from us and moved to be seated. Astra and I remained standing, awaiting orders.

Mother nodded to us. Dinner had begun. "Astra, pour the wine."

Samson's mother shook a finger at Astra. "None for my son."

We were all silent. Finally Mother spoke. "Your son does not take anything with his meals?"

"My son does not drink wine or strong drink. If you have milk, he will take that."

I could not help but giggle. This enormous man-beast Samson drank milk with his meals like a babe. He looked unhappy with his mother but said nothing.

Mother shrugged in deference. "Astra, when you are finished with the wine, pour our guest a nice bowl of milk."

Astra drew up a ladle filled with scarlet perfection from our wine crock and filled the bowls one at a time, setting them on the table. Neither of us missed the scowl Samson's mother made when Astra set a bowl of wine in front of Mother. As if she was tainted because she drank wine and they did not. Astra poured an extra full bowl for Father.

"Olive oil, bread, and chickpeas, please," Mother commanded. Astra and I moved to serve the feast, carrying the dishes from Mother's work table to the dining table, laying out a straight row of delicacies right down the middle of the table. A normal meal for us was just one thing—stew, perhaps, or bread and olives. Tonight we got to sample a little bit of everything, plus Mother had clearly splurged on tonight's wine. The bite of fermented grapes stung my nose and made it twitch. We Philistines were known to our enemies for our use of iron and weapons, but to those as well cultured as ourselves, wine making was our best achievement. We had yet to find another culture that could make a wine to rival ours. Not even the Egyptians, with their chemists and magicians, had been able to summon enough magic or technology to overtake us in this most important of achievements. Without good wine, my father often said, life's labors were too much for any man.

Samson's mother took a sip of her wine and raised a fist to her mouth to hide a cough.

Mother leaned forward, concerned. "Are you all right? Is the wine too strong for you?"

"Too strong? No, that is not it. I am used to the Hebrew wines, that is all. Our grapes are better. We have the best elevation."

Only Astra and I would have recognized the flexing of Mother's jaw muscles and known how that comment riled her. The Hebrews occupied the higher ground to the north and the hills to the east so that they looked down at us. Not a day went by that we did not feel their eyes trained on our homes and our land. Everything had been fine, Mother told me, until the Hebrews came. They wanted our land but could not drive us from it, unless they had decided to make us so miserable that we would leave.

"Yes, the wine of the Philistines is quite different."

I beamed with pleasure. Mother offered such a gracious reply. She could handle this woman.

"Don't feel badly about that." Samson's mother brushed off the comment with one of her own. My shock at her poorly veiled hostility made me almost drop my plate of bread. I glanced at Astra and noticed little beads of sweat rolling down her temples.

Father was still too busy, sitting at the end of the table with Samson's father, to realize anything was amiss. Samson himself sat at the far right end, the three men making a horseshoe around the end of the table. I noticed that the seat to Samson's left was empty. Astra or I would have to sit there when we were done serving.

Mother turned to me. "You may bring the roast."

I was not going to let him near Astra. I nodded to her, marking the other seat with my eyes, the seat next to Mother. She understood, and I went to fetch the roast.

Mother had purchased a roast already finished, marinated in vinegar and scallions, with a crisp brown crust sealing in the juices all the way around. The warm scent had filled the room and carved out a hollow in my stomach, making me keenly aware that

I had not eaten all day. I lifted the plate and carried it to the table, letting the aroma settle my nerves. If nothing else, I would get a good meal tonight. I set the roast down and then took the spot next to Samson, before Mother or Father could indicate where I should sit.

Astra finished refilling the wine bowls and sat next to Mother, across from me. I was in between the man-beast and his impossibly old mother. I looked across the table at Astra and almost had to sit on my hands to keep from reaching across and strangling her. I did not know why this Hebrew had come back, but it was her fault.

I sat rigid, careful not to turn my neck and catch sight of the Hebrew. I dug into the food right away, scooping a handful of chickpeas into my mouth before I realized the trouble had begun. None of the Hebrews were eating. They were staring at their food, and then at us. Even Father stopped talking long enough to realize there was a grave problem.

Mother cleared her throat. "Forgive us. We have neglected your needs somehow. What may we do for you?"

Samson's mother sat straight, her shoulders squared. "We wash before we eat. And give thanks."

"Wash?"

I could tell Mother was aghast. We had not prepared baths for them. That would take all night. I blanched at the thought of the Hebrew naked on my roof. I would never even touch the washbasin again if he used it for his naked body.

Samson's mother deigned a smile, as if we were ignorant. "We wash our hands before meals. Of course, it is also customary among my people to wash the feet of guests when they enter, but I did not mind that you neglected us. That ritual is really one done more for good manners than purity. But we will insist on washing our hands before eating. Even though you are a Philistine, you can understand, yes?"

Though the sun was low outside and the oil lamps were the only source of light, I could tell that all the blood had drained from Mother's face. Her knuckles clutched the edge of the table, turning white as a forced smile found its way to her face.

"Of course." Her tone was as cold as the winter winds to come. "Girls, fetch a bowl of water and a clean cloth. Do you require anything else?"

Samson's mother shook her head, a peaceful expression on her face. I knew that look. She thought she had won.

Samson leaned forward to catch my attention, taking hold of my arm. I could not rise. Astra stood still, waiting for me, until Mother snapped at her to be quick.

"You never told me your name," he said.

Mother's eyebrows shot up. I spoke quickly.

"My mother neglected to introduce me; yes, you are right. I am called Amara."

"Amara."

Every girl loves the sound of her own name, but when he said it, it somehow sounded dirty. I wanted to catch it and give it a good scrubbing and make him promise not to say it again. I looked at my parents, but they had not heard anything amiss in his tone. I did not want to provoke him. I smiled and turned to look at him, to keep the pleasant pretense as best I could while Astra fetched a crock of water. She went out the front door, which was not a good sign—we must have been near empty. I hoped she could borrow some from a neighbor, rather than have to run down to the well. I wanted desperately to be saved from Samson.

This moment was my first real look into Samson's face, his expression lit by the wide flat flames of the oil lamps. A shiver passed through me though the room was warm.

In the flickering light and shadows, his hair was no longer the first thing I noticed. Instead, the light focused on his face, illuminating it for me, so that I looked into his eyes for the first time, startled. He had a kind face, a handsome face. His eyes were wide and brown, reflecting the flames as he watched me. He was young, too, younger than I had first supposed, being no more than eighteen or twenty, if I guessed right. And although I was embarrassed by my own animal nature, which seemed to appear as if on command, I leaned in, just a bit, and inhaled through my nose. I wanted to know what he smelled like. Every animal has its own smell.

He smelled clean. His hair, though long, must have been well cared for. His teeth were white and whole, and his breath was warm and sweet, as if he had been chewing on cloves.

I shook myself from such dangerous contemplation. This man was a Hebrew, and a strange one at that, and he had a grudge against us. We did not even know why he was here.

He leaned closer in and inhaled through his nose, keeping his eyes on me, those playful eyes that showed me the laughter he hid inside. He was making fun of me. I couldn't have helped being curious about him. He had such an outrageous appearance, of course he must have been used to curiosity.

Samson turned away to address my father. "You know how I like the sash you are wearing. I had one myself a while back. Where did you get it? I would love to buy another."

I made a wide-eyed plea to my father to say nothing, but of course he did not understand. He waved an arm across the table. "I'm a merchant, my son. You have no idea the treasures I come across every week."

"I am sure."

Astra came through the door with a crock of water and a clean linen cloth. I wanted to jump up and kiss her for such timing, but I sat, hoping the hand washing would give the man-beast something else to focus on.

His mother took the crock first, dipping her hands in and then wiping them on the linen. She passed the crock to me as I turned to receive it, her piercing eyes accusing me of some unknown crime as my hands touched hers. I passed the crock right over to Samson. Dirty man that he was, he laid his hands over mine as I held out the crock to him, not releasing me, as together we set the crock on the table before him. When it sat there, he slid his hands off mine, slowly, his fingertips stroking the back of my hands. I clenched my teeth together, with my eyes narrowing and my nostrils flaring up.

Furious that he touched me so boldly, I jerked my hands free and tucked them under the table. My thighs went weak and hot as I stared at his face, which was already filled with stifled amusement.

He knew the effect he had on me, and he held me in no respect. I balled my left hand into a fist, and when he leaned over to dip his hands in the crock, I turned my body toward him as if to speak, landing a hard punch right in his stomach. He coughed, nearly knocking the crock over.

Astra gave me a stern look of rebuke, which I returned viciously. She had thrown a stick at this man's head. He wanted compensation, all right—wanted me to pay with a little fleshly affection. If he thought I would receive his advances with anything other than disgust, then he knew nothing about Philistine women and our opinion of the Hebrews.

Samson's father washed his hands next and then spoke to my mother.

"You are a kind and noble woman to accommodate us. Please, now, allow me to give thanks."

Mother nodded to acknowledge his offer of thanks, the wonderful praise she was due, but he bowed his head and lifted his hands, as did Samson and his mother.

"Almighty God, who looks upon His people with favor, thank You for this meal."

At that, he ate with vigor, as did Samson and his mother. My family and I were slower to reach for a plate or bowl. Had this man really just thanked his god for this meal, when it was plain that my mother and sister and I had prepared it? What had his god done? Where had his god been when I was oiling the table and trimming the wicks?

Mother sliced the roast into small slices to be eaten by hand. She served herself then passed the plate to Samson's mother, who held up a hand.

"What animal is this?"

"Pig," my mother replied. "Seasoned with vinegar and scallions. That is what gives it that beautiful dark crust."

Samson's mother looked pointedly at Samson and her husband, a sour purse sealing up her mouth. She turned back to my mother.

"Pigs are unclean. We do not eat them. It displeases our God."

"Didn't your god make them?" Astra asked. Her smile was too sweet. It hid something.

"Of course He did," Samson's mother replied.

"Then why did He make them taste so good?" Astra asked.

Samson laughed, but his mother stopped that with one look before training a cold, sharp gaze on my little sister. I curled my hands into fists once more. Rugs or not, no one was going to scold my little sister right in front of me, in my own home, even if she was trouble.

Samson rested a hot palm on my thigh.

Samson's father stood up then and bowed to my mother and father. "We should go. It is harvest time, after all."

Samson's mother rose. "At harvest time, my people work. We do not entertain. Only fools would waste this season." She glared at her son.

Mother stood very quickly—happy, no doubt, to see them gone. Astra and I stood as well. Samson's mother made a move toward me.

I thought she wanted to say good-bye, but instead, she plunged her fingers into my ribs. I squealed in shock, jumping back, but she clucked her teeth at me and kept searching. She ran her fingers along each rib's indentation, and then grabbed the sides of my hips, patting them firmly, as if testing them. Taking hold of them, she spun me around and dug her fingers along my spine next.

My mouth was open, and I looked at Astra in utter disbelief. Astra's face mirrored what mine must have looked like. Her mouth hung open, and her eyes were wide. She looked frozen in shock and disbelief that a stranger could handle me like this, in my own home, right in front of Mother and Father.

I looked at Father for help, but he watched, with a strained look. I think he wanted to stop her, but he didn't.

Samson's mother released me, pushing me to the side to address her husband. "She needs a good flushing. If this comes to anything, remember that."

With that, they left. Samson allowed his mother and father to pass through first, before turning and thanking us for our hospitality. I made a fist, hoping he noticed. He winked as he tilted his head in my direction, and was gone.

I had no idea what she meant by "flushing" me. I did not think it could be good.

When Samson was a child, he ate the brightest grapes first. It did not matter that they were bitter. He ate with his eyes, always.

I saw a lean wisp of a girl, her light green eyes sparkling like the Evening Star against the dark cascading night that was her hair. Though it pained me to admit it, she was beautiful, perhaps even more so because she had no sense of her own beauty. She still moved like a shy girl, with no awareness of her body, no awareness of her effect upon men. Her name was Amara, and she wore an amulet around her neck to ward off evil. A superstitious abomination.

When we left at last, Samson spoke not a word to me. Only after a long while on the way to our lodging house did I look at Samson, a searching look. Why had he done this to us? Why had he chosen a Philistine girl to marry? Had he seen her tonight, seen the careless evil of her people?

My stomach began to roil; blood rushed to my face. The strange blue mist, the mist that had signaled God's power resting on my son—this mist had settled upon him, now, but Samson did not see it. He smiled to himself and paid no notice to my changing condition as he whistled a tune to himself. I had to duck quickly behind a home so my men would not see me.

I vomited up the little I had eaten.

In his face, I had seen it. He was in love with the enemy. And in that mist, I saw this, too: God was still with him.

I pleaded my case, to Samson and to God, using my native tongue—guilt. I sat in the ashes, tears staining my face. I had not applied my beauty lotion in two days. Samson rolled over, trying to sleep, so I moaned again, loudly.

He sat up, resting his forearms on his knees to watch me.

With one hand resting against my heart, I used the other to scoop ashes from the crockery beside me. I dumped the ashes on my head.

"I think I'll see if anyone needs help with the plowing," Samson said. Manoah did not rise up from his pallet. He wanted nothing to do with this battle.

"At this hour? Everyone just went to bed," I protested.

"I'm not sleeping." He stood and threw a heavier tunic on before leaving.

Manoah sat up after Samson had left. He cocked his head to one side, watching me.

"No use fighting him," Manoah said. "Samson's strength is too much, even for you."

"She is a Philistine! This cannot be God's will for our son!"

"Samson says God told him to do this."

I grabbed my head with both hands to keep it from bursting like a melon. "This is all wrong."

Manoah got up and dragged a crock of water over to me. Sitting down beside me, he took a sea sponge from the crock and began washing my face. He was slow, holding the sponge over the bowl, warming the water in his hands as errant drops splattered back below. The dripping sound was the only noise in our home, save for our own breaths. Beyond us, a lion roared in the night. I hoped Samson had stayed in the village. He was strong, but strength alone was no match for a lion's wrath.

"Will you come to bed now?"

I took the sponge from his hands and wrung it out, setting it beside the crock. It needed a good airing in the sun tomorrow.

"When I took you from your mother's home, could you have imagined any of this?" Manoah asked.

I chuckled. "No."

"Then you cannot imagine what He may be doing now. Hold onto what is good, and trust God."

A smile played on my lips, thinking of my belly in those long ago days, that improbable swelling at my age. How the other wives talked of it, and nothing else! At my age, with age spots on my face and hands, my knees sore and a back that was already bending forward, at that age God gave me a child. Syvah, my sister-in-law, the one who would later bear two sons herself, rejoiced with me. She had a full, soft face with a wide blunt nose and sparkling brown eyes. She was not beautiful, but her smile could make you forget that.

"A miracle!" Syvah and the women had said, holding their hands against my belly.

"More than a miracle!" I had told them. "A gift to all our tribes! He is sent for all of them. He will deliver our people from the Philistines."

Manoah yawned. I lifted my ash-soiled tunic over my head. Manoah rose and took a clean one from next to my pallet and lowered it over my head. I accepted his help quietly. Then I went to our pallet and lay down. As I rested my head against his chest, he spoke.

"I leave for Timnah in the morning." He was going to make arrangements to get the Philistine girl as a bride for our son.

"Why do you give in to him?"

"Do you remember when the strength first came upon him?"

Wise Manoah. There was one memory that always stayed with me.

It had been an early spring day, just before the wheat came ready for harvesting. The sun was not out. Several tribes had sent warriors to a nearby Danite camp for training. Danites were, of course, the fiercest tribe. We wanted nothing given to us; we preferred to fight for what we wanted. It was our nature.

This day, a mercenary from Egypt was in camp. He was a big man, by our standards, with dark thighs as wide and rippled as tree trunks. He wore a leather shirt that wrapped around his chest, crossing over each shoulder, and a short blue and white kilt tucked in at his waist. He had on more jewelry than all the Hebrew wives combined: a nose ring, bracelets, a necklace with odd dangling amulets, and fat gold rings on his wide fingers.

Our enemies hated the Egyptians, and for good reason. Long ago, the Philistines had left their ancient homeland across the sea and gone into the waters searching for a new home. When they landed in Egypt, it looked good to them, and they made claim.

The Egyptians beat them so badly, all that was left of the Philistines in Egypt was a memory, a little sneering joke. Our men were eager to see what the Egyptian could teach us. If the Egyptians had defeated the Philistines, we could learn their secrets.

We women watched the Egyptian man closely and covered our mouths with our hands as we spoke to one another. Syvah, so young and bold, spoke without covering her mouth. "He has no hair!" I smiled to see her bulging stomach. She was soon to deliver her second child. Her first, Liam, a boy not yet two years old, played near us.

"They shave themselves—everywhere!" another wife answered. We spoke at once, over each other and too fast, as we did when we had a rare moment to sit together.

"Oh!"

"He looks like a newborn!"

"If the wind picks up his kilt one more time, I will run for the hills. It's too early in the morning to see that much of Egypt."

We were in for a wonderful day of gossip and laughter and freedom from work. Syvah's husband, Joash, sat with Manoah. They were brothers. Joash was the eldest. His hair was pure white, and his hands shook when he ate. Syvah married for the birthright, I suspected. He would die not four months after that day, passing quietly in his sleep.

Dark gray clouds, gaping holes in each, hung low in the sky, pink and yellow sun just now beaming to the earth. The men lined up, listening to the Egyptian talk about his weapon, his strategy, his military prowess. I yawned, tired from the walk. We had risen so early for this. I wanted to sleep, but how could I with this suffocating weight in my lap? Though a child, when Samson sat in my lap I was sure he would snap a bone.

The Egyptian called out. "Give me your best man. We will spar. You will see why Egypt has no equal."

A Danite stood first. Of course.

They had swords of equal length. I would have thought they were evenly matched. But the Egyptian moved with a fierce speed—like lightning, brilliant and fast. He slashed open the Danite's tunic, an unspeakably rude act. Tunics were expensive. Often a man could only afford one.

Murmurs and low curses rumbled back toward him in response, but he only threw his head back and laughed at us. Before I could stop Samson, he was out of my lap, striding toward the Egyptian with all of the arrogance of a ten-year-old boy who knew nothing of life and war.

Samson bowed to his Danite elder and motioned for the man to bend down and listen. The man did, much to the delight of the crowd. A strange light, a shimmering like the reflection off distant water, hovered over Samson. I glanced around. No one else seemed to notice.

The Danite handed my son his sword. I jumped to my feet just as Samson whirled around, holding the sword up.

"Samson! No!"

Syvah grabbed my arm.

Samson bowed politely at the Egyptian, who looked highly amused.

"A Hebrew girl! She's lovely!" he exclaimed. A few of our boys snickered. I gritted my teeth at the stupid joke about his hair. All our men had long hair, down to their shoulders. Of course, Samson's now reached his waist, but they had no right to embarrass him.

"Are you a Hebrew?" Samson asked, with the tender voice of youth.

The Egyptian spat at Samson's feet. "No."

Samson swung the sword with a strength and power that no man was capable of. In an instant, the sword rested against the Egyptian's groin, in a very delicate, particular manner.

Samson glared at the man. "Do you want to become one?"

The crowd roared. The Egyptian sweated profusely as Samson made him apologize and promise to pay for a new tunic out of his fee.

When Samson lowered the sword and walked away, we had all forgotten the Egyptian. We had a new hero. We yelled his name; the men slapped one another on the back. Samson's young cousin toddled over to stand with the men, who were in awe of their clansman.

The Egyptian, though, he was not happy. He must have been an honest man, because he did take money out of his belt bag and hand it to the Danite, before lifting his sword and lunging at Samson's back.

My scream was still in my mouth as the Egyptian's head rolled to my feet a second later. Samson had turned and cut him down in a blinding flash. Only then did I release the scream, hearing it echo across the plains. Birds cried back in fright, flying up through the heavens.

Not a soul moved or said anything else. Samson cleaned the sword by scooping up handfuls of the pale, dry earth and rubbing it across the blade until the blood was gone. When he handed it back to the Danite, the man shook his head.

"You have earned it, my son."

"I do not like the feel of a sword in my hand."

I thought, on that day, he meant he would not use his strength for war. I thought he would deliver the people in some glorious new bloodless way.

But there is no deliverance without blood. This is what an old woman knows.

So now, I settled in beside Manoah and waited for sleep. My only prayer was that God, in His mercy, would stop Samson from making this mistake. If He loved my son, He would. God's will could not include a Philistine wife for my son.

I had so much to learn about God, and my son.

The Day of Atonement had passed. Samson, Manoah, and I had suffered together, denying ourselves food and water from sundown to sundown. We had each repented of our sins.

At sundown I folded my arms and looked at Samson. "Well?"

He shrugged. "What?"

That was how we began the week of the Feast of Tabernacles. We had no bond. We had a truce. Our people were celebrating, though the harvest had been lean. Still, they danced and sang, late into the night, every night for seven days. On the morning of the eighth day, Manoah had departed for Timnah.

I pleaded with Samson to run after him, to stop him.

He pressed his hands to his forehead. "Stop nagging me!"

"I'll stop nagging you when I stop loving you. They go together."

My neighbors, the people of the village, even Syvah, young enough that her waist still curved, were bloated and sleepy from the feasting. Only I looked thinner.

"Are you well?" some asked. I wiped tears away, nodding in the direction of my son. He turned away and made new conversation, wherever he was.

But by the end of that day, two evenings after the feast's end, I sat on a high rock as the sun set, watching Samson in the fields. Manoah had not yet returned. Samson and his cousins amused themselves with the other young men from the village, the same way they had every year since Samson's strength was discovered. Syvah's sons, Kaleb and Liam, hitched up two oxen to a plough, then they hitched Samson to one that sat in a trench parallel to the oxen team. With a loud cry, Kaleb signaled the start of the race. Liam drove the oxen hard, lashing them with his voice and his whip. Samson lowered his head and grimaced, charging forward.

I could not help myself. I yelled out his name, urging him to victory. My son was not going to lose to a couple of oxen.

Beyond him, the sun was setting, washed in pale orange. Clouds floated on the horizon, soaked in yellow. Samson won, and there was time for one more race before the sun washed away. Samson reversed direction, and Kaleb and Liam turned the oxen team. I could hear much yelling and laughter from my perch.

Other mothers watched too, though they kept their distance. I pressed my lips together. No matter.

In the morning, we would begin plowing the fields. We had to sow seed after that, each of us. Next winter's bread started tomorrow.

But after the plowing and the sowing, came the rest. Our labors would be done until the spring. The air around me had turned cooler, another reminder that the year had flown by.

I watched my son, muscles straining under the yoke, dust blowing back behind him as he tore up the earth. Though this was the season of celebration, my joy in the harvest was bittersweet, as every year is when you have a child at home. The turning of the seasons reminded me that time was passing. My son was no longer a child, but if I closed my eyes I could still believe that I might again cradle him as a child in my arms. He was young and soft in my mind, a tender boy who hid behind my legs and cried when I refused to cut his hair.

The children's laughter made me open my eyes again, but Samson was not among the laughing children. He was sitting by himself, watching the children run, witnessing their delight at being set loose to play at last in the fields with no worries of damaged grain. Samson turned to me and smiled. I nodded back, grateful he was no closer. When he looked away, I wiped the tears from my eyes.

His cousins and the other young men from the village were making a bonfire. They all talked to each other with intensity, sharing their petty secrets and jokes.

I looked back at the horizon. The sun was sinking away, its last brilliant burst of orange illuminating the lingering clouds. The day had passed. Time had passed. All that remained now was deepest night and the long watch for dawn.

Fall's gentle sun did not last. Her gold empire evaporated into white clouds and morning mists. Winter was coming fast. We worked late into the night, every night, putting up the last of the harvest, pulling out the olives and grapes and wheat kernels that split during the walk home. We collected baskets of these to feed our goats and went out every morning to check their bedding. Some families let their goats sleep with them inside, on the lower floor, and the family kept their beds on a floor just above. We didn't do that. Maybe it's because we kept pigs sometimes too. Mother wanted a separate pen near the house, and we bartered space in it for extra food. Sirena kept two goats of her own in it, but Father made her keep her bucks with another family. He said he didn't trust males. Our three goats were pregnant anyway; we knew by their swollen backsides and bulging bellies.

Like our goats, we were at the mercy of time now. We did not control our lives. The fields did. They determined when we worked and when we rested. And right now, we were working.

Already exhausted from harvesting in the warm weather, there was still more work ahead of us as it turned cold. We went out into the fields once more, readying them for the rainy season. We turned the dirt over and over, deepening and airing out the rows, working the fertilizer into the earth. Like most Philistines, we used a combination of manure and menstrual blood. Only at this moment did the blood of a woman's moon cycle have good magic, as the ground cried out to be fertilized. Mother saved the soiled linens, and we worked them deep into the soil, knowing that what cries out for life to us would cry out for life for our crops. This same blood, if brought into the fields after they had been fertilized, brought death, a miscarriage. We had to sow this powerful magic while it favored us. If Mother noticed that she did not have so many rags to suggest Astra had gotten her cycle, she said nothing.

With our field prepared, we hired ourselves out to neighbors in our own village and the rest of the valley. How I loved this last, sweet labor! Seeding did not require me to bend over or lift a tool. All I needed was a basket around my neck for seed. I took off my sandals and stepped into the soft give of the soil, dipping my hand into the silky little seeds, scattering the seed along the rows. I walked slowly and breathed deeply, knowing the end of all our labors was at last here. The blessed rest of winter was coming, when Astra and I could lie under our blankets and tell stories, when Father would nod off to sleep after breakfast and Mother would pat him softly on the shoulder, letting him rest. The fire outside would feel delicious in its warmth, and we would only sweat if we wanted to, by getting close to the flames.

If there was a dark spot on the glorious white mists of winter, it was this: Word had spread through our village that Father and Mother had offered hospitality to Hebrews. Astra and I could endure the insults from other children, but Father had lost business.

He had taken a large share of money from his sudden wealth and invested it in another load of rugs from a merchant, yet he had sold not even one.

He was silent at dinner most nights, and not just from exhaustion. Finally, last night after dinner, he had said what we were all thinking.

"That money was a curse. We were happier before we had it. Now we've lost both it and our contentment."

"What can we do?" I asked.

"What should we do? Pretend it didn't happen?" He sounded exasperated with me.

"You didn't have to tell anyone that the Hebrew bought the rugs!" Astra came to my defense. Perhaps she felt guilty.

"You think I brought this trouble to our door? Are you so naive?" Father said.

I stood. Rain or not, I would spend my night on the roof.

He grabbed me by the wrist.

"Adon, no," Mother scolded him.

He became a different man as I watched. The hard lines from all the lean years surfaced in his face as his eyes emptied of all compassion. "I work until I am half dead. I scrape and scavenge like a dog, rent out my wife and daughters to work the fields like they are oxen, and for all this, look at us. Look! Who had enough to eat tonight? Who wears a tunic without patches? Even the wineskins look better than we do, and they'll get thrown out after one season!"

A cold, hard lump burned in my throat, an agony I struggled to soothe by taking soft, steady breaths. I could not bear to add to my father's shame with tears of my own.

But Astra was already crying, her head bent toward her lap. She was too young to practice any kind of restraint. I wanted to reach out to her. She would think this was her fault. That was true, but I didn't want her to suffer.

My father had not released me. He pulled on my wrist, getting my attention.

"Do you know who came to see me today?"

I shook my head. Astra looked up in alarm.

"Manoah, the father of Samson."

Astra jumped up. "I did it! It's my fault. I will apologize to him if he will listen."

Father looked at her as if she was a fool.

"Girls, go up to the roof," my mother said. "Leave me alone with your father."

"No. It is done. She should know about our arrangement."

What had gone on between him and Manoah? What could they have arranged? They were Hebrews. Any pact was an admission of both our poverty and our ambition. We were Philistines, superior in technology, learning, and power. These poor Hebrews worshipped a god that had promised them a land he could not deliver. Whatever Father had promised to them, it was a better deal than they had ever gotten from their own god.

Father didn't even take a breath or try to prepare me. His eyes looked at me without seeing me, as if his soul had evaporated during the dinner.

"Samson wants you."

"For what?"

"A bride."

Astra fell down, crumpling to the floor in shock. Mother jumped up to tend to her.

Father picked his teeth with the long nail of his little finger, as he looked at the far wall, his chin trembling.

"Please tell me this is a joke." I barely had enough breath to be heard.

"What did you expect me to do?" He looked at me, his brows tightly knotted together, deep lines of anger springing up on his forehead.

Mother helped Astra to sit upright, holding her, before screaming at Father again. "A Hebrew! You pledged my daughter to a Hebrew!"

"Name me one Philistine who wants her." Father's voice was cold.

Mother opened her mouth then closed it, her nostrils flaring. She slammed her hand on the table, palm flat, making the bowls jump and clatter. The noise made my heart jump, and I burst into tears. Father was a good man, but a poor one. He had only done what he had to do. I was going to become the bride of the man-beast of the Hebrews, the freak who made everyone stop and gasp in horror. The thought of the Hebrew man-beast reaching for me under the stars on his own roof, while his parents slept in the house below us, made me sick.

"How much did you get for me?"

Astra stopped crying, her eager expression showing me that she was hungrier than she even admitted. Even Mother leaned closer in, anxious to hear a good number.

"Four pieces of silver."

Mother's hand flew to her heart. I ground my teeth as the good number burned into my heart. My price was better than I could have imagined.

Oh, Dagon.

MOTHER

Samson and I passed the Sabbath together in peace. We remained in our beds later than we usually did, and when we rose, I made him a big breakfast of his favorite foods. We ate curds and honey and bread in our cool, quiet house. We could hear birds alight on the roof and sing as the sun rose.

I didn't want Manoah to return. It was a sin to think it, but I did more than allow the thought to pass. I prayed it. I prayed that time would stop, that God would stop His relentless push toward a new day and allow me this one day, this peace, forever.

Samson dipped a piece of bread in oil and handed it to me. "You're not eating enough. You're too thin."

Only he had noticed.

I accepted his gift and ate. The oil spread in my mouth, and strength flooded into my bones again. I swallowed and closed my eyes in relief.

"Here. Eat again." Samson was holding out another piece of bread dripping with the green oil of our olives.

"You're still growing. You eat it."

"No. It's for you."

I accepted it and ate. He had soaked it; I could not open my mouth quickly. He had set a clever trap.

Samson settled back and watched me. "I have to do this. I can't explain why."

I nodded.

"It doesn't mean I don't love you. My path was chosen for me, before I was even born. You have told me that all of my life. And this marriage, it is part of that path. I am sure of it."

I looked down at my hands with their spots from sun and age, and deep crevices across the knuckles. My life was fading, and Samson's was beginning its long, glorious burn.

"I have lost many friends because of the prophecy."

Samson nodded in acknowledgment. "I have never had any friends to lose."

"Do you hate me? Do you wish I had turned the angel away, or run from him?"

Samson reached across the distance between us and took my hands in his. His hands were warm. I had not realized how cold I was.

A tear slid down my face. I was like a cold, trembling child. Samson was indeed strong. He leaned toward me.

"Do you ever wish you had been made the deliverer of our people, instead of me?" he asked.

I laughed, a deep chuckle from my belly. "You know what I would do? I would start in Ashkelon and work my way to Gaza. I would smash the temples of Dagon into rubble and destroy every altar that had ever held a sacrifice made to him. I would deliver anyone who had ever suffered from this idol."

"Why do you hate the Philistines' god so much?"

"You're too young."

"Mother."

I rubbed my forehead awhile before answering. "Philistines believe a man teaches the gods how to act. If you pray to Dagon, you must show him how to answer you, or he will not know. And what do men pray for more than anything else in this world?"

"Money."

"Yes. And money comes from what?"

"Trade."

"And what are they trading? Think, Samson."

"Lumber. Jewels. Wheat, wine, olives."

"They are trading God's gifts. They grow rich and do not bless Him."

Here, I had to pause for a deep breath. To explain such things made the food in my stomach pitch and roll. I wiped my forehead before continuing.

"And there is more. The greatest gift of our God, this one they destroy. The next time you go to a festival, look in the gutters outside the temple of Dagon, and tell me what you see. I did it once, as a child. I have never forgotten the sight." I narrowed my eyes, willing him to ask me what I had seen. "When we claim that land, we will have to build a lot of graves."

Samson stood up, needing more distance between us.

Manoah opened the door. Samson and I looked at him but did not speak, the weight of our words holding us back from him.

Manoah frowned, looking between us. "Well, it is done. You have a Philistine bride."

Samson glanced at me. I was careful to keep my face still, to say nothing with my eyes. I would not give my blessing.

My son walked out of the house, slamming the door behind him as he went.

Samson was coming. He would bring his parents but no one else for the marriage. As was the Hebrew custom, he would throw a feast for seven days. I could invite anyone I chose. For seven days, he would entertain and feed my guests, but it was on the evening of the first day that I would go up on the roof and become his wife.

We said nothing of the marriage to anyone in the city. Sirena noticed the deep wells under my eyes, the dark circles from mourning all through the night. I told her nothing. Talos and Neo asked Astra many questions, but she fled like a doe back to my side, and we glared at them until they shrugged and walked away. The gossips would find out the news soon enough anyway. They always did.

At night, though none of us had brought home much from the harvest, we did not count the grapes or weigh the wheat. We knew that our family would survive the coming year, not because of the harvest, but because I would belong to a Hebrew.

On one of these last sorrowful nights, when we had extinguished all but one oil lamp, we all remained on our pallets in silence. Golden light flickered against the walls in the darkness, making shadows leap and dance all around us. Astra must have trimmed this wick; she knew just how to angle her cuts to make the flame dance for hours.

Father spoke, and I listened. His deep soft voice joined the leaping shadows, until in the shadows I saw the tale he told spring to life.

"I have learned the tale of Samson and his people. Let me tell you of the man you will marry and the tribe you will join. Learn their ways, daughter. Become as one and live. Forget us and prosper. I could ask no more for my daughter.

"Twenty years ago, this man Samson was born under a strange star, and his tale is a strange one. A spirit appeared to his mother one day as she worked in her fields, and the woman conversed with the spirit freely. The spirit foretold of the child and extracted promises from the woman. She would be the one to guard his magic.

"This woman, you should know, is a Danite, the warrior tribe of the Hebrews. Though the Hebrews have twelve tribes, although they all look alike, we know them to have very different temperaments and to make very different neighbors. The Danites are born serpents. This was their blessing, pronounced by their forefather Jacob, a man known for stealing his own blessing. Jacob pronounced that the tribe of Dan would be a tribe of serpents, horned snakes resting on the path of their enemies.

"Forget us, daughter. You will dwell with serpents. Be as happy as you can. Once you leave, never return."

"Why?" It was Astra who spoke. "Why does he want her? He won't get any land with her."

I was too numb from pain to take offense. I knew my beauty was not a logical answer.

Father sighed. "There is more to this tale, a strange turn. That fierce serpent, the tribe of Dan, refuses to strike. They were gifted the land of the Canaanites by their god and by their forefather Moses, yet they refused the gift. Why do they watch us, that serpent in the road, and not strike?"

A terrible silence dwelled with us as we contemplated his question.

Philistines had been always been anxious to strike, dealing a savage blow once to the fierce Hittites, burning their capitol and slaughtering their women and children. We devoured them so completely that even the pharaoh of Egypt, Ramses the Third, was awakened. He came after us with six-spoked chariots that glided across all the sand and rocks between us as if on air. And while it is true that we could not overcome him and lay claim to Egypt, we did not consider our prize to be a small one. We settled here along the Mediterranean, eating fish for our supper and watching the sun set over distant empires that traveled to us, begging for iron and knowledge.

Knowledge was our crown, and skill gave us a throne that none could take from us.

The Hebrews came to us before every harvest, asking us to sharpen their harvest tools. They used to come to us with their killing blades, held flat on their palms, asking us to sharpen them too. How could they make war against us if we were the ones who made their weapons work? Every year we sharpened fewer blades and more tools. The Danite warriors became craftsmen. Perhaps it was their real destiny; their god had asked their tribe to build an ark for him, to carry his belongings in. They said he traveled with stone tablets inscribed with his laws and a branch from an almond tree.

I giggled. What a strange god.

We were not fools. We watched their eyes when they walked among us. We watched them working out in their minds the layout of our cities, the location of our storehouses. We forbade them from watching how we sharpened their tools and blades. We watched them, as they waited in the open road for us.

"The Danites will attack us someday. The serpent will lift her head and strike," Father said.

In the leaping flames, I saw a vision of that terrible, coming day. Astra threw a blanket over her face in dread.

"That is why, daughter, when you leave this house, you must forget us. You will become the mother to a brood of vipers who will rise up and strike us. If you do not remember us, your heart will be spared much grief." Father's voice sounded so cold.

I rose up, my face illuminated in the flickering light. "I will never forget you! How can you tell me such a tale and ask such a thing? What evil have you brought upon me?"

Father sat up to face me. The shadows played under his face, the soft glow of his gentle eyes turning to stone as I watched. Mother must have sensed the change, for she, too, sat up, resting a hand on his arm.

Father stood and fumbled in the darkness for his sword, a short blade that he wore only in times of urgent threat. He opened the door to the night. As moonlight flooded in, Astra gasped at the image of Father with a knife to his throat. Mother leaped from her bed and took the knife away, whispering comforting words. She looked at me, accusations in her eyes, and my thin robe left me very cold.

I stood in my house, thankful for the mercy of rain. The air was lifting, growing colder and lighter, and the heavy rains could at last break through the clouds and pour down on us. The heavy rains meant that the women did not linger when baking their bread. We covered our faces in the rain and scurried between house and oven, house and pen, house and refuse dump.

Several weeks had passed, and I knew everyone had heard of my shame. Who can know how such secrets escape? But they do. Secrets are not safe in Timnah. Sirena wept as she baked her bread then fled from me. Talos and Neo looked stricken every time they saw me. I was marrying another race, which was bad enough, but to marry a freak? The shame would never lift.

Astra opened the door and pranced outside, making her way to me, lifting her tunic to keep it clean.

My heart rose.

Astra sat beside me, nudging me over with her bottom. She dug her toes into the sand next to mine and shivered. Her tunic was old and thin. I put my arm around her, holding her close.

"Are you scared?" she asked at last.

"Yes. And no. What must be done, must be done. I will get through it."

"You sound very brave."

"I do not feel brave. If I love Father at all, if I have love for any of you, I will obey and go."

"And you will forget us."

"Oh, no, Astra. No. I cannot forget you."

She began to cry. "I will never see you again," she said. "It isn't fair! Don't go. Father will find a way to earn more money."

I pressed Astra's head into the crook of my neck. Releasing a deep sigh, I tried to breathe through the pain in my chest. The agony of waiting for the wedding only gave my mind time to think fearful thoughts. I groaned and looked away to the hills just beyond us. What I saw made me swallow a cold, giant stone. It tumbled down into my stomach, sinking, sucking all the air out of my body.

"What is it?" Astra gasped, righting herself. She looked at my face then turned her head around to look at the hills. She saw it too and raced back to the house. She did not mean to leave me there alone, I knew.

A donkey picked his way down the hill, carrying Samson's mother. Beside it walked Samson and his father.

Today was my wedding day.

Astra and I crept up to the roof. Samson and his parents were outside in the courtyard. Everyone from our little village was here, the men gawking, the women clucking their teeth.

Astra and I clutched arms as we watched Samson's mother for a clue as to my days. Samson would have my nights, which was for me the stuff of feverish, shameful nightmares, but this wrinkled old crone would rule my days. I would bake her bread, empty her toilet pot, wash her tunic, wipe her mouth.... If I lived a year it would be a gift from Dagon. Or a curse.

My attention was drawn back to Samson. Closer now, he announced he would teach the boys of my village how to hypnotize a bird. Samson caught one of our fowl by her feet and swung the poor squawking thing round and round over his head, then placed her gently on the ground. He took a step back, and the confused bird followed. Wherever he stepped, she followed, mesmerized by the confusion he had caused.

My face burned hot as I watched the coarse gestures that accompanied the demonstration. I was to be his little bird, no doubt.

MOTHER

The Philistines had a nasty surprise for us.

I had clearly instructed Amara and her sister on how I planned to serve the meal, and to whom, when a group of two dozen men or more walked up, uninvited, settling themselves at my table. Samson had been watching the hired men roasting the pig—that fatty, dripping abomination—but was at my side in a moment. He grabbed me by the arm, cautioning me. Were it not for his hand on my arm, I would have started the great deliverance right then. Arrogant, ill-mannered pig eaters!

Amara looked at me with both fear and admiration on her face when she approached. She did not like the men, either. I frowned at her. She blushed and went back to her work. I debated how best to ruin her wedding night. I decided to test her by asking Samson to serve her a brimming bowl of wine. She drank, and well.

I knew I had won. *Drink,* I willed her with all of my being, *drink deeply.* Again, I nodded and he poured. And she did drink, finally becoming so drunk Samson had no other honorable choice but to carry her inside and face the taunting men alone for the rest of the feast.

No matter. He had spent his life surrounded by taunting leers. My deliverer needed deliverance, but not from them. From a straight-hipped, flat-chested girl snoring loudly on her pallet inside that rat-infested house not twenty good steps away from me.

"If you will excuse me, I have to go and shake the hand of a dear friend of mine," Samson announced to the men, who roared too loudly with amusement and pointed Samson to the latrine.

I hurt all the way into my bones, a deadening exhaustion overtaking me. Syvah had been complaining of weariness too, but mothers with young boys are always tired. They grow tired just watching their sons. My exhaustion came not from my body but from my heart. Fear wears a woman out.

I gave up fighting sleep, at last. Manoah led me back to our lodging. Samson had chosen his path, and the time had come for me to return to mine. I was his mother, not his conscience. Manoah had been at my side since I was a child; he would be there when I died. It was time for me to focus on him once more.

As I hid on the roof, my wedding feast took shape below.

I had no appetite.

Samson's mother requested that my mother give her the names of anyone we wished to invite. Mother was not anxious to celebrate her downfall, so she insisted that the only guests be Sirena and the other families we shared the oven with.

The tables boomed like thunder as the men rammed them together. I jumped from the shock of the sound. Samson had briefly retreated to his lodging house for a bath while his mother and father stayed behind and saw to all the details. I stole a glimpse as she crumpled her nose at my villagers. She avoided touching them too, but I saw a glimmer of hope in that: She might not slap or hit me once I was her daughter-in-law. Samson returned quickly, surprising me. For a people concerned with cleanliness, he did not take much time at his bath.

Nausea rolled up in my stomach, and I shut my mouth, trying to stop from heaving. The thought of his seed in me, his child growing large and violent within me, finally tearing itself free, made the sky spin around me hard and fast.

Why had Mother not stopped this marriage? What if I died when he took me? What if I tore, and he did not stop? What if I cried and he laughed, or I suffocated in all that hair? I did not want to become a wife, especially not his. I did not want to do those things that wives did. I did not want to be disrobed and touched and forced back on a pallet while men snickered at the feast below.

I couldn't stop myself this time. I rolled over and vomited into a crock. Mother would probably have to break it and throw it out when I left.

The hired men set a bonfire at the far edge of the courtyard, partly for warmth, I guessed, and partly to keep the lions away. In the lean harvest years, lions were as hungry as we were. Fewer grains and grapes on the ground meant fewer rabbits, fewer small sweet things scavenging for their supper, and lions that came looking for us.

I could always walk past the fire into the night, my arms extended before me, making soft weak clutching sounds. I could be eaten by a lion. Better to be dragged away to my death by a lion, who would kill me within an hour, than to be dragged away by Samson. There was no humiliation in being eaten by a lion. I would not die a thousand deaths before I flew away to the underworld.

I was considering this death when the steady fall of heavy footsteps startled me. Talos and Neo had come, and they were not alone! With them was a group of Philistines; some were men from the village young enough to wield a sword, but not old enough to consider staying it. I gasped, and Talos looked up, by magic, smiling broadly at me. I went down to welcome them without a smile. Samson's mother would think I had done this to her.

But these men had come uninvited, wearing knives at their sides and swords in their hands. Their hair was slicked back, and the red feather headdress of war sat on their heads. Red stripes had been painted under their eyes, and each had braided their beards into two rows, tied off with a bead. They had come to the feast prepared to die or defend me. I did not know which. Perhaps it was not really for my sake, either.

They still counted me as a Philistine, even in my shame! Samson parted the men and walked right through the middle of the pack, which was at least thirty men as I made a fast count.

Samson's father was already asleep at a table, his head face down. The journey had been hard for the old man. His mother had her arms crossed, sitting beside her husband. She turned and spat on the ground, pronouncing a curse on my people.

I slunk back a little, unwilling to hear her words.

"What is this?" Samson's voice was soft, disinterested.

Talos took a step forward. "We've come for the feast."

"With your swords and knives? Really." Samson twisted and looked up at me.

A smirk played on his full mouth, underneath those thick long whiskers. The scratchy cheeks that would soon be under my palm, and the lips that would be on top of mine. What would his mouth feel like?

Sweat beaded along my brow. I was two people at once, one filled with dread and terror, the other curious. I was a Philistine, though. I was born for the pleasures of the flesh. I was dying right here, leaving behind the girl I was forever, becoming a true Philistine, a goddess of pleasure. But I didn't know it would all be for a Hebrew's touch.

If I ever felt desire for Samson, I would have to carry that secret to my grave. Whatever he wanted, I would resist becoming. I would remain a Philistine in my heart, always.

But what was done, was done. The bitter reality shook me once more. What good were any of my secret pledges, my refusal to see my destiny? Just because I didn't look at the horizon didn't mean the sun would refuse to set.

The men were drinking and laughing. Astra and I hung back in the shadows, refilling wine bowls when summoned, lugging heavy crocks of beer to the table when we spied men frowning at their bowls.

My arms ached, and my stomach growled again, louder, filled with rancor at the closeness of food and my inability to eat any of it. I was terrified to eat in front of Samson. The act would reveal too much of myself. He would know that I was hungry. He would watch me choose what suited my tastes, and then watch my fingers pick the food up and carry it to my lips. He would know what I did with it, chewing, tasting, swallowing, wanting more.

His mother, who had grown no younger by the firelight, approached me in the shadows where I stood.

"Come here, girl," she said.

Astra's hand grabbed mine, and she pulled me further back into the shadows under our roof.

Samson's mother stood there, one arm extended. She shot a horrid look at my mother, who was standing behind my father at the far end of the feasting tables. Mother pointed a finger into the shadows where we stood and then moved her finger toward Samson's mother.

It had already begun. I was becoming the property of this old woman.

I pried Astra's fingers off my hand and stepped into the fire's light.

"Closer, please," she said.

I crept toward her, uncertain of my fate.

She rolled her eyes and walked to me, finishing off the distance between us. Grabbing me by the arms, she spun me around and dug her fingers into my spine, testing it up and down, then digging those same bony of fingers into the space between each rib. I could hear her huffing in disgust.

"You've lost weight. You needed to flush out."

My blank stare infuriated her. Her nostrils flared. "Flushed. Made fat. Like our breeding goats."

I stopped breathing completely from the indignation, my breath frozen right in my chest. This woman wanted me fattened up, just like we fattened our goats before breeding. We checked the goats for the amount of fat between their ribs and along their backs. I was not a woman at all to Samson's mother, not even a girl! I was a goat. I was livestock for breeding her little Hebrew half-beasts.

The men's laughter died down as they watched us. Aware of all those glittering eyes on me, the darkness of the night, and the snapping of the fire, we all grew silent.

I moved back into the shadows and settled into Astra's arms. I didn't want to do those things that are done in the night, not with her son, and I didn't want to breed his strange children. Breath flowed again into my lungs, cold night air, and I burst into sobs. Astra held me tightly.

Heat burst through my tunic from a huge hand resting on my shoulder.

"Why are you crying?"

I did not move. Astra turned me to face him. Samson stood before us. I felt like a child standing in his shadow, with my tear-stained face and running nose. One of his thighs was bigger than both of mine put together. And he had a strange gift, a magic that stole over me, making me feel safe and terrified all at once. He made my stomach forget its food and wince from sharp new pains, pains of a hunger that was strange to me.

"Do you want to tell me?"

I realized I had not spoken. I opened my mouth but could not make any sounds. I shook my head and looked away from him, at the ground. He reached for my hand and brought it to his lips. His lips grazed my hand, the gesture of a kind man, and my legs almost went out from under me from the shooting pains that attacked my thighs when he touched me. His lips were soft, softer than anything I had ever felt, and warm, and his whiskers scratched the skin where they touched me. Goose bumps rose all over my arms.

He did not release my hand. Instead, he led me to the feasting table and made room for me. He poured a bowl of wine and handed it to me.

Under the flickering light of a torch, I saw Samson's mother smiling at me as I accepted the wine. She nodded in approval, and I understood. This was what she expected of me as his wife, although I did not understand the significance. Maybe wine brought fertility. I would ask my own mother tomorrow.

Little fool that I was, I smiled back at her, grateful to have perhaps earned her approval. I drank the wine and grew warm, letting the weight of so many emotions overtake me. I was unable to think, unable to act. I leaned against Samson and drank another bowl and waited for him to take me.

Samson did not lie with me on that first night of the feast. I was drunk for the first time in my life, so that much of what I remembered about the rest of the feast was told to me by Astra. I do remember the men dancing with women from the village, women who had crept near the bonfire, hoping for a bite of free food. I remember the moon, huge and white, lighting the whole night sky, like a bridal gift from Dagon.

I remember Samson's warm skin, his arms like iron that slipped under my knees and around my back, lifting me when I began to doze off at the table. I rested my head against his chest like a child and heard his heart. It sounded like my own. That was a revelation to me, under that bright round moon. His tunic flapped open at the neck, revealing his tanned, taut skin and a few dark hairs from his chest.

I abandoned myself to him, rubbing my cheek against his flesh, letting myself be carried to our bridal bed. My mind told me to give in to him, to know why the women giggle at the bread oven when they speak of their men. Let it happen. You are too drunk to fight him off anyway.

Samson carried me into the house and to my pallet, ignoring the lewd comments from the men. He sat down next to me, leaning over me as he smoothed back my hair. He asked if I needed a blanket to keep warm or anything to settle my stomach. He had not seen me eat all night. Surely I needed something? Astra said I rolled to the side and curled up like a disappointed child, saying nothing. He laughed and found the blanket at the foot of the pallet, laying it over me. He sat there with me, she said, for a long while, just watching me sleep. He smiled as he did. He did not leer, she promised, or laugh, but smiled, like a man bewitched.

"I think he will be a gentle husband," she added, as she dipped the linen in the crock of water and washed my forehead. I was still on the pallet, feverish and ill after too much wine last night.

"Where are Mother and Father?" I tried to sit up, but the weight of the room pushed me back down. The walls were moving in on me. My pallet was rolling side to side, too, I could feel it.

"Cleaning up. The men will return this afternoon at dusk. The second night."

"Five more to go," I whispered.

Astra slipped the linen cloth into the crock and lay down beside me, resting one arm around me. I closed my eyes, praying for relief.

"Five more to go," she whispered back.

MOTHER

"Your wedding clothes," I said, pointing to the pile on the floor.

He pulled off his tunic, tossing it onto his bed. He rummaged in the pile, finding the tunic, dyed blue and soft as a morning cloud. It suited him well. Next he pulled out the fringed wrap, and I turned my back to give him privacy. It was meant to wrap around his waist, under the tunic, and hang down to his knees.

"Done."

The last piece of his wedding clothes was a woven shawl with a serpent across the shoulder, the symbol of our tribe. I draped the center of the shawl over his left shoulder so that the image of the serpent hung down onto his chest, then pulled the ends across his body, knotting them together over his right hip.

"Be gentle with her. She is young. And undress in the dark, or you'll never get her into bed the first time."

Samson groaned.

"What? I cannot tell my own son how to behave on his first night with his wife?" I said.

Manoah came in just then. He glared at Samson. "Did you tell her?"

"What did you do now?" I asked.

Manoah stepped between us. “He bet the wedding guests that they could not solve his riddle. He bet them thirty sets of clothes.”

Samson rolled his eyes. “It’s an easy riddle. The Philistines have the answers painted on their pottery. They’re even drinking out of bowls with the answers painted on them.”

Samson had bet a fortune, our fortune, on a riddle, to amuse himself. My head was throbbing, and dark specks floated in my vision. Manoah rested his hands on my shoulders, whispering that I should remember to breathe.

But this one riddle would change everything.

"Do you know what this would cost me?" Talos was yelling at my father. I heard their voices through the walls of our home. Astra was sleeping peacefully next to me, so I slid myself off the pallet trying not to disturb her. Her arm, which had been around me, shifted back and forth around the pallet. Even in her sleep, she knew when I was gone.

I tucked the blanket into the crook of her arm. She pulled it close and sighed.

My sandals were near the door, but I did not pause to put them on. Cracking the door open, I leaned my head out to listen. The sun was setting. My stomach lurched as I thought of last night and what must surely happen tonight.

"My family will kill me if I lose that much money!"

"Then shut your mouth and solve the riddle. Did I force you to accept the bet?"

"Is this your idea of a dowry? Sending Amara away with wealth from all our families?"

My father shoved Talos down to the ground. I ran out to stop him from kicking him, too.

"Stop! What are you arguing about?"

Talos stood up and spit at my feet. He walked off without looking at me.

"What happened?"

Father glanced at me and sighed. "Last night, your Danite made a bet with our men. If he wins, they have to provide him with thirty sets of clothes. Your friends accepted before hearing the riddle."

"My friends? You blame me?"

"They think we set them up to get money out of them."

"I didn't invite them." I looked from my father to Talos, accusing. Neither cared, nor met my eyes. Talos was done with me.

"A set of clothes can mean a month without food. And they are our guests! Wish us luck ever getting work again in harvest time or selling any more rugs. What did you say to him?"

"Nothing! This is not my work!"

Mother returned, carrying fresh water in a crock. I hoped she had warmed it, if it was meant for me.

"What is all this noise?"

Father made a fist and slammed it into the frame of our door, near my head. I screamed and ducked out of the way. I stumbled as I did. My legs were not solid yet.

He gestured at me.

"The riddle Samson posed last night? The bet? Every family in the village is furious with us."

"That's Samson's doing, not ours. Not hers." Mother took a step toward me, out of instinct, I was sure. She knew what it was like to be given away.

"If you don't want to see your family ruined, then get your groom to cancel the bet. He can tell all the riddles he wants, but he can't extract money from our villagers. He knew you had no dowry before he accepted you," Father said.

"No dowry at all?" I did not hear right. My ears were not working after my first drunken night. No girl ever married without a dowry. Even the poorest man saved something to send away with her. What man would take a bride who had nothing to offer?

❦

I sat, naked, my back to the door, as Mother washed me. The water was freezing, and I shivered, an involuntary protest, but she insisted it was a good remedy for my ills after last night.

"The only remedy we can afford, you mean," I corrected her. I sounded cross.

Astra brought in a small basket of herbs to weave into my hair. She sat it down next to us as Mother laid her hand on my shoulder.

"Never mind your father. He is ashamed. This bet makes it worse for him."

I was glad I did not have to look at her.

"What kind of man takes a bride with no dowry? Why did Samson choose me?"

She dipped the sponge back into the crock. I winced as I heard her wring it out, bracing myself for another cold shock against my skin.

"My greatest regret, daughter, is that I will lose you to a Hebrew. I do not know why Samson insisted upon you, or why your father allowed it."

"I love her."

Samson's voice boomed through our tiny home, making us all gasp. Mother jumped up as Astra hid behind her. I was naked, with nothing to grab for cover. I held my hands over my nakedness and did not turn around.

"I chose her because I love her."

"But you just saw me once, on the roof." I was emboldened by my mother and sister, and by my modesty in avoiding his eyes. Would that I could cover my back and buttocks. I hoped he wasn't looking at them. I knew he must be, though; they burned with embarrassment.

"I saw you once, on the roof, yes. Any man that needs a second look at you to decide his intentions is no man at all. I look forward to our second night together."

I heard the door sweep across the floor and close. Mother and Astra stood frozen, but when they met my eyes, my blush of embarrassment was so quick that they laughed at me. They laughed despite the new little tears that sneaked out of my eyes, the small, mean tears of surprise and embarrassment.

I was not going to drink tonight. I had to be alert, to speak to Samson if I could, and ask him to cancel the bet. I would persuade him to wait one more night to touch me.

Besides, I wanted to hear the riddle.

Samson's cheek brushed against mine as he bent down to speak in my ear. Goose bumps rose along my arms as his hair fell forward, touching my arms and bodice.

"Are you ready?"

My stomach twinged with these strange sharp pains that were not from wine or bad food, but strange hot pinching pains that shot down my thighs whenever he touched me or his gaze lingered too long. Would all of married life be such agony? I did not think I could take another hour of shivering at his touch, and certainly not a lifetime.

It was wrong, I knew, to feel these things about a Hebrew, but there was no Philistine man or boy that was anything like him. Samson was a new race of man.

"Did you hear me?" he asked. "Why do you seem far away?"

I shook myself, biting my cheek. If he knew my thoughts, I would die of shame.

He continued. "Out of the eater, you'll find something to eat. Out of the strong one, you'll get something sweet."

I shoved him away. It sounded lewd. I didn't want to reveal my utter ignorance, but neither would I be made a fool.

He leaned back and roared with laughter. Everyone watched us. That was not a new feeling. Everyone had watched us all night, looking, no doubt, for hints of my complicity with Samson's bet, as if I was plotting with my groom to rob them all.

"Samson. That riddle cannot be solved. It's not fair. You should call off the bet."

"The answer is nearer than you know. Besides, the men accepted my terms before they heard the riddle. Was that wise?"

I floundered, keeping my eyes on my plate lest I start a fight among them all.

"No," I admitted at last.

"Let them suffer."

"But they are angry with me."

"You are my wife. Not theirs."

Our whispers did not carry, though the men strained to listen. I was grateful for the musicians who had come tonight. The music made everyone's heart lighter. A lyre player and harpist sat together, while the lute player circulated among the guests, enticing us with his melodies, begging among us for a dancer.

Samson stood, the wide, white moon behind him, lighting him around the edges like a god. He extended a hand to me, and I stood too, his huge frame casting a shadow over me. I spared only one glance at anyone else, and it was at his mother, to read her face. Her eyes narrowed as she lifted her bowl of beer and gulped it down. Odd that she drank beer and not wine, but I would learn much more about her people in days to come, I knew.

Samson led me away from the tables, closer to the fire. The lute player followed, and men who could find partners joined us. Talos sulked away alone, but I could not think of him. I could only think of this man Samson holding my right hand, standing so close I could feel his breath on my neck. He spun me in a slow arc, then pulled me back in, closer this time, so that the fabric of our tunics touched. I sucked in my stomach, a feeling like fear shooting through it, unwilling for him to touch my body, even through my tunic, afraid to touch his. The buzzing in my head was relentless, drowning out all thought and reason. There was only his breath on the soft, bare skin of my neck and the warm, soft flesh of his palm pressed into mine.

I couldn't breathe. He lowered his face to mine, and without thinking, without meaning to offer myself, I lifted my mouth to his. I closed my eyes and shivered. His lips grazed my forehead—my forehead!—and not my mouth, and he held me a moment more.

The lute player had changed songs. Samson was leading me to my home. Panic stabbed through my stomach as I bit my lips to keep from crying. I heard bowls being raised in a lewd toast.

Where was Astra? Or Mother? I tried to steal glances back over my shoulder, but I was too embarrassed for any of the men to catch my eye. I saw Samson's father instead, who was watching us with a kind expression. Old as the dirt we stood on, with sparse white hair and hanging white brows, he nodded at me and raised his bowl.

I wanted to die. I was going to die, before Samson even had a chance to undress me. I could not breathe when he touched me, not even when I was in my tunic.

He released my hand at my door. "Good night, wife."

"Uh." That's all I could say. I had thought he would take me tonight. I had been drunk, I understood, he had been kind, but he was surely going to take me tonight. Why was he not going to take me tonight?

That same cursed smile played on his lips. "You were expecting something else?"

He leaned his right arm over me, leaning against the doorframe of the house, imprisoning me under his huge, overfed frame.

"My wife is disappointed with me? So soon?" Samson asked.

"Don't." It was a warning.

He loved it. He laughed like I was the wittiest girl he had ever known, a rare gem.

"I was joking. I only brought you home so you could change."

"Change?"

"I want to take you somewhere. Change. We will take my donkeys. Unless you prefer me to carry you."

I flung the door to the house open to escape the horror of such a thing. He probably would do that, too. However, I had nothing to change into, and we had never owned donkeys, so I didn't know why I had to change my tunic to ride.

The length. Probably the length of my tunic was too long. I rummaged through Mother's basket and found her best sash. Wrestling my own off, I wrapped hers around my waist twice, tying it in back. A splash of cold water on my face and a finger scrubbed across my teeth were the only other grooming tricks I knew.

I opened the door, and he was waiting.

❧

The donkey plodded up the road into the hills with steady good humor, despite the huffs from nearby lions and the screams of the badgers.

"Your donkey is a good one," I said, ending the quiet truce we had kept since leaving the feast last hour.

"He is not my donkey."

I turned, finally having the nerve to look at him.

He had been studying me during the whole ride and smiled to see me finally look back. "He's yours. For the return journey."

"He's sweet." I didn't know how to judge a good donkey, but I had to say something. I couldn't believe I was alone with Samson in the valley under a full moon, and all I could talk about was donkeys.

If he had any wisdom about choosing wives, he'd swat the donkey and send us both fleeing into the hills, away from him.

"Where are we going then?"

He smiled. "Away for a few hours."

My stomach was knotting up. I had to relieve myself terribly badly. The more I thought about it, the worse it got. Sweat broke out all over my face and chest. How did wives say these things to their men? Or was I to always keep these things a secret, an honorable silence? I did not know.

"Listen." Samson stopped the donkey, stroking his muzzle. The donkey turned his head and pressed into Samson's stomach for more attention. "We're near the stream of Sorek."

In winter, the stream was full and wild, with daisies blooming at the edges and ktalav trees nearby.

"Do you need to stop?" Samson asked.

I didn't know if I should lie. "If you do."

He laughed, which I did not understand, but he found much amusement in things I said or did. He pointed to his right. "The river is just beyond these trees. Do you want to go first?"

I nodded, slipping off the donkey and walking away. Insects shrieked and sang all around me, and birds called to one another in the trees above my head. I did hear the river now, and as I parted the last clasping pair of evergreen branches, I saw it.

I had a clear view up and down the banks. No matter where I attended to myself, he could see me if he peeked. Just across the banks, rising above me, was a cave set into the gentle hill. It didn't look like a bad climb. I lifted my tunic and plunged into the freezing cold water, slipping on the stones at the bottom, pushing against the currents to get across. I climbed out and up the slope, and picked my way up to the cave.

From this perch, I could see the faraway lights of my village. The bonfire must have been one of the little burning yellow lights I saw twinkling back at me. I had never seen my village from this distance. It looked so small. Or was it me? Had I grown so much bigger?

Samson whistled for me. I whistled back, to confirm I did not need his assistance.

Lifting my tunic again, I ducked inside the cave for certain relief. The mouth of the cave was several feet above my head; it was a small cave, which was a good sign. Large caves were used by the wealthier farmers for storing grain. The caves were close to the fields, dry, and cool. But a small cave like this would be of no use to them.

I let my eyes adjust to the darkness, then carefully placed one foot in front of the other, sliding my sandal side to side to be sure of my footing. Moving this way, I slid away from the mouth of the cave into the darkness. I chose a suitable spot and was standing back up, finished, when I heard a rustling noise near me. And another, followed by a tight little hiss. Something touched my hair, lifting a section up before dropping it. I saw the light at the mouth of the cave as if it were a thousand leagues away, and my legs would not move.

A rush of hisses and chirps swept past me, my hair flying in all directions. I screamed and ran for the mouth of the cave, my tunic still tucked in my sash.

I stumbled out of the mouth of the cave with Samson watching below as the horde of bats swept over me and into the night. Breathless, I clung to the edge of the cave.

He didn't laugh. "Are you all right?"

I stared at him, waiting for the rebuke of laughter. He just watched me.

"Yes." A smile twitched at my mouth. I saw the same smile working at his lips, too. I giggled and hid my face with my hands.

"Come down."

Though the night chill was creeping in and goose bumps rose up along my arms, I did not feel cold. I felt … like a child. But this was not a childhood I had ever had, of adventure and freedom at night. I had never been allowed to roam at night, for fear of wild animals.

Now here I was with the wildest one of all. I giggled at the thought as I took his hand at the bottom of the slope, happy to have one last secret.

Once back on the donkey, he led us to a spot nearby, under a ktalav tree with soft moss all around. I slid off the donkey while he spread a blanket and motioned for me to sit.

I was going to be sick. I did not know what to do, or what he wanted. Or what he wanted me to do. Or what to say. When I did not move, he brushed the hair away from my forehead and led me to the blanket, sitting with me. He no longer had the amused twist to his mouth. His mood had changed. He was quiet; his face I could not read. He was impassive. Or content. In time, I hoped I would learn the difference.

Samson pointed to the dark canopy above us, radiant with shimmering white stars.

"Do you know her name?"

"No," I admitted. His thigh was touching mine as we sat side by side.

"The Greeks call her Venus, the goddess of love. Canaanites call her the Queen of Heaven."

"What do you call her?"

"The Evening Star. Sometimes she shows herself at dawn too, and then we call her the Morning Star. Now, look to the right, lower."

He pointed to a long sweep of stars. "The Archer." His finger moved straight in front of us. "And there, the horizon kisses the sky." He drew his finger back and pressed it against my lips.

I turned away. His fingers rested against my cheek, and he gently turned my face back to his.

"Are you afraid of me?"

I could not answer. I was afraid of being touched. I was afraid of not knowing what I must do. I was afraid that his skin on mine, our bared bellies touching and sliding over one another, would kill me. I wouldn't be able to breathe from the pains of desire that would overwhelm me.

"Do you know why I brought you here?"

I shook my head.

His hand touched the knot in my sash. One finger played over it as he studied me.

"All the men that attended the feast …"

"I did not invite them."

"They are lewd. Making coarse jokes."

I let a little more of my weight lean against him, trying to thank him without embarrassing myself through words.

"The only sound I want you to hear tonight is the sound of my voice."

He brought his hand up to my lips, brushing a finger across them. I gave his hand a furtive, small kiss. It was bold of me. I thought I should do something.

"I do not know what you must feel," he said, bringing both hands to my sash, grasping the loose end and pulling. I felt the tug as the sash slid along my back.

He removed my sash and tossed it into the darkness beyond us before reaching for the bottom of my tunic. My hand shot down and caught his, my heart plunging into my stomach.

"I am afraid of being naked in front of you."

He showed me that amused curl of his mouth.

"You won't be in front of me. You'll be under me."

⁂

We returned at dawn, a fiery sun rising at our backs, pink rays streaking overhead. The horizon was deep purple, the color of fortune. I would not smile at this thought—that would not be modest—but I had found mine. It did not matter that fortune was tinged with scandal. I had thought I must force myself to accept this disastrous turn of fate, but I was wrong. I didn't have to force myself to do anything. Samson was a good lord, a gentle lover who was patient and tender and whose bare stomach pressed against mine made my mind swim so fast I feared I would die.

"Wait!" I said, turning in the saddle to look at Samson. "If I am your wife, must I worship your god?"

Samson nodded. "My mother will insist."

"If I worship him, will I have to cut something off?" Even now, after hours of intimacies, I could not bear to place a name on any immodest body parts. I hoped it would be enough that I knew where they were.

Samson frowned, lost. "Cut something off?"

"Never mind."

If it came to pass, I would worry about it then. Not today. Not when I could see Astra waving from our rooftop, spying my arrival. I lifted a hand in return, then lowered it to lightly touch my cheek. My face was chafed, rubbed raw from so many kisses with my hairy groom.

"Will you be all right?"

I dropped my hand and looked at him, not understanding the question.

"In four days, you will leave your home. And Astra. Forever."

I stroked the neck of the donkey as he plodded along. I had no tears. My body hurt from so much emotion and so much love. I knew the heartbreak would be fierce, and that it would come no matter how I tried to hold onto my happiness here. Perhaps we should leave, I thought. Right now. Perhaps trying so hard to love Astra and tend to her as much as I could right now, to soak in our final moments together with my mother, perhaps that was stupid of me.

Samson's hand rested on my lower back, a soft reply of its own. "If I could give you my strength, just for that day, I would."

"Why me?" I don't even know why I asked that question, at that moment.

Samson did not react. He just studied the horizon, keeping his pace.

"Why not a Hebrew girl?" I was getting bolder with him. He had known my body; why could I not know his thoughts?

"Tell me about Dagon."

Had he not heard my questions? Why did he ask me this?

"He is the god of the fields, of the harvest."

"Have you ever talked with him?"

I giggled. What god would talk to a girl?

Samson stopped and stared at me, hard and cruel. "Dagon is a block of wood, a worthless piece of sculpture. He does not care about your fields, or your harvest, and he will never care about you."

My mouth fell open as I started to take fast gulps of air. I was going to bawl like a child.

"The truth makes more enemies than friends. So, before you ask me the truth again, be very sure you really want it. I don't want to talk about Hebrews and Philistines."

We continued the rest of the journey in silence. I swallowed back my tears and all my other questions.

A few moments later I slid off the donkey, with Samson holding one of my hands for support, and hugged Astra. She had come bounding out of the house, anxious to have a word with me. We embraced and over her shoulder I saw the bonfire, almost dead by now, a huge black pit that smoldered and smoked in the heavy dawn air. Talos sat, his feet in the ashes for warmth, watching us. A big man, maybe from Gath, still sat at the table, picking at a greasy bone, ignoring us. A few other men from our village lingered near the houses, deep in conversation. With winter here, and nothing to harvest but a few winter figs, men often had such long negotiations and discussions.

I sighed in contentment and released Astra.

"I thought you had left!" she scolded me.

"No." Neither of us said what we both thought. I would leave. If not last night, then soon. Sometimes Hebrew men let their wives stay with their parents, but only until they were pregnant. Then the wife came home with the husband. I did not judge Samson to be a patient man, though.

"Wife."

I stepped aside from Astra to face my lord.

He kissed me, on the forehead, and took his leave.

Astra stared at me, wide-eyed with the scandal. I had done it. I had slept with the Hebrew. I was his wife forever now. My hand went to my belly, a strange new reflex. I would bear children from this man.

Samson walked away, leading the donkey with him. A patch of greenery surrounded the houses, just on the other side of the road. Samson slapped the donkey's haunches, pointing him toward his breakfast, before Samson took the road leading to his lodging.

As soon as Samson disappeared from view, Talos stood. The big man from Gath threw down his bone and stood too, wiping his greasy fingers on his tunic. The men stopped their conversation and walked toward me, as one.

The big man spoke first. "So."

I shrugged. I did not know how else to reply.

Talos watched the older men. I could not read his face. He had changed so much since we were children. His once-full cheeks had leaned out, and his beard was coming in. His eyes had changed more than any other feature. Where once there had been softness, there was a fire now, an anger I did not understand. He held up one hand and addressed me.

"Do you know the answer?"

"Answer to what?"

He pulled back his hand as if to slap me. Astra yelped and grabbed me, pulling me back.

The big man from Gath took one slamming step toward me. His footfall made the earth shake. I felt it in my knees.

"What is the answer to your groom's riddle?"

"I don't know." Panic was rising in my stomach. I clutched Astra's hand, whispering out of the side of my mouth. "Get Father."

"Your father won't be coming outside today," the big man said.

My heart froze in a tight pinch.

He took another step toward me. "I will make you the same offer I made him. Either tell us the answer to the riddle, or die. I myself will kill your family, one by one, even as you watch. I will stack the bodies in your home and throw yours on top, and then I will destroy your house through fire."

I stumbled back. My feet landed on top of Astra's feet, knocking her down, and I fell on top of her as the men laughed. We scrambled toward our door, tripping on our tunics as we jerked up, trying to get away quickly. Not a man moved to help us. We ran for our door, not looking back.

Once inside, my eyes adjusted to the darkness, and by the light of our oil lamp, I saw Mother and Father sitting at our table, hands folded, faces down. They knew. They knew what those men were going to do. They weren't getting up either, or stirring to comfort us. A bleak distress settled in the air, tainting it with a soiled, sour smell.

"Mother? Father?"

They did not move. Mother pressed the back of one hand to her mouth.

My legs moved with great effort, invisible shackles weighting them down. I walked to my pallet and lay down with my face toward the wall. Over the hours that passed, my mind, frantic with fear, settled on three outcomes. I could flee tonight with my groom, never to return. Perhaps if Samson did not collect on the bet, my family would be safe. Or I could stay and let the men suffer the punishment for their rash stupidity, which would mean certain death for my family, but not for me. Finally, I could flee with Samson as soon as they paid the debt, and we would have even greater wealth thanks to his shrewd tale.

The only outcome I could imagine that did not lead to my family's death was Samson losing the bet or forsaking his claim to it. And perhaps this was a test sent by the gods, not just for the men of my village, but for Samson himself. I would know the man I married by the decision he made. Which did he value more: my happiness or their money?

I sat up on my pallet. Astra was asleep next to me, clinging to a blanket for comfort. Mother and Father were gone, perhaps off to seek counsel or mercy.

I would know soon who Samson truly was and what he most wanted.

I set to work brushing out my hair. I had to give him every reason to desire me more than money.

That night at the feast, I watched as crooked yellow teeth flashed in the mouths of the Philistines while they ate our food. Thick calloused knuckles scratched those flea-infested heads as they tried in vain to solve the riddle. I watched their faces turn hard and angry, their chewing turn to tearing, their hands clasp and unfurl, wishing for a dagger.

Amara appeared at my elbow, whispering in my ear. "Mother, would you walk with me?"

I agreed with reluctance.

"You have heard Samson's riddle?" She roped her arm through mine as we walked past the houses.

"Yes."

"The men from my village are very angry."

"If the men from your village are anything but complete idiots, they'll solve the riddle soon enough. The answer is plain."

"But if they don't …"

"Amara, if you want to be a good wife, you must do as I do. Stay out of the affairs of men."

"It's very hard."

I patted her hand. "You have no idea."

AMARA

Samson stood. I followed a few steps, at a discreet distance, until out of earshot, then grabbed him by the arm.

"Amara. Stop."

"Why won't you tell me? Do I not please you?"

"Amara, I'm going to relieve myself. Either let go, or come watch."

I dropped my hand, outraged. Had I not made myself irresistible tonight? Had I not served him without complaint, attended to his every need with plain adoration and subservience?

"I am only asking for the answer to a riddle."

Samson walked off several more paces behind the houses on the left, to the trench where men relieved themselves. His back to me, he answered.

"I haven't even told my father and mother."

"I am not your mother. I am your wife."

Samson turned back to me, adjusting the sash at his waist. My face was hot with anger and embarrassment. I had never stood behind a man as he did that. I prayed I would never have to again. My donkey made a quieter stream and did not sigh with ease as he did.

"And as your husband, I command you to stop pestering me."

I bit my lip to keep from shaming myself further, even though tears streamed down my face, cold in the night air. Samson strode past me, stopping a few paces away to offer his arm.

"Coming?"

I narrowed my eyes and made the angriest face I could. Did he not see my tears? Did he not understand what he had done to me, to my family? How could a man be so utterly blind and insensitive?

"My God wanted me to marry you."

"What?" I was confused.

"You asked me last night why I married you. I will answer that riddle. I married you because I am in love with you. God struck me with love for you the first time I saw you."

With that, he was gone. Back to eating and drinking and swapping lewd tales, slapping his thigh to the music. I hung back in the shadows, and when the fire began to ebb and he stood to look for me, I lifted my tunic with a huff and walked inside my home.

Nothing made sense. But I made one decision in the chaos of the evening: If he did not give me what I wanted, then I would not give him what he wanted. This was marriage, was it not?

A full three days passed in this same manner. Samson refused to tell me the answer to the riddle. I refused to stop asking. I tried tears. I tried teasing with my body, trying to hint at pleasures as I leaned over him, pouring his wine. If I dared follow him past the bonfire to have a word in quiet, he grabbed me and pressed his mouth to mine before I had a chance to say anything at all.

The men saw that. I knew by their lewd shouts. How could they not understand I was trying to help them? I was trying to get the answer. They had accepted the bet, not me. Why was I threatened if I did not save them? And why did Samson insist that I must not have the answer?

The seventh day arrived. My eyes were swollen and my vision blurred. My whole body felt used and raw, exhausted from anxiety and shame and lack of sleep. Tonight the men would admit they could not solve the riddle, and they would be indebted to Samson. One set of clothes per guest. No small fortune in a lean harvest year.

I washed my face in the cold water sitting in the crock near my pallet. Wiping my eyes dry with my hands, I had to force myself to decide the answer to my own riddle.

Would I choose to live and flee with Samson? I would not hear my family die. I could pretend it did not happen. Samson's family was wealthy, and thirty more sets of clothes would make us the wealthiest family I had ever known. I could be rich. No more work in the fields, with bleeding fingers and tired, aching feet.

I had to choose.

The door swept open, and in walked that ogre, Samson's mother. She did not look surprised to find me alone. Saying nothing, she came and stood over my pallet, her arms crossed.

"You are unhappy with my son?"

I looked down at my lap.

"I see that you are not packed for the return journey. Do you intend to honor the marriage?"

"Why did you force him to marry me?"

The words flew from my mouth without restraint. I could not believe I was raising my voice to his mother.

She tilted her head. "I forced him?"

"He said he loved me. That cannot be true! And now he is going to rob my villagers by this riddle!"

"I would never have wanted Samson to marry you."

Her voice was sharp and cruel.

"We are both prisoners, then. Help me. Please. Get Samson to tell me the answer. I will serve you like a slave all of my days."

"Why is this riddle so important to you?"

"If I do not tell the men the answer, they're going to kill me and my family and set us on fire and burn down our house! We'll never even enter the afterlife!"

She threw her arms up in the air in disgust, rolling her eyes in exasperation. "I told Samson you were a horrible choice. Not only are you a Philistine, you're still a child."

She walked to the door, and I heard her muttering about the foolish imagination of girls. With one hand on the door to pull it open, she turned back to me.

"When you are in my home, I will see to it that you have plenty of work. Tired girls do not have energy to invent wild stories."

"It's not—"

"Do not talk back to me!" she screamed. "I will have respect!"

"What you said about Dagon? I believe it. I believe what you said."

Samson was at the fire's edge as we waited for the feasting hour to arrive. He looked at me, frowning. His eyes were watery. But how could it be that those words could make him cry? I was just trying to make peace between us. He had not taken me into the hills since the second night, nor had he tried to get me alone for any reason. It was possible he could take the money and leave me here forever.

"If I reveal the answer to my riddle, you must make me one promise."

"Anything!" I stepped closer and took him by the arm. How had I broken his resolve?

"Do not tell my mother. Ever."

"Do not tell her you gave me the answer?"

"No. Do not give her the answer. Ever. She must never know the answer."

I wanted to take the answer like a stick from the fire and twist it in her side for all the grief she had given me. I was not the only one with a wild imagination, if Samson was afraid of what she might do. All over a riddle, no less.

"I promise."

Samson wrapped his arms around my back and drew me in, in plain sight of the men arriving.

"Promises are sealed with a kiss." He bent down and sealed my promise. I relaxed into his arms, without meaning to, my body grateful for his touch again. I had held out for days, resisting the furtive, dark pains that made my thighs tremble when he was near. I had been strong. And now I had won, though I did not know how.

I let myself fall into his arms, letting his mouth sweep over mine, his breath hot and wet against my cold cheeks.

I do not know how long he kissed me, only that I was grieved that he stopped.

"Do you remember when your father first invited me to dinner? On that day, I was walking on the road to your village when a young lion came roaring out of the trees. But that is the wrong place to start."

"There was a lion? And it was going to attack you?"

He sighed, looking out at the horizon. "I am not like other men."

I wanted so badly to laugh at him, with those heavy dreadlocks hanging to the ground, his body twice the size of anyone else's. He was so very unlike other men. Did he think I had not noticed?

"No, you are not."

"My mother was alone in a field many years ago when a messenger of my God appeared to her. He foretold my birth."

"You are a god? Is this what you're trying to tell me?" I had heard of such things. It made sense, given his size and appearance. What would our children look like? I hoped our daughters were not big like him.

"I am no god. My God comes upon me, and I am helpless to stop Him. His might overwhelms me suddenly, like a raging fever. I do things other men cannot do, cannot dream of doing."

"You are blessed then."

"No. Strength is not a blessing." Samson was lost in thoughts I did not understand.

I wanted him to return to me. "What of the lion? Did he bite you?"

"The lion? Oh. He's dead. I caught him by the throat and broke his neck. Then, because so much strength flooded my body, I tore his body apart, limb by limb. Then I dropped the carcass and the limbs on the side of the road and went on my way to find you. On my return journey here, I saw the same carcass, and there was a hive of bees inside the rib cage. I stuck my hand into the heart of the hive and scooped out the comb, dripping with honey. I ate it."

"'Out of the eater, something sweet.' Yes. I understand!"

"Why was it so hard? There are lions and beehives all over your pottery."

"But not a beehive inside a lion."

"Do not tell my mother. You must promise me that."

"Why? Is the lion sacred to your people? Will she be angry you killed it?"

"No. She'll be angry that she ate the honey."

"Ah. Another riddle?" I tried to prod him with a gentle joke.

"We broke the law of our God. We touched the dead." Samson pointed to the feasting tables. "One last night. We leave at dawn."

I left him, going to the tables to begin the wine service. I had the answer to his riddle. I thought it would make my choice so much easier, clearer. But some decisions were best made before riches came. Now I knew the men of my village could never solve this riddle; it was unlike any we had ever heard.

Samson was going to win the bet. And he would take me home to his god, a god I did not know.

After pouring everyone a brimming bowl of wine, I excused myself to fetch more. I looked frantically for Talos, who had not yet arrived. Running to the edge of the houses, I saw him coming down the road. I picked up my tunic and ran. I had a negotiation of my own to conduct.

I woke on this morning to a gentle tapping on the walls of the lodging house. I pulled the blanket tighter around me. Manoah was on his back, one arm flung over his head, mouth open wide, asleep. Samson was on his stomach across the room under the window. I saw beads of water running down the walls above him. The innkeeper needed to shut up his house for the winter now that the rains had come.

Tonight was the last night of the feast. The men had not solved the riddle. My son was going to begin the deliverance through cleverness, not strength. The last battle would begin with money, not swords. Perhaps all battles do.

We spent the day in between sleep and attending to the preparations for our journey home. Manoah talked to the innkeeper and settled our debt, making arrangements for our donkeys to be saddled and ready to leave by dawn. I never thought I would say this, but I was going to be happy to see my donkey again.

We walked to Amara's house just after the fifth hour of the afternoon. The sun had not shone today, staying tucked away in gray clouds overhead. I wrapped my shawl around my shoulders and in between my arms. Samson noticed it and put his arm around me.

He stood a foot taller than me. He could not have been comfortable, but he kept me warm.

When we arrived, he went to talk with Amara, leaving Manoah and I to work.

After an hour, we had the tables and benches in place, a goat roasting and the bread delivered. Amara had left Samson, going I know not where, but he did not move to help us. He just stared into the fire.

When the men arrived, I could tell they were already drunk, with stained faces and broad grins. They laughed, licking their lips when they saw Samson.

I saw a flick of black hair as Amara fled into her house.

The Philistine beast from Gath spoke first. "What is sweeter than honey? And what is stronger than a lion?"

I closed my eyes to stop the thundering in my heart. Amara must have gotten the answer from my son.

Samson lifted his arm from my shoulders, taking a step closer in, moving until he stood toe-to-toe with the red-headed beast. "You're too stupid to have solved it on your own."

The beast lowered his face. He stood a foot taller than Samson, which was a miracle in itself. "You're calling me stupid?"

"If you hadn't ploughed with my heifer, you would never have guessed the riddle."

The beast just laughed, looking at the other men, who snickered and drank and nodded in satisfaction.

Lightning flashed behind Samson, illuminating the edges of his body and the strange shimmering madness that was pouring down upon him, like the breath of God. The white of Samson's eyes turned to a searing silver, and his flesh shone so brightly that he burned pale blue.

I had seen this before. This madness was Samson's gift. I braced myself for the burst of wrath, the destruction of these filthy men. I thanked God I had made it to this moment, when I would see the deliverance begin for my people.

Samson exhaled and turned to leave.

I trotted after him, calling his name. "What are you doing?"

I looked back in confusion at the men we had just left. Every one of them was still alive, still laughing. At us. At Samson and his defeat. On the roof of her house, Amara stood, her black hair whipped by the wind, a final lash of lightning illuminating her.

Samson said nothing to me, nothing to Manoah. He stomped and brooded, and when we got to the lodging house, Samson untied our donkeys and handed the reins to Manoah. "Take Mother home."

I grabbed his arm. "Amara betrayed you. I did not."

"Yes, you did. You thought I married her out of foolishness. It was God, your God and mine, who wanted it. Not me. I obeyed, and you gave me nothing but grief for it."

"No. God would not have wanted you to marry a Philistine."

Samson glanced at Manoah, who said nothing to defend his son. Samson shook his head and turned left, toward the coast, toward the heart of the Philistine empire, the five sister cities that ruled our people.

I called out after him. "Where are you going?"

"To make you happy."

The bag for my journey was by the front door.

But Samson did not return for me. He had walked off into the night without a word, his mother and father trotting behind him. He had taken the road out of the village, the glow that surrounded him fading as the hour went past. A log had snapped and split in two, collapsing into the fire, just as a flash of lightning streaked through the sky while I watched him go.

His god was angry with me. And my marriage was dead.

MOTHER

We rode through the night.

By the fourth hour of darkness, the air grew heavy and smelled of salt. The grasses turned from low grasses good for grazing into high grasses that shifted in the wind, the grasses of the sea.

Samson did not speak. I watched the back of his head, those cords of hair spreading out across his shoulders.

"They cheated you," I called ahead to him.

No reply. Manoah looked at me and shrugged.

We were alone on the highway for most of the night. A caravan passed us, five camels laden with bags, probably spice merchants going east into the Judean Hills to make a profit. The camels towered above me as they passed, their heavy eyelids and soft brown eyes studying me with gentle curiosity. The merchant rode a sixth camel behind them, quietly urging them on. He wore a dusty turban, and his face was wrinkled up in brown folds. He tipped his chin to me when our eyes met, and then he was gone into the night.

Toward dawn, we were still on the main highway. We had not turned from the path for even one minute. I had needed to make water, and Manoah had waited for me, but my poor donkey paid for my weakness. I had to run him to catch back up to Samson, but what choice did I have? At my age, on a donkey, all night?

Samson led us deeper into Philistine country, toward one of the five sisters, the cities that the Philistines ruled in. Traffic along the highway picked up now, with merchants heading into the cities and families coming in to buy what they needed. By mid-morning, I saw the high arched gate with the two mud-brick towers on each side, the wide blue sky above and the strong smell of fish in the air.

We had arrived at Ashkelon.

The city looked as if it was built on a hill, but it was not really. Instead, a long steep mud rampart was built around the city as far as the eyes could see in either direction, and the city wall was built behind that. The wall was a giant, slow curve; Ashkelon was open on the other side, open to the sea.

The highway ran off down the coast toward the south, toward Egypt, but we turned on the road leading up to the main gate. This road was wide, wide enough for two chariot teams to ride side by side.

As we neared the gate, a horned altar stood outside, perhaps forty paces from the gate, with a silver statue of a bull calf. Travelers laid offerings on the altar before passing through the gates, probably praying for success and blessing in the day's trades.

Samson paid no mind to the roadside idolatry. He led us through the gates. I saw him shiver once inside; the gate was wide enough for one chariot at a time to pass through, but taller than three men standing on each other's shoulders. No sun illuminated the interior of the gate; it smelled of dead sea and mildew, and it was cold.

When we stepped out into the sun a few minutes later—for the gateway was longer than you can imagine—we were almost run over by a driver lashing his donkeys. They carried a load of pottery to market, the pots covered in red and black bull calves and heifers, a symbol of the Canaanite deities, and the colors of the Philistines.

Women shuffled past us wearing gold scarab toggle pins on their tunics that flashed in the late morning sun. They had Egyptian eye paint on, and I suspected those fine hairstyles they wore were nothing but wigs. I put my hand to my own hair, smoothing it back. I had not brushed it today, but at least it was mine.

In the distance, narrow Egyptian ships sailed into the harbor, their red and yellow painted sterns rising up and down, breaking the waves. Egyptians were quick to forgive enemies with money. Judging by the number of Egyptians, there was quite a bit of money here.

To our right, facing the sea, was a temple to Dagon, which I remembered as a brothel and nothing more. I remembered this city from a visit here as a child, when my father had risked my mother's wrath only once by bringing me here as he traded. I had to ask him what the inscription meant, the one over the doorway to that house where all the beautiful women leaned from the windows. He had turned red and mumbled the answer. "Enter and enjoy," he had said, and I had not understood the reason for his blush for many years. I had jumped from my donkey to retrieve a pin that fell from my sash, I caught a glimpse of what hid under the gutters. As soon as I looked up, Father saw my face, and we turned for home. He begged me to never reveal what I had seen.

The brothel had a latrine dug all the way around it, covered over to keep the smell down. It ran out to the sea. I turned away to keep the memories from surfacing. If you want to know the heart of a city, look at what it throws out.

Samson veered to the left, toward a row of shops, one with jugs and dipping spoons for wine and date-palm liquor. Alongside it were a butcher shop and grain shop, their tables out front, customers already yelling about the prices and inspecting the scales with a critical eye.

It made sense now, of course. Samson had lost the bet. He owed the men of Amara's village thirty sets of clothes. Ah, but that would kill us. The expense!

"Why did you drag us all the way to Ashkelon?"

He was ignoring me, wandering through the crowds, as if looking for something. He had the frown of a man who has one item to buy, and only one, which was lost in a sea of options.

And then he walked right past the shops. I was off my donkey at this point. I had to; my hip bones were going to pop out of their sockets if I didn't stand up straight for a while. I grabbed Samson by the elbow and tried to turn him to face me.

"You've gone past the market."

He pulled away, cocking his head as he looked at me, the look one would give a bold stranger. He ducked to the left, behind the last stall, where merchants threw their refuse. I covered my mouth and nose with my tunic, making my eyes wide and angry at Manoah. He did nothing. Of course. So I followed, and as I turned round that corner of the stall, I saw a man I did not recognize.

It was my son.

Samson stood over a dead man. The man's head flopped back, blood spurting out of his neck, a high red arc that sprayed me as I stepped too close, so shocked that my body moved against my will, moving me closer to this horror and not away from it.

A splash of hot blood hit my cheek.

"Help me," my son said. He began lifting the tunic from the man.

I could not move my own legs or arms.

Samson reached up and took my hand. My eyes moved to look at him, to look into his eyes. I was seeing him for the first time, this other man.

"Help me," he said.

I pulled the wrap skirt from the man's waist, almost uncovering his nakedness. I took the skirt and held it out, as innocent as a baby. Samson took it from me, folding it over his arm, over the tunic that he carried. He grabbed my hand, and we moved on, into a dark stairwell built into the city gate, where guards could climb into and out of the mud-brick tower. Samson pulled me into the entranceway to the stairs, and we were not ten steps up when a Philistine guard came down the stairs. He frowned in surprise at seeing Samson, with his strange appearance, and me, an old woman with blood on her face. Before the guard could draw his sword, Samson had sprung up the steps separating us and had the guard on his back. I saw the flash of metal and heard a gurgling sound like a child trying to swim.

Samson untied the breastplate on the man, then lifted the tunic off of him. The man's head and arms flopped about as Samson grunted with effort. The guard had been a big man. Now he was a big, dead man.

"Help me."

I remembered. I took off the wrap and folded it over my arm. "Give me the tunics," I whispered. Samson handed me the two tunics he was carrying, plus the other wrap. I folded them neatly over my arm, smoothing them down.

What can I say? I had watched my son kill two men. My son kill other sons. All my life was reduced to this moment, this one simple, pure, clean fact: There was Family, and there was Not Family. But there was not Choice.

I carried out the clothes like they were nothing more than laundry and followed Samson up the stairs. Two more guards were in the tower. Samson drove the knife into one man's side, and as he fell, Samson drove the knife into the neck of the other guard as he reached for his weapon. The blood spilled and pooled and as he yanked the tunics off, Samson slipped in it, coating the back of his legs with thick hot red blood that dripped as he moved. I made him wait at the mouth of the stairs while I cleaned him off. Some had gotten in his hair, too, and this I cleaned with the only spare cloth I knew of, which was the loincloth from a dead guard. I did not look as I removed it and was careful to touch no bodies. I was a good Hebrew.

I was a new woman, too, a woman I did not know who could do these things. I followed Samson back down the stairwell and back into the bright morning sun. It might have been the noon sun, or the third hour sun; I no longer could tell. I had no bearings for this new world. Manoah was wandering the market, still holding the reins for our donkeys. He looked relieved when he saw us. Relieved!

Samson took the clothes from my arms and loaded them on the donkeys, then turned to his father.

"Get her out of the city, Father. Now!"

"I will not leave you here!" I shook my head, glaring at Manoah. Manoah looked in confusion between Samson and me, waiting for explanation. Samson turned in the direction of the next entranceway to the towers, on the other side of the shops, and I followed, hurrying behind. Manoah called to us, but I did not turn back around.

There were guards in this tower, too—four this time—and Samson killed each of them as I watched. He took off the tunics, I took off the wraps, then folded everything neatly over my arm.

We went back down the cold dark steps, Samson holding my arm to keep me from slipping on the blood dripping down, and returned to the light. Manoah tried to flag us down again, but there was no time. Again, Samson took the clothes from my arms and loaded them on our donkeys, then picked the next man to slaughter.

He chose the wine merchant. I grabbed Samson by the elbow, and when he turned to look at me, I saw recognition in his eyes. This new man, this murderer of sons, knew I was still his mother.

"Not a merchant. It will attract too much attention."

Samson nodded. We moved down the lanes toward the administrative building, easy to see from any direction with its wide pillars and men lounging on its steps, waiting to be heard by the lords of the city. Samson walked past them, immune to their snide whispers about his hair. Inside the building—its mosaic floor of brown and red stones so cold on my feet even through my sandals—where every word spoken reverberated across the domed interior, Samson chose an inner room and opened the door.

He had chosen well. Around a low bench sat a gathering of men, the oldest of which wore a large signet ring. He was, no doubt, a Philistine lord. He had white hair that flew in all directions as Samson cut his throat, and I noticed he had a bump in the middle of his nose. His eyes met mine as he breathed his last. A younger man with this same distinct bump lunged at Samson and as he died, I understood, of course. Samson had killed a father and son, and he killed the other three men, who were in their middle years and had nice fat stomachs and balding heads that smeared wildly with blood.

Now we had twelve sets of clothes. We were not even halfway done.

The thirteenth man was the easiest kill; he was a servant who walked into the room carrying a platter of fruits. He, too, slipped on the blood, and Samson drove his knife through the man's back.

Because the hour grows late, I will not tell of the fourteenth man, or the nineteenth, or any of the others. When we got to twenty-five, we had exited the building and saw a city squirming in chaos. Men were shouting, warriors were running, women were keening for the dead being brought out of the towers.

"What is happening?" Samson asked a woman hurrying by with her children.

"We are under attack!" she screamed. "They are shutting the city gates!"

In the chaos, Samson did not have to be as careful. We did not have to work in the shadows. He killed the twenty-sixth man right there on the steps, and as we worked our way through the panicked masses, back to the market, he killed off his twenty-seventh, twenty-eighth, and twenty-ninth man, letting them fall in the streets. I had to work fast to get the wrap off. If people noticed, no one called out. People in shock do strange things.

We found Manoah standing at a table outside the shops, where he had been eating a sweet bread as he waited for us. By now Samson was carrying the clothes. How could I? Our pile had grown too heavy. Manoah, gasping and spitting crumbs in his confusion, helped us load everything onto the donkeys, and we fled for the gates just as men began drawing them closed, mothers inside the city screaming at them to hurry.

As we entered the long dark tunnel again, Samson killed his last man, as a young pregnant wife watched. Her eyes met mine as she stood still in disbelief, her grief falling on her like the city walls, her life ending with his.

We looked into each other's eyes, and I prayed. I prayed she would not have a son.

With that, we were through the gates just as they closed. The metal hinges groaned shut behind us as screams echoed through the tunnel.

We turned for Timnah.

Samson and I spoke to each other in the low whispers of criminals. I walked in front of Samson, my spidery old legs surprisingly fast. Manoah held his tongue, saying nothing, his face bug-eyed and red, until the travelers along the highway thinned out and we could speak without being overheard.

"What happened?"

Neither Samson nor I answered.

Manoah trotted his donkey ahead of us, turned, and held his hands out. We stopped. I looked at him as if he were a stranger to me.

"What happened?" His words were soft and sharp, cutting across the blaze of the afternoon sun.

I wiped my brow and shifted on my donkey.

Samson walked in front of me to answer his father. "I killed thirty men. Thirty Philistines, thirty Ashkelites. Now we're going to Timnah to pay my debt."

"What? What have you done? We could have bought the clothes." Manoah's voice was shrill.

"What would you say if I told you it was God's will?"

Manoah's face registered his total disbelief.

Samson gave him a grim smile, taking his reins, leading Manoah's donkey to face back around, then swatting it on the rump.

Manoah held on tight as the donkey trotted away. He turned and looked at me once, his face white with confusion and shock.

Samson looked at me as he passed. His face was smeared with blood. A riverbed of clean lines ran down his cheeks from under his eyes. He had been crying.

I pressed my lips together and looked away. Night was coming. I hurried my donkey along.

We stopped at a shepherd's well not long after midnight. Our donkeys were exhausted. Every bone in my body ached from the ride. My jaws ached, my teeth hurt, even my hands were sore, the knuckles throbbing from holding the reins, the palms burned and raw from the reins slipping through as we rode.

My good and kind son, the one I knew, came to me first, extending his hand. I accepted his help and slid off the donkey, hobbling a few paces, praying for blood to return to my legs. A moment later, it did, and I cried out.

Samson was helping Manoah get off his donkey. Neither seemed to hear me. Falling to my knees in the dirt—for we were well out of Ashkelon now, and the sand had become dirt once more—I panted through the pain, like a woman in childbirth.

I was alone in my pain, just like my first night as his mother. That night the village women stood outside my home and listened for my screams. Every scream had seemed to them a miracle. An old woman giving birth? Was it possible that God still moved in the lives of women, that God still opened dead wombs and heard silent prayers?

And they worshipped, they told me later, worshipped outside my window while I screamed in pain and fear, the burst of hot fluids and the swell and stretch of a child forced into this world. He cried as the midwife pulled him from my womb. How he cried.

Samson came over to help me, but it was too late. I hobbled to the well. He and Manoah followed, watching me with wide, moonlit eyes as I lifted the water up in the bucket and poured it into my dry, open mouth. I lowered the bucket again, and raised it, offering it to Manoah next.

He drank and backed away, still watching me as one watches a stranger.

Again, I lowered the bucket and lifted, ignoring the red stains my palms left on the rope. I held it out to Samson, who sighed and drank, water running down his beard, leaving pink stains in the dirt.

Finished, he handed the bucket back to me, but I grabbed his arm and pulled him near. I filled the bucket and dipped my robe in the water, then set to work washing his face. I washed the blood off of him, washed away those tears, washing him tonight as on that first night so many years ago. He submitted to me without argument, but his gaze never left the ground.

This was his destiny, the destiny I had bragged about to my sisters of our tribe? Blood and tears?

When I finished, he wrapped his arms around me like a child.

"Are you sorry I gave birth to you?" I spoke harshly. I had to know what he thought, who he blamed.

"Are you?" he replied.

I grabbed his arms and shook him. "We will find a prophet of the Lord. We will ask that your vow be completed and that God release you."

"You should be dancing, Mother. Singing. I have begun the deliverance. Thirty Philistines lie dead by my hand."

"No. I will not lose you. God can find another way to deliver His people."

"It is too late." He sighed like one dying, and walked ahead of me into the night. I called his name but he did not answer.

I lost sight of him in the darkness.

"Samson has returned for you!" Astra was so excited, so eager to heal my heartbreak, that she bounced as she squealed the words. "He is coming! He has brought the clothes he owed the men! Come! Come!"

I rose from my pallet for the first time in three days, since the night Samson had left me. Splashing my face with water, I rubbed it dry with my tunic while Astra combed my hair. She was too quick, though, and I yelped when she hit a tangle.

"We must hurry!" She was nearly breathless.

I followed behind her, and saw other villagers coming out of their houses to see Samson's return. All would be forgiven. He would know how loyal I was, how I had acted shrewdly. And he was a real man, a man of uncommon strength indeed, honoring this debt. There was no husband like mine, not ever.

Having no city gate, the elders met him at the end of the main traveling road. Samson walked alongside my donkey, which carried a heavy load of clothes. I smiled broadly.

The elders watched, with folded arms and haughty expressions, as Samson lifted the clothing and presented it at the feet of the elders.

Then he turned and walked away, leading the donkey back to the road.

"Wait!" I called out, running to the elders, trying to get through. "I am here!"

Samson did not turn back. I did not understand, but I had no chance to ask anyone what was happening. A great cry was growing behind me, curses raining down on Samson and all those of his household.

The stench made me wince. Turning to the elders, I saw them holding the clothes up in the morning light, crying out to Dagon for justice. The clothes were red, all of them, a dark dry red.

"Blood!" an elder screamed at me, shaking the garment at my face. "Blood on Philistine robes!"

I looked for Astra, but she was running back to the house, frightened, as the men closed around me in a circle.

"A curse on you and your father's house! May you be barren all of your days!"

MOTHER

The almond trees have budded, a sign to our people that God is watching, to bring all His promises to fulfillment. Other mothers think it is safe to dream for their children, of what they might do, of how they might serve the Lord. I see these white flowers bursting open and they seem to me like burial shrouds, reminding me that my son's destiny is found in a grave.

Thirty graves, a guarantee of wonders to come.

My people danced when Manoah whispered the story at our well. Their scowls of suspicion changed into admiration, even worship. Women who crossed the path to avoid Samson when they walked alone now pushed their daughters toward him with open smiles.

He stepped back, behind me, as we walked through the village. I walked faster, not acknowledging him. He wanted to be a child again. I did not want a child. Not anymore.

Baking bread the next morning, after the news had spread, Syvah hugged me in celebration. I noted her thin frame, how her bones were sharp under her robe, how her eyes were yellow and her breath smelled foul. Death was closer than anyone knew.

The fields were empty. Spring was coming, and soon we would be picking the barley, but for today, no one was in the fields. I walked, calling out, hissing, whistling, raising hands in supplication to the sky. The angel did not return. I sat, determined to wait.

Samson joined me. He walked tentatively at first, trying to get me to nod in approval, to welcome his company. I turned my face.

"Are you angry?" he asked, as if such a thing were incredible.

"Why would I be angry? Because you broke your holy vows? You drank wine, you touched dead bodies, you ate honey from a carcass and gave it to me and your father."

He stood as his temper burst out. "How did you think deliverance would happen? Were you that naive?"

I stood up and slapped him, hard. Shock registered across his face, then a long, cold glare. He stepped closer, and I edged back.

His voice was low. "You thought only of yourself, of the glories for your name."

As the crescent moon rose above me, I fell to the ground and wept. How had I lost him? How had my hopes for glory, for honor, withered so quickly into fear and confusion? Why did God hide His face, His will from me?

I wept until my stomach ached from the effort, until my eyes burned dry and I needed a deep drink of water to soften my raw throat. I stood and turned for home.

Passing a bonfire at the edge of our clearing, I saw Syvah's sons and all the youth of our village eating and dancing and celebrating. I peered closer and saw Samson in the middle of it all, lifting a wine bowl to his lips, though it was forbidden to him. He drank with savagery, red wine flowing out the sides of his mouth, down his chest. I marked how everyone watched him, their strange savior, with pleasure, with curiosity. He did not hide his sneer, disgusted by their affection.

Samson sensed me out there in the night. He must have, for he left the group and walked to the fire's edge, staring into the darkness, searching for me now. I knew he was blinded by the flames, and, taking advantage of his temporary weakness, I hobbled away in silence.

Months had passed. Perhaps as many as six. I did not remember the first weeks, or count them, so great was my sorrow. This morning I was out in my fields, inspecting our harvest. My hair rose and fell slightly, and I looked up.

Flying low in the morning sky, raptors migrated to distant lands. They made no noise as they flew. Only the tussle of my hair gave them away. The almond trees had bloomed in a white explosion across our land, and I remembered how I had smelled the tender blossoms as I laid awake on my wedding night weeks ago, while my husband snored softly next to me. They had been a balm to my broken heart, spring's promise that beauty would always find its way back.

The barley harvest was almost over by now. Soon we would begin harvesting the wheat, our greatest and most profitable crop. Spring gave me fresh courage every day. I rubbed my belly, wishing it to be full, wishing for curses to be broken and life to come to me at last. I had earned it, had I not?

Pero, my husband, was eighty years old, and the most senior of the townsmen. He had slept through my first wedding, content to stay home. I do not know if he even believed the tale, that a Hebrew man had claimed me first.

I wrapped my shawl around my shoulders. The winds, especially early in the day, could still be chilly. A stinging breeze blew past me, making me wrinkle my nose in curiosity. My husband stopped moving, lifting his nose to the air. He looked at the horizon behind me and cried out.

Smoke was in the air, too much smoke to be an oven or even a roasting fire. Something was burning that should not be. I ran to my husband to help him to safety. He had to get out of the fields, but he swatted me with his stick, urging me back.

"Go and see!" he wheezed. "See what is burning!"

I lifted my tunic and ran, grateful at that moment that Dagon had not heard my prayers and had not made my belly swell with child. My feet were quick down the narrow dirt path between fields, a steady flat pathway through the valley. As I ran I heard shouting and the screams of women and a horrid high pitched yelping.

Something hit me in the shins, and I fell forward, catching myself with my palms. Rolling onto my hips, I looked for what it was but could see only cinders and ashes floating in the air, like butterflies carried by a little breeze. The cinders were everywhere. I watched as one fell on a stalk of ripe, dry wheat, making a black circle that began to grow white, and then white turned to red and burst into flame.

A pair of foxes tore through the wheat at my left, torches bumping along the ground behind them, the flames burning too close to their tails. Their eyes were wide in terror as I instinctively reached for them, to comfort or save or stop. It was too late. They charged around me, into the wheat. The flames followed. I stood up, raising up on my toes, and saw smoke rising from fields in every direction.

If we lost our crops now, we lost our food for the year and our seeds for the next. The frail people would not survive the winter, and the strong would not survive the second year.

The flames closed off the path behind me, as flames began to take the fields on either side of me. I did not return to my husband. I ran to my family.

I did not question the goodness of the gods that this was the only path left open to me.

Father and Mother were at their table, crying. Nothing could be done. It was all going to be destroyed within a few hours: the grain, the olives, the vineyards. Their food would burn, and there would be no work in the fields.

"They did not want to watch," Astra whispered, hugging me when I came in. I nodded.

"Pour them both a bowl of wine."

"We must save it!"

"Pour it. They need it right now."

I unwrapped my shawl and sat beside Father, saying nothing. He lifted his hand and placed it over mine. Mother placed hers on top too. Astra began pouring the wine, setting out an extra bowl for me. I shook my head no. I would not be a burden to them, not anymore.

We sat in silence for a great while, vaguely aware that the screams outside our door had turned to quiet moans.

"The fire must be dying down," Astra whispered. I would have answered, but a heavy thunderclap shook our front door. Footsteps on our roof made Astra scream, and we all looked up in confusion. Something was dragged across the roof and dropped, making the walls shake all around us. Dust swirled through the air as Father and Mother jumped up. Father ran to the front door and Mother to the roof stairs. Both tried to open their doors but could not. Mother began beating at the door at the top of the stairs.

"Open this! What is happening?"

Father yanked against the door with all his might, but it did not move. Men's voices from outside cursed us. The walls shook, threatening to collapse as he pulled on the door. Astra screamed and grabbed his tunic, trying to stop him. I stood at the table, a hand over my mouth. I alone knew what was happening. I alone knew why. I had done this. I had killed us all.

Terror boiled in my stomach as footsteps landed on our roof again, running away this time.

The flames took hold of the roof first, little burning embers falling down all around us, singeing my soft bare shoulder, stinging my scalp. Astra clung to me next, screaming, her little hands trembling violently. I threw my arms around her, shielding her face in my bosom, screaming for her to close her eyes. There was to be no escape.

The village men waited outside. If the flames did not kill us, they would. I did not want to leave her for them. I would choose the death that would rob them of any chance of pleasure. Better to feel pain now, better to die in pain, my dear sister, and die alone, than to let them have us.

Father slumped facedown on the floor, rocking and keening prayers to Dagon. "Why?" he moaned. "I offered Astra to him. She is so much prettier!"

My mother pounded his back, screaming. She wanted him to get up, to save us. This was not how her family would end, how her daughters would die—barren, betrayed, burned to death by the same villagers that helped raise us.

I clutched Astra and lifted my face to the flames above. I had done this. I had lit this fire. I had chosen to betray my husband, to save my family, and for that, they would all die.

The smoke grew thick, rolling in through cracks in the walls and gaping holes the fire made in our roof. A red cinder fell from the ceiling into our jar of oil, which was still full to the brim from the wealth Samson had brought us. The clay jar exploded into flame, and the heat began to roast us alive as the flames dropped to the floor and ate our home.

I coughed, my lungs filling with the smoke. There was no more air, and there is nothing more of my tale to be told.

What was done, was done.

PART TWO

BRIDE OF DESIRE

Three Years Prior to Amara's Story,
in the Philistine City of Ekron

The god of ice sent his sign.

By noon, the elders sat together at the city gates of Ekron, clucking their teeth.

Ice fell from the sky, a wonder not often seen in my village. Each elder sat wondering what dangers it foretold. The oldest among them, a white-haired man named Selanius, told them the story of a Hebrew god, one that sent a plague of ice on the Egyptians many generations ago. He proved to be a strange and troublesome god, Selanius said.

I squinted, looking up at the sky to see the face of this god. I could not find him. I finished my purchase—a bit of kohl for my mother—and hurried home to see what Father thought of it all.

"Why do you care?"

My brothers looked up from their bowls and snickered. I had three brothers, though since all wore the same crude expression around me, it seemed that I had only one brother who was in many places at once.

The ice god's message would be lost on my family. I felt shame for them, speaking ill of strange and marvelous gods, as they crouched behind closed doors.

"I'll bring in the sheep," I offered.

No one answered. The steaming porridge Mother had ladled into their bowls must have been especially good. No bowl was set out for me, of course. When they slept tonight I would sneak down the ladder and roll each foot, ball to toe, quietly across the dust and straw. I could move with a cat's silent grace. When I reached the pot, with my fingers I would sweep the edges and bottom, and in the darkness, eat.

When you only have a little, a little can be very good. Were I given a whole bowl of stew to eat, I told myself, I could not enjoy it. Everything tastes the same after the fourth bite. My way, the way of hunger, made the pleasure of each tiny taste almost unbearable. If I was not so hungry, food would not taste so good. In this way, I feel sorry for my family, who probably never tasted Mother's cooking the way I do. Already, I have riches they knew nothing of. I know how to find treasures in the ashes of this life.

I watched them eat. I may eat in darkness, but I taste the food and they do not. I breathe deep and easy at night, with no eyes upon me, no hands brushing me out of the way, no lashes across my back for disrespect and laziness.

Then, after tasting the bowl, I always stay down here below and sleep, right with the animals. They nuzzle me while I rest, their beating hearts a familiar old story passed between them in the dark. As I slept nestled between my two ewes, they wove my heart, too, into their moon tale.

This is how these ewes came to be in my story, and I in theirs:

The city had been quiet for weeks after the pinch-faced Hebrews came. They always came into the city after their festival of sleeping in tents. Their god drove them out of their comfortable homes to sleep in tents and get bitten by sand spiders.

I did not understand their devotion.

But as always, they had arrived, stinking, tired, and irritable (mothers with young children most of all) and bought up everything we had, except the meats. Hebrews didn't eat what we did. They said we eat unclean animals.

Have they ever seen a clean animal? Every animal is unclean.

They came into our city, Ekron, which is a lovely place as I see it. There is an upper city and a lower city, which does not refer to a direction, but the height of each part of the city. One end is noticeably higher than the other. I don't think that is much advantage, unless you want to spy on pale old women bathing on their rooftops. The lower end of the city collects more rainwater and has more fertile gardens.

We lived in the upper end, which was why my father often took his whip out after us. He had to drive us all, he said, even the land. He had one enormous problem. Me. I was born a girl. Father wanted to collect great wealth, and my brothers wanted to inherit great wealth. A girl was a liability, a little thief that stole food from the boy's mouths until the day she married and the father had to give away even more of what he had saved for his sons. Every penny he spent to keep her alive, and to finally get rid of her, all went to another man and another man's family.

"Did you see the field I planted today?" my brother—as I said, it matters not which one since they are all the same snot-nosed soul—had asked as we waited for a Hebrew woman to count her coins. She was buying a sash I had woven.

"Yes."

"You sit all day, weaving, while I labor in the sun. And while I am sweating and hungry, all I can think about is that we're going to have to pay to get rid of you!"

"It's a dowry. It's not payment."

"Shows what you know."

My brothers did well that day, as did I. They sold the Hebrews plenty of roasted grains to eat as snacks, plus honey for strength for their walk home. I was not allowed in the fields or gardens, as a girl with soft hands brought a better bride price. I obeyed in every instruction my father gave me in this regard, hoping he would weigh the coins in his mind and realize perhaps he could profit from me someday too.

So I worked with a loom and kept my skin smooth and pale. I brushed my hair every night and rubbed a finger over my teeth after eating. I did what I could for my looks, and I worked to sell the Hebrew women enough sashes to buy my father's love. My hope came in the form of two ewe lambs, with fleece like you've never seen or felt. Their fleece was so dense and smooth, like running your hand through cream. I had spied the young ewes for sale at the market. Every day I had prayed that Dagon would keep them for me, and he did. I paid for the ewes and walked them home, head high.

"More mouths to feed," Father grumbled when he saw them. I do not think he really meant it.

"Pigs offer nothing but meat," I said, keeping my eyes on the floor. "Once you eat them, you're done. But with this wool, think how much I can charge for my clothing."

A sheep can give wool throughout its life, plus lambs, and you can eat lambs or sell them.

"I'm not going to feed them. I can barely afford food for you."

I had thought of my entire plan. I was ready.

"I don't need you to." I ducked so he wouldn't hit me, thinking I meant disrespect. I spoke faster. "You can have all the money they earn. I will do all the work, and you will have all the money."

His face did not remain angry, so I knew I had won. Brother, however, glared at me. All of them.

One night about a week later, as I slept between my two ewes, I heard someone clumsy stumbling through the darkness inside the home. Moonlight blinded me for a moment, and I squinted to shield my eyes. What I saw was my brother opening the downstairs door to sneak out. He turned and walked toward my sheep and gave one a good kick.

I sat up and yelled. "What are you doing?"

"Shut up down there!" my father yelled down.

"You're going to lose," my brother hissed.

"What are you talking about?"

"You can't be anything other than what you are."

He turned and sneaked away, out into the night. He had money to spend from market. At night, very different wares were offered.

I sat back down between my sheep, stroking their soft fleece, whispering little encouragements. It was almost winter, and the nights were getting cold. I stared at the door, the moonlight searing through the edges and cracks. No sheep would live through a dark winter night out there.

As if Dagon himself agreed, a cat of some kind screamed in the night air.

"May my brother be eaten tonight for kicking my ewe," I prayed silently.

I would make my father rich. He would love me and praise me. What did any man value more than money? I ran a finger through my silken black hair and wondered.

I fed my lambs whatever grains I could steal—and yes, I stole often. Every night, I slid between the moonlit cracks of the door, slipped across shadowed streets, sneaked into homes, and felt in the dark for barrels of grain. I held a hollow palm up in the darkness and filled it with the cool smooth stones of life, the emptiness of my life erased. I moved with ease as sweat beaded along my neck and forehead. No one ever heard me, and no one knew. Silence was my gift. My legs were no more than feathers sweeping across the dirt floors.

My ewes were hungry all the time, bleating when I returned before dawn. I fed them fast to keep them quiet. I did not know why a ewe would demand more and more food. During the day, I led them out into the low hills above us, but there was not much good grazing left before the harsh rains of winter. Sometimes, they slept instead. Sometimes, I did too.

I had to steal from more houses, and steal more than what fit in my palms. If only my father had offered to buy grain.

But of course I still had my sashes and my loom, and one afternoon as I fought to say awake, a god took my side in the battle. (I do not know which one.) I saw in my mind how a sash could be made into a bag, and yet still look like a sash. I could steal much more. I set to work at once to make it.

“It is good to see you work with vigor,” my mother commented.

She rarely said anything to me or anyone else, which is why I have not mentioned her before. She hid behind her hair and did not make friends with other women. Or me.

That night, as everyone slept, I once again slipped out the door. How fast my heart beat to see my sister the moon again! How blessed the darkness that holds all our secrets! I was not the only one with a shadow life. I heard others on some nights, caught sight of their robes as they disappeared into other houses, or the house of Sehna, our harlot. I even made a game now of watching in the market to see who yawned most in the afternoon. I began to suspect the most startling citizens—men and women alike—of living shadow lives.

But this is not their tale. Not yet.

That night, I crept into a home with many barrels. They would not miss what I stole. I was a kind thief, careful never to burden any one family. That’s what I promised myself and the god who watched over me. I thought my kindness would be rewarded.

I eased the wooden door open over the dirt floor only a few inches, as I turned myself sideways and slid like a moonbeam between the cracks into the home. I unwound my sash in the darkness and glided to the barrels, dipping a hand in and filling my sash. The sash could hold more, so I dipped my hand in again. Moonlight flooded around me, and I turned, trying not to cry out. A man with a shadow life had returned to his home and caught me.

I could barely see his face in the darkness. He stood there a moment, then walked to me, taking me by the hand and leading me out. He led me down the street and into an enclosed garden, where fruit trees hid all from view. Just before he turned to face me, I closed my eyes.

He did speak, of course. I shouldn't leave that out, or you'll wonder why I did not run or scream. He reminded me of the punishment for thieves. (My hands would be cut off.) He reminded me that he saw my face clearly, knew who I belonged to. He could demand restitution from my father, besides my hands. So I surrendered underneath the fruit trees, their bare branches hanging low.

I thought about those branches as I walked home afterward. I thought of nothing else, to keep myself from screaming. I forced my mind away from the blood smearing across my inner thighs, away from the strange taste of his mouth, away from the terror of being known. I thought of the branches. The fruit was gone. They were bent and brought low. But nothing should have stopped them from rising back up and finding the sun. Nothing but memory stood in their way.

I ground my teeth together.

That is why I can tell you so much and fly away from it all so freely. The earth has lessons to teach us all, if we but listen.

The sun began slipping away sooner every day, off to her own secrets. Winds caught women by the ankles, making them shiver and press their legs together as they sat at their booths in the market. Fish and pork had been salted and pressed, set aside for later sales and meals when women were too tired to prepare them fresh. The last of the fruits had been eaten or hung from the beams in homes to dry. Grapes were crushed, and each wife had set about making her own wine, boasting to her neighbors that her grapes had been blessed by Dagon, that her wine was the secret to long life and good teeth.

As I lay awake in the darkness one night, I heard heavy footfalls, the thump of something hitting the dirt outside our door, and fast, scuffling steps away into the darkness. I lay still between my ewes for the longest time, not knowing what to do. Everyone above me slept.

One ewe nuzzled me, sensing I was awake.

Above me, a great groan reminded me that others had their own bad dreams. Mine did not matter.

I crept to the door. Pressing my ear against it to be sure, I heard nothing. I rested one hand flat against the wood and pulled gently with the other hand, easing the door open.

A huge sack sat on the ground.

I poked my head out like a turtle, looking this way and that. The street was empty and quiet; I could hear no noises from the other homes. Creeping out and crouching down, I opened the mouth of the sack. It rattled, a sound like a snake redoubling on itself, the rasp of scale on scale. I jumped back, holding my mouth to keep quiet.

The sack did not move. I kicked it with one foot, and the mouth tipped open, the contents cascading in a little clicking stream on the ground. It was grain. A sack of grain. Worth a week's wages, at least, if the worker was a strong man!

I looked up and down the street again. Nothing stirred. I reached out to grab the sack and saw a dark shadow lift from the wall of the furthest house and slink away into the night. His scent carried on the night wind.

I knew then who had left it, but I did not know why. I did not know what men felt about these things, what laws they lived by. A woman's life was not a man's.

My ewes would be hungry in the morning. I had no right to starve them because of my foolishness. I dragged the bag inside and tucked it in the corner where I kept my weaving supplies.

After this gift of grain, my ewes began to get fat. At first, no one noticed but me. They were so fluffy that no one could tell where their wool ended and their bodies began. But one night my father stopped eating, his hand in mid-air, the bread dripping juices back into his bowl, and he stared at me as I led my ewes back inside and to their stall.

"They have gotten big," he said.

I beamed, and trembled, afraid to say anything. I was worth more to him than ten sons.

"Should they be that big?" He was frowning. "They're too big," he said to my brothers, who glared at us all.

That night, I understood his alarm. As I slept, my hands drifted across the belly of my ewe, and something stirred beneath my hand. My heart quickened, and I pressed my palm against the belly. Something hard rubbed against it from the inside.

"Oh no!" I gasped.

I rolled over quickly and pressed my palm into the other ewe's belly. Nothing. Nothing moved. "Thank you Dagon thank you Dagon thank you," I whispered, resting my forehead on her side.

Then something kicked against me from inside her belly, too. I bit my lips to keep from screaming. Oh, no, I cried in my heart, oh no oh no oh no. My ewes were pregnant. Both of them. Both of them would deliver in winter. But they were too young to mate, I knew. Too young! How was it even possible? I thought I had been so careful watching over them. I napped sometimes when they grazed, I admit, but I did not worry about them mating. They were too young. No male should have been attracted to them for another full season.

It was my fault. My bones turned to ice from the coldest fear yet. I pressed my palm into my own belly. I forced all the breath out of my body, wanting to feel only my belly, wanting to know if disaster had come to me, too. I felt nothing.

I did not sleep the rest of the night. In the morning, when it was time to lead the ewes out and make water, I vomited against the side of the house.

I thought it was dread that had made me sick.

❧

"Why are you in a hurry?" my brother called out this morning. "The damage is done! What can you save now?"

I ran out without my breakfast. I did not want to wait until my brothers were done eating, and see what crumbs they left me. The smell of their breakfast, and their fetid breath, was too much for me. The room seemed very small and filled with hot, penetrating stenches, and so I ran out to get away from them all, the boys and the smells. If indeed one could separate them.

I heard my brother's coarse jest as I leaned over, just outside the door, trying very hard not to heave. I hated throwing up this yellow fluid every morning, and I worried very much that something was terribly wrong. I had no one to ask.

I set out to graze my ewes in the flat areas just below us to the east. If I walked long enough toward the sun, I could get them to a sweet, quiet place where the only men were tired old shepherds who wouldn't bother me. I walked with heavy steps, feeling old myself today. Old and tired, as though I had lived many more than my fourteen winters.

I wanted nothing more than to lie down in the soft green grass, with the morning sun warming my face and the cold winter air blowing against my cheeks, and sleep. I could sleep all day. If the shepherds were in a kind mood (and Dagon, please may it be so) they might leave me a bit of dried pork or fruit. Not all men were cruel. I seemed to have a special charm with the old ones, I noticed. They did not want to hurt me. They looked sad when they saw me, as if they saw something in me that I did not, and what they saw made them feel a great sorrow.

If I had the courage to ask, I would ask this: "What fault do you see that makes you sad?"

I had so many questions.

❧

"Look how she swells."

A man was gesturing to my ewes, as his wet lips parted as he grinned at me. My father threw his hands in the air. "What else could I expect? When a female is in heat, the men find her."

Several men laughed, and I felt heat rising in my face, as if the conversation were not really about my ewes. I pulled at the side seams of my robe, trying to get it to fall straight to the floor. I did not want these men to see the outline of my body. I did not want them to know anything of me, not the length of my legs nor which places swelled like a grown woman's body.

I wasn't just getting breasts and hips, and quite suddenly, but I was also getting fat. My mother eyed me with distaste as I bathed now. I had to hurry to put on my robes and get out of the house. I had been leaving, leading my ewes out to graze, but Father was already out, talking with our neighbors near the upper well.

He was going to brag on me one day, the daughter who made him rich.

I realize I have not told you enough of Ekron. You know that part of it is raised, part of it is not, and that there are families, and men and women, and secrets, and we worship Dagon and have a market. But one principle attraction of our city was our prostitutes. Women were available for purchase on every corner, under every archway, in any booth. Not all men wanted to travel to Gaza or Ashdod, where the temples of Dagon stand and beautiful priestesses were available. To worship this way, with a beautiful priestess, costs much more, but my brothers whispered that the rulers of Ashdod and Gaza are more careful than other lords, making sure the girls do not cheat the customers and are always clean and sober. On the street here in Ekron, men took their chances but paid much less. For some, the gamble was worth the reward. Some men love their money more than their own flesh.

Everyone lived this way, and at peace, the elders said, until the Hebrews moved into our territories. They were always terribly uptight as a people. The wives hissed at the prostitutes who called out to their husbands, and the mothers swatted at the hands that wanted to reach out and touch the face of a child.

I wish the Hebrews weren't so cold to those women. Hebrew women are always cold. Father hates them. I never thought much of it, except that this was the way of the Hebrews, but today I came to understand much of this problem.

After I tried to graze the ewes (and they refused, preferring to sleep, so eventually I led them home), I went to the market below us. As I wandered from booth to booth in the late afternoon, a beautiful woman watched me.

Each time I glanced up, her eyes were on me. I tucked my face down and smiled, wishing to show her that I was not a rude child, but neither did I have anything to say to her. Even at my age, all of fourteen winters, a girl could be shrewd and earn money. There was more than one way for women to prove their worth.

The beautiful stranger bought a handful of dried apricots and held them out to me. I pressed my lips together. They looked so good, and I was hungry, hungrier than I had ever been, a new kind of animal hunger.

She smiled and held them further out to me. I refused, my eyes wide. I didn't have the money to buy them. She held them out to me, nodding. There was no reason I could think of for such kindness.

My animal hunger did not care.

I grabbed and ate them in a rush of need and intense satisfaction. My teeth were thick with the orange meat as I grinned at her. She laughed and motioned for me to step closer. And then she did the most remarkable thing.

She put her arm around me.

My body stiffened to feel a gentle touch. I concentrated on keeping my back straight and to keep looking straight ahead, but really,

I wanted to sink into her motherly touch. There was more than one kind of animal hunger. Tenderness was a need as real as any food.

"Your name is Delilah, yes?"

I nodded.

"I am Tanis. Do you know who I am?"

I shook my head from side to side.

"I am not ashamed. You can look at me."

I stole a little glance. She was beautiful, even in the winter's late afternoon shadows.

"I am Tanis, a priestess from the temple in Ashdod."

I nodded in acknowledgement.

"Delilah, who has lain with you? Who has fathered your child?"

"I do not have a baby!" I even raised my empty arms, letting my robes fall back, to prove my point. She took hold of one hand and pressed it into my stomach. Though I looked around for help, everyone was ignoring us.

"What are you doing?"

"You have a baby in here."

I felt something move under my hand. I cried out and pushed her away, pushed her arm away from me. She must have done magic on me. A man glared at us both, and she swept one arm back around my shoulder, leading me to a quiet, empty booth.

"You did not know?" she asked.

Tears were filling my eyes.

"Delilah, how could you not know? Has not your mother told you these things?"

I stared at the ground.

"I was going to ask you what made you so bold, walking around the market like this. But now I know. You aren't bold. You're ignorant. And Delilah, you are in great danger, my dear."

"Why? From who?"

"An unmarried girl who is with child can be stoned to death. You are of no worth to your father, Delilah. He cannot marry you off, not for a good price. No man will want you now."

"What do I do?"

"Find the father and insist he marry you at once."

"I do not know who the father is."

Her eyebrows rose, and I could tell this answer displeased her. I did not know why. I decided to tell her everything. And I did.

"I never saw his face, not really. Just a certain scent that I remember," I finished. "He did leave me some grain for my sheep. I think it was him. Was I wrong to take it? Am I in trouble?"

She pulled me in and kissed the top of my head. I trembled from the effort of holding myself in, keeping myself from bursting into tears and curling into her lap. We sat there like that for some time, her soft, painted hand stroking my plain, unbraided hair. She smelled of myrrh and incense, of cinnamon perfume and cedar. For that moment, I wished she could have been my mother. I think she did too, for she was not eager to release me.

"Delilah, would you like to come and live with me at the temple?"

"As your daughter?"

She sighed. "No. A servant. Of sorts. You have known a man, so you can work."

My mind led me to where her words pointed. I stood, smoothing down my robes. "I could never … I don't mean to be rude, or harsh. You're very kind. But I do not want to be a prostitute, even in Dagon's temple."

"I am a priestess, not a prostitute!"

"I am sorry."

"There may be no other way for you. Not if you want to live."

"You're wrong. I own two ewes. They have the softest wool you have ever touched, a fine hand, thick and full and like cream. I will use their wool to make the softest fabrics. Plus they are due to have babies soon."

"In winter?"

"It will be fine. I will take good care of them. And I will earn money, lots of it. My father will be pleased to keep me."

"I am sure you are right." She sounded sad.

"I will earn a lot of money. And money changes a man's heart."

"Yes, it does. But it can also make people do bad things, Delilah. Mean things."

"You do not know my father. He will rejoice when he sees how much money I make for him."

I turned to leave, but she called out softly to me, one finger rubbing her chin.

"Delilah, how much does your father expect to earn from the ewes?"

I stopped. I had not put a number to my dream before. I calculated, biting my lip as I held up fingers. "I think each lamb will bring in a drachma. And another three for the wool, come spring."

She smiled, although there was no happiness in her eyes. "Five drachmas. Go on, then. And may Dagon bless your plans."

When I returned home, everyone had eaten and climbed up the ladder to bed. My eyes adjusting to the darkness, I saw with dismay that my ewes had discovered the hidden sack. They were stuffing their faces down inside it, jaws chomping furiously.

I was overcome by hunger too, and stepped quietly to the pot left near the low table. Sticking my hand in, I was unexpectedly blessed. It was full! I scooped out a handful of porridge and smeared it into my mouth, then proceeded to sit down on my rump and pull the pot right between my legs, hunching over it and eating with snorts and swallows like a great ox. I heard something above and looked up to see my mother peering down on me. When she caught my eye, her face withdrew into the darkness above again.

I wondered if she had done this kindness for me, and why. There was no time to consider this mystery, however, because my fatter ewe stirred and stood. She had a panicked look on her face and glanced about, as if deciding on a direction to flee. I jumped up and tried to hold out my hands to her, as if to quiet her, but she gnashed her teeth at me. My calm and dear friend was overcome with something I did not understand, and she began wandering around, her head butting anything that stood in her way. I glanced above, praying she didn't awaken anyone. As she trotted past me, I saw that her backside was distended and red, and I began to panic, too. Something was wrong, with her or maybe the lamb she carried, but I did not know what it could be.

My father muttered something above us. If he came down that ladder, we'd both get a beating. I did what I could, which was to open the door and let her out into the night, and I followed, closing the door softly behind. Instantly I regretted my haste, as the night wind had turned cold and sharp, cutting through my robe, even cutting through my thin legs to pierce my bones. I followed my ewe as she trotted in circles and began bleating. Something froze against my cheeks and I looked up at the sky, expecting to see ice, but there was none. I was crying, the tears freezing against my cheeks.

My ewe flopped to one side and bleated, and I stroked her head, praying. "Please Dagon. I don't know what to do. If you are there (forgive me for my doubts!) please help me. If you are there, bless my ewe and me."

She grew very still, almost as if she was dead, but her breath clouding out around her muzzle told me she was alive. A sack pushed through on her backside, and my mouth fell open. There were two legs hanging down toward the ground. Two perfect, white legs. I scooted around to her backside and witnessed such a miracle as I will never forget. Following the two perfect legs came a perfect white head, followed by the whole lamb. As she gasped again, she pushed the whole lamb out and I scooped the baby into my arms. There were fluids all around, pooling out from the mother's backside, covering us all. Steam rose into the air, and we were enveloped in its white cloud under the silver moon. I hunched over, trying to keep the baby warm, my heart beating wildly with awe. My ewe had given birth!

That was the last moment of peace I would ever know.

The mother stood and trotted away, looking frightened by what she had just brought into the world—startled by its perfection, its miraculous entrance on a dark night in this cold world.

I did not know what to do. Shivering myself, I rubbed the lamb clean of the fluids, seeing the steam rising all around it, stealing the heat of its body. I chased the ewe, offering her lamb to her like I was holding out a loaf of bread at market. She had a wild look in her eye and refused to let me come near. But I knew this: she had enough fleece and enough fat, to last for several hours out here. The lamb could not survive this world without warmth. It had moments to live perhaps, though I could not be sure. I ran back into the home with it, nestling the newborn against the other sleeping ewe. The newborn bleated for milk.

I thought hard of our home, of what was in it, what I could use. I thought of nothing. I had to get the mother in here, nursing, or the newborn would still die. Bile was so high in my throat I could taste it. I wished I had not eaten so much. My first full meal became a curse for me now.

I decided to apply more force to the situation. I ran out into the night, to find the ewe and drag her back. Clouds rolled over the moon, making the way difficult. Stones cut into my bare feet, and I twisted my ankles against rocks as I ran, looking behind shrubs, running further from home, calling softly. I did not want to call a wolf or lion, only my poor scared ewe. I looked for more than an hour, I think. Maybe more.

A bleat came to me on the wind. I grew completely still, opening my ears, willing my whole body to do nothing but listen. Then I turned to my right, and walked in that direction. Parting a pair of low bushes, I saw her. She was on her side, her eyes wide and white, like two perfect moons. Her mouth hung open, her tongue hanging out, touching the ground, covered in sticks and dirt. She did not pull it back into her mouth. I think she recognized me. I don't know. It could have just been her eyes widening as she died.

Behind her, steam rose to the heavens and departed. A dark pool spread around her haunches as I bit my lip to keep from crying.

Edging forward, I looked at her. Hind legs hung out of her birth canal. A second lamb had been coming. She must have panicked when the birth became too hard. That is why she ran from me. She did not know how to have a baby. She did not want to have a baby, not in winter. Even a stupid ewe knows that is disaster, with no fresh grain to feed the mother, nothing for the lambs to graze on after they weaned. They had all been doomed to die. She ran from me out of fear and anger, I knew. I had done this to her.

"I am so sorry," I whispered, reaching out to touch her muzzle.

A high growl made the hairs on my arm stand up. A cat was nearby, perhaps a lion or mountain cat. Blood was in the air, and everyone was hungry. No one waited for spring.

I do not remember walking home. I do not remember if I cried, but I know it would have made no difference. What would happen to me next was already written somewhere far above, where my cries could not be heard.

The newborn lamb was already dead when I returned. The other ewe had not known what to do with it. It froze to death, wet and hungry, surrounded by my sleeping family. If they had heard it bleating, they did nothing.

The next morning, when the sun revealed my stupidity, my father's face was grey like ash from a cold fire.

"How am I to get money from that?" he said, gesturing to the lifeless lamb. I swallowed and looked at my toes. They were flecked with blood. He did not ask.

"And where is the ewe?"

"Outside."

"Dead?"

"Yes, Father."

"So she ate my grain, gobbled my money, and died. You let her mate before her time, before all natural order would have it, and now ewe and lamb are both dead."

I said nothing of the second lamb, my third victim. *Let the lion eat them both, before my father finds them,* I prayed. *Take away the evidence of my sin.*

Father grabbed me by the robe and dragged me across the dirt floor until my face was just under his.

"You are a curse upon this house!"

I whimpered without meaning to. He slapped me.

I put a hand to my face and turned away, but he moved his hands to the center of my linen shift and tore it open. My swollen belly was plain to see.

I heard my brothers snicker above me in the loft. "No different than her ewes."

"At least we can shave the ewes," another replied, and they broke into laughter.

My father raised his hands to my throat, choking me, the anger in his face a mystery to me. My guilt felt a part of me, like a second heart. I went limp, willing my father to kill me.

"Shame!" he screamed. I meditated on that word in the darkness I swam in, as I lie dying on the dirt floor. I could smell my ewe, the surprising, sharp smell of birth and blood. Feet ran past my head, with a strange metal clapping between the steps. Stars fell all around my head, little bells that sparkled before hitting the earth.

Someone touched my neck, tenderly. Anger swelled up in my darkness. I did not want my death to be interrupted. Not all murder was sin! Some murders were grace!

"We had an agreement," a woman's voice said.

I opened my eyes, groaning. I wanted to stop her.

My father spit in my face, his final good-bye. Strong arms went under my back and legs, lifting me to a woman's soft chest. It was Tanis; the perfume of the temple gave her away. I could not look up at her face. I was dirty. I did not want to be saved dirty. I wanted to swim in the darkness, a little further, and disappear from everyone. But I was saved nonetheless. I closed my eyes, squeezing out tears. Everything I did was cursed.

Tanis carried me out and into the streets. She paused only once, setting me down in a doorway to remove the chains between her ankles. She caught me staring at them and shrugged.

"When I heard you were in trouble, I did not take them off. No time."

"Why do you wear them?"

"The chains make me graceful. Men like women who sway with each step."

Her ankles were red and raw. I wanted to cry for her. Why did I bring grief to everyone?

She patted my shoulder. "No one makes me wear them."

"What's going to happen to my other ewe?"

She studied me for a few moments, sitting on her haunches. "Don't you want to know what is going to happen to you?"

"No. No. I don't."

"Your father will most likely kill the ewe and eat her."

The sun rose over our shoulders to the east, casting a prim yellow light over us. I saw Tanis's face clearly, the morning sun harsh on her kind features. Now I saw there were wrinkles around her eyes, deep lines, the scars of time, marring her beauty. I glanced up at the sun, hating it for touching her, for allowing me to see her this way. I closed my eyes and looked down.

"Everyone will be awake soon. We should go."

I did not understand.

She stood, holding out her hand to me, her chains dangling from her other hand. I accepted her help and stood, and together we fled through the quiet stone streets, our feet making a soft beating noise as they landed against each stone. To me, it was like the sound of a heart beating in the stillness of the city. Tanis rescued me in my death, and a new life was given to me.

I did not want it.

"Is this Delilah then?"

A man sat upon a high-backed chair at the top of marble stairs with crouching lions resting on each stair tread, daring the unwise to approach. He was bald, with a stern face and broad shoulders. His legs were bare, easy to see under his robe as he sat. They were covered with coarse black hair. It made me uneasy.

Tanis nodded. We were dirty from the day's walk, and my feet hurt terribly. I braced my knees to stand straight and proud.

"Go and sleep, Tanis. I will watch over her."

Tanis nodded and bowed, exiting through doors that were rimmed in black and white stripes, with bold blue mosaic centers. Inside each center was a golden lion. The walls all around these doors were covered in the same blue tiles and rimmed at ceiling and floor with the same black and white pattern.

As the doors opened and then closed behind her, I peeked into the room. There were golden couches with lifeless forms of women draped across them. Beautiful fabrics covered the women, linens dyed for hours until they made your eyes dance. None of the women stirred. Tanis lay down on a couch, pulling a blue linen over her feet, and closed her eyes.

"So, Delilah. Welcome to Ashdod, and to the court of Dagon."

"Thank you."

"I am Hannibal."

He stood, and I took a step back, holding in my breath. The room was shifting under my feet.

"You will make a wonderful sacrifice. I am sure Dagon will think you are tasty and ripe to eat. We'll only have to roast you a short while since you are so young."

"Yes."

My knees were trembling. I pressed them together to make them stop, watching him as I did.

He cocked his head, grinning. "I'm making humor, Delilah. Tanis saved you for a reason. She has a good eye. She's brought me most of my girls, did you know that? Any girl Tanis picks for me has served Dagon well."

"I will be a good servant too. Should I start now?" I exhaled, hard, to clear my head, looked for a door I could run through and pretend to fetch mending or cleaning rags. Any door would be a good one. I had to get away.

"You are with child. I will not put you to work yet. Let me bring you some wine. And bread. Food is always good, yes? Food and wine, first thing in the morning, makes the whole day more pleasant."

I did not know if this was a trap. Or a test. I did not know this man.

"No, thank you."

He stopped and turned to look at me, as if I had admitted some great crime.

"Not eat? Not drink? Nothing?"

"I'm not hungry. Or thirsty. But thank you."

"If I did not know your story, I would never guess you were lying. You are very good at lying."

He clapped his hands, and a servant appeared. He whispered something to the servant, who looked at me and grinned before disappearing again. A moment later, the servant returned with two others, each bearing a tray stacked over his head with foods and wines. There were fruits (though at this time of the year, this surely was some magic trick), and nuts, and breads, and oils, and vinegars for dipping, and slices of meat, and raisins, and a bowl of milk large enough to bathe in. The servants set these down on a table near me and exited.

"Sit there," Hannibal said, gesturing to a stool in front of the table. I obeyed, trembling. My stomach lifted and lurched, wanting me to bury myself face-first in the foods. I sat on my hands to keep myself strong.

I sat here, not moving, trying not to breathe and taste the foods in the air, until a single tear rolled down my cheek. Hannibal circled behind me, and his hand wiped the tear away.

"Do not lie to me again, Delilah. You are hungry. And thirsty."

I nodded, my throat burning.

"Eat. Drink. There is no shame here."

If he said anything else, I didn't hear it. I was eating from a bowl, from a table, in the light, for the first time in my life. I could not believe how dazzling the wine looked, how pure and calm milk could be in a bowl, like a cloud had been caught! How the bread was brown and crisp and how the darker spots made it crunch in my mouth. My eyes had never eaten with me. It was a new world.

Hannibal sat across from me as my eating slowed, sooner than I wanted. My bulging abdomen sometimes left me no room for food, though my appetite raged unaware. I licked my fingers and laced them under my stomach, holding it up. Had I ever been so full?

I clenched my jaw to keep a yawn from escaping. I would not sleep yet! I did not want to close my eyes. The food was too beautiful. I wanted to clutch the bread to my chest like I saw lovers holding each other.

He saw my longing and grabbed the bread, pressing it into my hands. "You might as well sleep with it. If you don't, you'll wake up and miss it."

I giggled, partly drunk with food and partly drunk with wine, and he broke into a wide grin.

"I have one thing I must do before you sleep here."

He reached into his belt, a wide sash tied at his waist, and retrieved a small dagger, its blade no longer than his palm. It glittered in the morning sun that was illuminating the chamber from small openings above. His hand reached out for my neck, and I whimpered as his other hand closed in. I felt a tug at my scalp then he stepped back.

He was holding a lock of my hair, its edges cut clean and smooth.

"Good girl. Now get some sleep. Everything will be all right now."

I could not look back up and meet his eye.

"I am very sorry," he said.

"For what?" I glanced up and around, for a clue as to what he was going to do to me next.

"For everything that brought you to me. Tanis did not bring you here to hurt you. She saved you. She has nothing but good plans for you. In time, I hope you will begin to heal."

My throat burned and knotted. I tried to bear my neck down, to push the painful lump back down. I could cry when I was alone.

Hannibal did not move any closer to me but gestured to the door that Tanis had slipped behind.

"Go and rest. We do not rise until after the noon hour. You will feel better after you sleep. Then I will tell you more of your new life here, yes?"

I started to nod but stopped myself, forcing myself to look up and into his eyes. "Yes. Thank you, Hannibal."

Hannibal's expression changed, first a frown, then a wide grin. He gestured toward the lion doors, and I went. I needed both arms to open one, but it was silent as it swept over the cool tile floor. No one stirred within. Soft breaths hummed in the air, like invisible wings beating all around us. Several couches along the sides of the room were empty. I spied Tanis sleeping on hers, and walked to her. Lying down on my side, I curled my knees up and tucked my hands under my head, preferring to sleep on the floor beside her than sleep in comfort apart from her.

As I drifted to sleep, I felt her hand reach down and stroke my hair.

❧

When I opened my eyes, I was alone. I sat up and stretched, blinking my eyes. The shadows in the room were thicker now; it was close to the time of the evening meal. But these women did not count time the way my family did. I did not know if they had evening meals here.

I stood and saw that one other woman still slept. She had long blonde hair, a rarity for our people. I wondered where she had come from to have such light hair. She might have come from some land far away, a land without sun, so that her color drained away. Sometimes fish that live deep within the water are pale like this. I've seen them at the market, stacked one on top of the other, glistening like a bed of pearls.

I crept out of the sleeping chambers without making a sound.

Tanis and Hannibal were arguing. I pressed my back against the door, thinking they might not see me. I knew they had not heard me.

"You defend her?" Hannibal said.

"She pleases her noble. He gives us ever better sacrifices. That is not a defense. It's truth."

"She disrupts our lives. She has no respect for our gods. She has no respect for any of us. It's a poison."

"She never had a family, Hannibal. She does not understand how to please us."

"She doesn't want to please us!"

"Because she sees no value in it. The more we love her, the more she will understand. You will be glad she is one of us."

"Tanis. She will never be one of us. That is truth too."

Tanis cocked her head, as if catching a scent. She turned and spied me against the door. Widening her arms, she waved me to her.

"Come here, little pet."

I ran to her, and she wrapped me in an embrace, letting me rest my head on her chest. Stroking my hair, she whispered to me.

"Did you sleep well?"

I nodded.

"Good. Are you hungry?"

I nodded faster.

Hannibal laughed. "This one eats like a gladiator."

Heat rose in my face, and Tanis shushed him. "She's too thin. She needs to fatten up."

"So we can sacrifice her." Hannibal wiggled his eyebrows at me, and I gave him a little smile. Tanis laughed and pushed me toward the table that still sat below the marble steps, off to the side.

Hannibal clapped his hands and conjured a servant. (That is how it appeared to me. The servant must have been waiting in a nearby room, waiting for this command.) My mouth watered at the sound of Hannibal clapping. A plate was soon at my mercy, and I ransacked it like the gladiator I was, leaving no survivors. I burped loudly and out of habit threw my hand over my mouth, glancing up to see if I had awoken anyone. Hannibal was sitting on his high black chair, guarded by those blind stone lions, and he laughed at my reaction.

"Seeing ghosts, are you?"

I smiled, having no understanding what he could mean. But I thought on it as I lifted the bowl and let the juices run into my mouth before holding it up to the light just to see that it was empty. Nothing was left. I glanced back up at Hannibal, and then I understood. My family was gone forever. I knew they lived, but they lived elsewhere, in a different world. When I crossed the threshold into the temple of Dagon, I had entered a new world, like one who died and entered the afterlife.

Hannibal clapped, and the servant returned. I hoped he would bring more food, but he wanted my empty bowl, and I gave it to him with much sorrow. Hannibal rose, scorn lighting his face, and I turned to see what made him so angry.

The blonde one had come out from the sleeping chambers. I got a good look at her now. She was tall and lean, with a square-shaped face that called attention to her high sharp cheekbones and full mouth. She had blood-red eyes that were probably blue if she slept well. She was a strange beauty.

Pressing her palms into the hollows of her eyes, she groaned and sought a place to sit. Noticing the chair next to me at the table, she stumbled over and slumped down as she sat, resting her head on the table. I thought she smelled like fresh-cut cypress wood. I was very sensitive to smells these days. I wondered if that man who put the baby in me hurt me some other way, making smells sharper to my nose.

"Why did you send someone to wake me? You know I'm ugly at this hour."

"You missed prayers, Parisa." Hannibal was still standing, his face pinched and dark. "And the noon meal."

She took a sack from her sash and tossed it on the steps below him. "Horace!" she called, wincing at using her full voice.

The blessed servant who had been feeding me nodded. Why hadn't I thought to ask his name?

"Yes?"

"Take this money back to Lord Marcos. Tell him I won't be seeing him anymore. I am needed here for prayers at dawn."

Hannibal crossed his arms, staring at her as Horace swallowed once with great effort and glanced between the pair.

Hannibal caved first. "You have no grace. You walk like an ox."

Parisa turned her back and stared at me, seeing me for the first time. "Who is this? And why does she get to eat at this hour?"

Hannibal came down the steps toward us, picking up the bag Parisa had thrown down and tucking it into the sack at his waist. "Tanis brought her in."

"She's a little big to be a foundling."

Some women left their babies in fields at harvest time, when they were sure to be found. I gave her a small smile.

She sneered at me and leaned over the table. "Stand up. I want to look at you."

I stood, and she leaned back in her seat, laughing at my protruding belly. She did not sound happy. "Tanis amazes me."

I looked to Hannibal, unsure what to do. I wanted to leave the room, but he gestured for me to sit. I did not want to sit down again at this table with this woman.

She grinned at me. "Do you know what she has gotten you into?"

"I know everything I need to know."

Hannibal raised his eyebrows.

Parisa narrowed her eyes. "Really? Everything?"

"I know that Tanis is good and kind! I know that she saved my life and I trust her and I know that you are a mean, hard woman!"

I jumped up and rushed from the table, running out the doors at the far end of the hall. My head was swimming with angry words. My heart was frantic, pounding fast and sharp, pushing away the awful things I had just said, the fear of what that woman might do next.

My feet hit warm stones, and I turned my face up from the ground to see a purple sky with no clouds or stars. People were milling about all around me, some leaning against an almond tree that had just put out its early blossoms. Some strolled arm in arm with women I recognized from the sleeping room, disappearing around corners, laughing or deep in discussion. The women often stroked the arms of these men—and the others were almost all men, I saw—encouraging more words, more time. Tanis should be here, with the others.

A few couples stopped when they noticed me, very different looks on each face. The men were curious. Curious and surprised. The women were surprised and unhappy, so I pushed my way through them quickly to find Tanis. I was a stench in the nostrils of some women here, and I did not know why.

I turned round a giant limestone pillar to my left and saw Tanis sitting with a finely dressed man in linen robes. She held his hands in her lap, leaning in to listen to him. As she accepted a kiss on her cheek from him, she saw me. I do not know how to describe what I saw in her face at that instant. Anger, perhaps, or fear. Those two are too similar to tell apart from a distance. She stood and yelled something in a language I did not know, as a guard moved toward me.

I ran out, straight past them all, into the busy main street of the city. I looked for a place to sit and unleash all these tears blurring my eyes, but where could I go? I ran toward the back of the temple. My belly began to ache, the baby inside pressing down, making it hard to stand. Using my left hand to brace myself against the wall, I edged along and around the side of the temple, where at least I was alone, if not comfortable.

Something else twisted inside me, something dark and painful. I hated myself. I bit at my nails, wishing I could bite all the way through my skin, destroy this whole miserable creation that I was. I wished I were a roaring lion, stalking the stupid little Delilah through a dark forest, knocking her down with one strong paw, then ripping her up and eating her until not a drop remained. I wished I were that lion. I wished I were anything but me, the girl so clumsy she was caught stealing grain, so stupid she did not even know what to do when that shadow man reached for her, so cursed that a baby sprang up in that same space …

I might have made a longer list, but Tanis found me.

I couldn't look at her. I only knew it was her by the voice.

"Delilah? Are you all right?"

I wouldn't reply, so she came and sat by me, lowering herself to the ground, her back against the wall like mine. We sat side by side until my breathing slowed and my body became flesh again instead of cold stone.

"I am sorry, little pet. I thought Hannibal was with you."

"He was. I ran away."

"Why?"

"It doesn't matter. I don't belong here."

"Are you a seer?"

"No." My tone sounded like an angry child.

"Then you don't know that, do you? I would say you know very little at all, Delilah. That is one reason I had to save you."

"What's another reason?" I knew she was going to say that she needed a slave. Or that Hannibal did. Or some noble. I didn't want to be stupid anymore. I wanted the whole truth, right then. All these things I didn't know were what hurt me. About men, about ewes, about lambs.

"I like you."

I turned to face her. "Don't lie to me, ever, ever, Tanis."

"I'm not lying!"

"Then why did you save me? What must I do?"

Her face grew still, her eyebrows coming close together. "You must eat. And sleep. And then when you are strong, you must have a baby."

"And then?"

She sighed, settling back against the wall but putting an arm around me. "Those are big enough tasks for any woman, much less a girl your age. You cannot take on any more than that for now. Promise me."

"Tanis, I said something awful to the blonde woman inside."

"Parisa?" Tanis laughed. "Did her face puff up and go red?"

"I don't know. I ran away."

"Don't provoke her. She's still a slave in her heart. Small and cruel. I think the gods must have set her eyes backward in her head. She doesn't see a big world with all its wonders. She only sees what she does not have, all the little joys she is denied."

"Did you bring her here too?"

"No. Parisa was brought here by a slave caravan five years ago. We saw her at an auction. She had passed through so many owners. I did not want her brought in, but Hannibal insisted."

"But you defended her to him."

"He has grown to hate her, but he needs the money she brings in from her lord. I only want peace for my girls, so we may work without distraction."

Tanis stood and turned to me, extending her hand. I accepted and stood up, not without some grunting, which made her grin. She rested her hand on my belly, and I saw a shadow of great sorrow pass over her face, like the shadow of a bird flying above, going to a land I did not know.

MOTHER

This is still my tale.

Although another woman would enter into my story, her time is not yet. Not in my tale. I was still unaware of her, a merciful ignorance.

On one of those ignorant days, I was working in the vineyard. I cleared my throat, not willing to spill tears in front of the other mothers. They watched me closely, looking for clues, hoping for a weak moment when I needed their comforts more than my own good name.

I would not give that. Our name is all we have in this world.

I grasped the next vine, slicing the fruitless tendrils, letting them fall at my feet. Tending the vines is not easy work, for the sun returns in glory after the dark, blinding rains, and soft, sleepy people who had rested in the coolness of walled rooms are forced out to face the sun. There is much work this year; the harvest is plentiful. All of Zorah has turned out for the first day of harvesting. All except Samson.

I tended the vines, refusing to acknowledge this, my heart almost crushed after tending to Syvah the day before. She was so pale, so thin, but she still expected to rise from her bed. I pushed her even closer to her death. I told her the truth. You should never tell people the truth. This is what I have decided: The truth kills as surely as the blade.

She had grasped my hand, clutching it between her cold, dry palms. "Why so much sorrow, sister?"

I was more than old enough to be her mother. She was being kind, calling me sister.

I removed my hand and dipped the cloth in the water I had heated. I washed her face, neck, and hands. I dipped a dry cloth in a little jar of olive oil I had brought and rubbed the oil into her skin, across her gaunt face and lips, careful to make her face shine. As if good health were that easy, as if miracles could be so simple.

"You are afraid," she said, settling back against her cushions. Her sons were working in the fields. We were alone. "You should just face the truth."

"And what is the truth?" I humored her.

"You were mistaken. No angel visited you. It might have been a dream. Samson is not the man of God you thought he would be."

I chuckled, not meeting her eyes as I moved down to wash her feet now. As I kneeled on the floor, she watched me with intensity.

She was right about Samson, in a fashion.

She sat up. "Why can't you love him as he is? Why do you drive him so? If you would only accept him, he would come back to you."

"I am his enemy, Syvah. That is the truth. And before you go telling me how I should face the truth, maybe you should face it too."

Syvah looked away, her chin trembling.

"You're dying, Syvah. You won't get up from this bed." I looked away now too, toward her window open to the afternoon sun. "Truth is no comfort to either of us."

When I looked back at Syvah, I was shocked at her expression. She was smiling, a strange radiance settling on her young features.

"Maybe we do not need comfort, not at this late hour of our lives. Maybe we should be asking for hope instead."

What hope could a dying woman hold onto? What hope was there for me, or for Samson?

I smiled as if I agreed, and left her there to wait for the hour of shadows.

I could not see my toes. If I looked down, I saw only full breasts and a bulging stomach. I couldn't sleep well, either. My throat burned at night, worse every week, and although Tanis insisted I sleep on a couch like the others, it did not make me comfortable.

No one else here was with child. I wished to ask someone if these changes were from the child growing big within, or if this was what it was like to become a woman. I was surrounded by women, and what use were they to me? Twenty girls lived in these quarters, but none had a husband. None would be able to tell me the answer to this mystery.

This morning I rose before any of them and sneaked out to find Hannibal already seated on his chair. Two male servants attended him, small men with no muscle. They smiled when they saw me and stepped aside.

I nodded to them and bowed before Hannibal.

"Good morning, Delilah."

"How may I serve Dagon today?"

"Do you hear that sound?"

I closed my eyes and listened. I heard the steady hiss of rain, as I had every morning this month.

"The rains, my lord. They are still with us."

"Listen more carefully."

I exhaled and placed my hands under my belly to lift it, to stop the constant ache from standing. I closed my eyes and listened, harder this time.

"It is softer today?"

Hannibal nodded. "The rains will soon be ending. Maybe one more month of rain, maybe less."

"Should I do something?"

Hannibal shook his head. "I'm trying to tell you that time is passing. You are soon to give birth."

I felt my expression freeze. I did not know how to give birth. What was he asking me to do?

"Yes, my lord." I did not know what else to say. I made a serious expression, nodding.

The door behind me opened. A cold morning breeze swept in, chilling my ankles. I shivered and looked behind me. Parisa stumbled in, her gait unsteady. She rested for a moment with one hand on a pillar, then wiped her forehead and continued her staggering walk toward the sleeping chambers.

Hannibal was on his feet, chains in his hands, walking toward her. His expression was that of an animal about to pounce. He stood in front of Parisa, and she tried to stand erect to face him. She couldn't, though. Her feet remained in one spot, but her torso waved and rolled like she was on a rough sea.

Hannibal grabbed her by the face, and she brought her arms up to pull his off. The servants moved quickly then, taking the chains and shackling her feet while Hannibal held her off balance. They all let go at the same moment, and she fell forward, whipping around to see what had tripped her. When she saw the shackles on her ankles, she shrieked.

"Get these off of me! I'll tell Lord Marcos everything!"

"Only if you want me to cut off your tongue," Hannibal answered. "I am sure even he has had enough of you by now."

"Get these off!" She thrashed, trying to kick the shackles off. The door to the sleeping chambers opened. Tanis came out first, wrapping her tunic tightly against her in the chill. The others girls came out after her.

Tanis saw Parisa struggling on the ground and turned to face Hannibal. "Hannibal …"

Parisa shrieked at her next. "Go back to bed, you stupid heifer! All of you!"

Tanis walked closer to Parisa, bending down to whisper. Parisa pushed her head up and spat in Tanis's face.

I could hear nothing. Even the rains seemed to stop in that moment. I cast my gaze down, so I would not see Tanis in disgrace. I saw her feet, though, as they moved away from Parisa, and I heard the door to the sleeping quarters close.

When I looked back up, they were all gone. Hannibal stood over Parisa, his arms folded. She had stopped struggling, looking up at him with unblinking eyes, every muscle tensed. A soft growl rose in her throat.

He stepped back and nodded at the servants. They paused, glancing at each other before obeying. Parisa gave them no fight as they took hold of her arms and led her to the sleeping quarters.

Hannibal watched, then looked back at me.

"She walked like an ox. It had to be done," he said.

I nodded. "Better to do it now, when she is weak."

Hannibal rewarded me with a smile, twisting his closed mouth up at one end. "You are a very smart girl, Delilah. You will not make her mistakes."

I nodded in agreement, and not just to please him. I knew this to be true. I would not make mistakes here, nor ever again. I knew that mistakes were made for one reason, and one reason alone: ignorance. And I would never be ignorant again, I promised myself this.

I would be proved a fool before the new moon.

Tanis sat still, her eyes closed, as I applied her eye shadow. I used an emerald green, sweeping it out at the edges. Most of the Philistine women wore red, and plenty of it, but the torchlight cast moving shadows, and red made a disturbing appearance.

"Tonight, may I bring you your wine?" I tried to keep my hand, and voice, steady.

"No."

"But you grow thirsty after the second watch."

"We have servants for that."

"But I can do it!" All I had done for weeks now was apply Tanis's cosmetics and watch as she slid out the side door to the private portico. I would sit in these sleeping quarters and listen to the familiar sounds of her night: men's voices, women's laughter, the sound of lyre and harp.

The bigger my stomach became, the less I was given to do. The other women did not even speak to me as often now, stepping to one side as I lumbered past, nodding nervously if I spoke first, seeming eager to move me along. I was an ugly sight, I decided. There were no mirrors big enough to take in all of my appearance at once, but I imagined how I must have looked to them.

Parisa had not left the quarters yet. She was always the last one out, preferring to go out only when called, and only one man ever called for her—Lord Marcos. Perhaps other men wanted to, I did not know, but Lord Marcos was the lord of the entire city, so no man dared claim her time.

I took a shank of lamb from my robes, laying it without a noise beside her couch. Her hand shot out and caught mine, and I cried out in shock.

"I thought it was you." She sat up and stretched, arching her back. I watched, biting my lip. She was beautiful, if you could pretend she had never opened her mouth.

Swinging her legs, still chained, off the couch and onto the floor, she reached down and grabbed the shank, bringing it to her mouth. She gave me a sly wink and began eating. Her eyes did not leave my face as she ate. I shifted from foot to foot, trying to pretend the floor held great interest for me, but glancing up over and over. My face was growing hot.

She nudged me with one foot, the chains sliding against the cold floor. "Why are you feeding me?"

"You slept through the last meal."

She stopped chewing, juice running down her chin. "Becoming a little version of Tanis, are you?"

"No. I don't know. It seemed right to feed you."

"You still have a soft heart. That's good."

But somehow, the way she said it, it did not sound good.

I doubled over, a cramp seizing my abdomen. I couldn't breathe. But as soon as it hit, it passed again. I looked up in confusion at Parisa, but she shrugged and went back to her lamb.

I wanted Tanis. I shouldn't have fed Parisa. It must have been wrong, and now I had a pain. I had angered Dagon. I was thinking about where else I could wait tonight, where else I could hide from Parisa until Lord Marcos called for her, when it happened. Warm fluid gushed down my leg, pooling under my feet. It smelled sweet.

Parisa squealed in disgust, yanking her feet back onto her couch.

"What's happening?" I cried.

"Oh, by the gods. You don't know anything. Go find Hannibal. Ask him."

But I didn't want Hannibal. I wanted Tanis. I looked down at the pool I stood in, turning cold and slick, and saw a trace of blood in the fluid.

I was going to die. My child, too. Dagon was fierce and fast in his justice.

I stepped out of the fluid and shuffled my feet along the floor, scared I would trip. Perhaps there was still a way to save the baby. I opened the great door that led outside, pushing my way through the couples huddled and flirting under the moonlight. My ears heard the men's voices, low and rich, like a buzzing in my head. The women who saw me made wide, angry eyes at me. I was not welcome here.

I moved between them all quickly, silently. The men hardly even noticed. The women, however—they wanted to kill me. It didn't matter. I was going to be dead soon anyway. I just wanted to find Tanis. I wanted to tell her I was sorry. I wanted to tell her thank you, for saving me that morning months ago, and please, save also my baby. If you can. No matter what happens, save the baby.

Tanis would find a way. All my faith was in her.

There was a stairway at the far right end of the portico, one I had never used. One I had never seen used. It had held no curiosity for me, and it had never been explained. Perhaps it held storerooms, or servant's quarters. I did not know why Tanis would be in those rooms, but I had to find her.

Another cramp hit as I reached the stairs. I grabbed the wall and grunted, lips pressed together. *Dagon, spare me a while longer,* I prayed. *Let me find Tanis. For my baby's sake.*

I stood and took the stone steps one at a time, out of breath by the third one. At the top of the stairs was another door, a plain wooden door. I heard no noises behind it, so I pushed it open.

There was a long, dark hall of rooms. Each room had a dark curtain drawn over the entrance, and the curtains closest to me fluttered from the breeze of the door opening. I heard awful sounds, sounds I would not want to describe. I did not take any further steps, and I did not pull back a curtain.

"Tanis?" I called.

Nothing.

I took a step into the hallway, testing the door first to be sure it would not close behind me. It stood, so I let go of it, creeping down the hall, listening for her voice. The noises I heard! I grimaced, my stomach rolling around, nausea coming in unbearable waves. I had heard one man make these noises once. I did not like the noises.

I reached for the curtain nearest me, my hand touching the soft material, gathering it in my palm, crushing it between my fingers. Finding my courage, I yanked it back.

A man and a woman were in the room. Each was naked.

It was not Tanis. It was Rose. I looked at her, not understanding. She screamed a curse at me, and the man shoved me back, yanking the curtain back into place.

A pain came then, so sharp I fell to my knees and cried out.

I don't remember as much as I should now. I think the midwife gave me something. Let me pause now for breath, and I will tell you of how I died.

It was a sparse room. There was a stool, a couch without pillows or linens, and a bowl for water that rested on a small, high table. None of the furniture was even painted or carved. Tanis stood over me as I squatted, and she wiped my forehead. I swept away the tears with my tongue, catching them before they rolled into my mouth. Tanis wiped my nose.

The midwife sat on the couch, rocking on her haunches, her face ballooning as she coaxed me into holding my breath.

"Like this," she crooned. I watched and did as she did.

It did not help.

"It hurts too much!"

"Shhh, now. Everything is fine," Tanis said. She was so good to me.

"No, I'm going to die. I can't do this!"

"Yes, you can. Just tell me when you must push, and we will deliver the baby together, okay?"

"Yes, yes," the midwife echoed. She was no help, I think. I only listened to Tanis. I held her hand as if only she could save me.

"It hurts!" I wailed, the pain splitting me up through the middle, a force so violent and oppressive I could not even vomit, though I retched without sound. I caught a cool, quick breath as the pain left, just as the new pain came and ripped through me again. I opened my mouth and squeezed my eyes shut. How long I did this, stealing breaths between waves of cruelest pain, I cannot say. The memory is strange to me now.

A guttural, animal noise came from my mouth, and I pushed against this child within so hard that bits of blackness floated in my vision. Again I pushed, and with one last cry, I was delivered of a daughter. She was born into my world red and screaming.

I laughed out loud when I saw her, her face screwed up in anger, her lungs drawing the first air of this new world to make her fury known. She was a miracle beyond comprehension. I had desired nothing, not the man who put her in me, not even her, and she was born indignant, unafraid of her own rage, or mine. In her first cry were all my lost words.

I did not wait for the midwife to clean her. Grabbing her slippery red body I clutched her to my chest, wrapping my arms around her, making soothing noises, even as one last pain hit and the last of the birth was finished.

I had not known I could be a gentle, good mother. But I was. The midwife wiped her, as best she could, because I would not surrender my girl, not even as I hobbled over to the couch, lying down.

When the midwife approached with a knife, I sat up in bed and gave her a look that made all the color drain from her face.

She handed me the knife, telling me how to do it. I tied the cord between us, and lifting the knife with a prayer of thanksgiving, I severed the living rope.

This is the moment I try most to forget.

Tanis stroked my hair afterward and kissed my forehead before she excused herself. She promised to return in a few hours and bring me something to eat. I looked around the room, but without windows, I could not tell the hour. Perhaps Tanis had to serve in the temple.

The midwife did not remain after Tanis left. She kept bumping into things, making apologies and speaking nonsense as she gathered her things. She left with loud, fast steps, closing the door behind her.

An oil lamp burned on the table, giving us our light to see each other through. A soft light, pleasant to my daughter's eyes perhaps. She stared up at me, quiet and serene. I ran my finger along her face. How had I been given such a treasure? She was more beautiful than any god I had ever seen. My soul grew quiet within me, too, as we stared at each other in the dim light of my world.

Tanis did return. She brought fresh barley bread and figs and a skin of wine. She pulled the table close to my couch and set them down, then motioned for me to hand her the baby.

I held my daughter tighter. Tanis looked down, then drew a breath and looked at me, steady and with much concern.

"This is not good."

"For me or the baby?" I would do what was best for the baby, if Tanis would tell me what to do.

"You are going to make a wound that cannot heal."

I held my baby and did not reach for the food. Her words were riddles. I did not like riddles.

Tanis looked grieved, shaking her head. "Delilah, have I been good to you?"

"Yes."

"I love you, like you were my own daughter, and I shouldn't. Love makes life more painful."

"Why do you say this to me?"

"I don't want you to hurt anymore. I want you to have peace. Love is your enemy, Delilah. Do not love this child."

"Get out."

"But—"

"Get out!"

And she did, leaving as tears came to our eyes, both of us. She swung the door open to the temple beyond us, letting a cold draft in. I shivered and held my daughter closer. Some time passed before I felt the hunger in my belly and reached for a fig. I was so hungry.

I did not even taste the poison.

MOTHER

I watched as the women prepared Syvah's body in her home. I had bought for them the round perfume jar and the spices, but I did not cross the threshold. I was no longer welcome in their circle. My son, the one I had so proudly proclaimed as their savior, had delivered no one, except his bride and her family unto death. The Philistines, angered now, were raising prices too, forcing some of our children to go hungry at night. All suspicions of Samson, no matter how dark, seemed to be confirmed by the rumors and hardships.

Which made his next move even more incomprehensible. My son, the man I no longer knew. The murderer, and now the judge.

The women washed Syvah's naked, thin body with oil, wiping away the grime of this life. Then they washed her with water and anointed her with the perfume and spices. I had bought the best—myrrh, and aloe, and balsam. They wrapped her frail body in a linen shroud, and, placing her on a stretcher, they carried her to the tribe's burial cave.

I walked behind them, each arm around one of her boys. Perhaps they should have been with the men, but they were heartbroken. They needed a mother as much I needed to be one. My hips were hurting as we climbed the rocky terrain to the cave. Inside, they laid her body, resting the perfume jar against it. One at a time, we entered the cave and said our good-byes to Syvah. The boys emerged, Kaleb's red face crumpling into great sobs. Liam refused to cry. He scowled at the women and walked ahead of us all. Other women gave me dirty looks as I comforted Kaleb.

As if I would ruin them, too, just like I had ruined Samson. Samson, who now sat in a chair at the center of our little village, judging. He accepted cases of all kinds: injuries, stolen livestock, husbands who sought divorce from barren wives.

"How can he judge others?" I had asked Manoah. We were eating dinner alone in silence until that moment.

Manoah set his bowl down and wiped his mouth, fixing me with a stare. "He himself is not judging. He is saving them from the judgment of God."

"He can't even save himself." I knew I sounded bitter.

Manoah went back to eating. "Still. His word is accepted."

Of course it was. No one knew what he might do if angered.

Manoah grimaced, forcing a last bite down. His lips turned darker, a blue shade, when these pains hit. They hit more often these days. I pressed my lips together in fear, and he tried to clear his throat to swallow and wink. He wanted to be my hero, even if God had given me Samson, too.

I shook my head, bringing myself back to this moment's fresh grief. Two boys needed me.

A messenger came running through the valley. His face was wide with fear as he ran. I had not seen Samson for days on end. My grief and my shame all turned to fear when I saw this panicked boy. Where was Samson? What had happened to him?

"Boy! What has happened?" I called.

He stopped, squinting up at us, glancing back at the direction of the village. He wanted to talk to the men. But I had money. I took a coin from my bag and held it up in the sun.

I went to him. When I gave him the coin, he gave us his message. "The Philistines are raising an army against the Hebrews. The Hebrew named Samson burned their entire crop, the standing wheat and the crops still in the field. Then he slaughtered a great many of them! Now they have an army and are coming against us all!"

"Go," I told him, motioning for him to run to the men. My stomach clenched in cold fear.

A woman stepped from the crowd and slapped my face, then spat at my feet. "You have done this to us! Your son has brought trouble to us all!"

They all stood, staring at me, their faces unforgiving and hard.

I took the boys and ran toward the village. Perhaps it was not all true. Perhaps the men would know more. They did not allow me to enter the home where they had gathered, but they welcomed the boys. I stood outside a window, pressing my hot face against the cool stone. My hips burned terribly, but I had no remedy. I had no remedy for anything.

The men did not speak in hushed tones, though they must have known I would listen. They spoke without restraint, without respect. And to think! Some of these men had flirted with me when we had been young together, in our green days, before I had accepted the proposal of my husband.

A tribal elder ended the council with a rap of his walking stick against the floor. "Raise, then, the tribe of Judah. We will bind

Samson ourselves and deliver him to the Philistines. In this way, we may avoid their wrath. May God grant us our petition."

"A judge of our people, turned over to our enemies?" Only one voice was raised in protest, and he was hissed into silence.

I turned my body, resting my whole face against the wall of the home. How had I gotten here? How had Samson, or my people, come to this? God wanted us to destroy the Philistines, and we had not. God had raised up Samson to deliver us from the Philistines, and now we would betray Samson into their arms? Samson would die a horrible, slow death, all so my people could live at peace with their enemies.

This was an abomination. God could not grant this petition, not if He was God.

DELILAH

I woke up slowly, the room smelling of blood. The couch was warm and wet, the blanket stuck to my legs. My mouth was dry and sour, and I rubbed my tongue against the roof of my mouth, trying to dislodge the strange bitterness. My body hurt, especially my hips and groin, like a bruise that went all the way into the bones. I tried to sit up but had no strength.

Falling back onto the couch, I remembered. I grasped at my chest and then, frantic, padded down the blanket, then the couch around me. I forced myself up with a cry of terror, looking around the room, trying to move off the couch. Had I rolled over on my baby? Where was she, if not under me?

Hannibal's face came into focus as he leaned over me, taking me by the shoulders, pushing me back onto the bed. I heard screaming and wailing, like one mourning the dead, and suddenly Tanis was there, telling me to hush, telling me to sleep. I fought against them until it was of no use. My body flopped, lifeless, back onto the couch, and as I closed my eyes, I saw my spirit take shape above my body and float away.

I was not there, but I watched from a far place as they wrapped my chest tightly and bound my breasts down with wet linen strips that would dry later into a hard cast. I never saw my daughter again.

Tanis or Hannibal, or maybe both together, had taken my baby. As the poison wore off, I returned to my body, determined to find her. She was mine. Nothing Tanis said could keep me from loving her. I breathed through my mouth whenever a servant entered my room, the breaths coming so fast and hard that I collapsed twice on that same day. I had to force myself to stay calm, to get my strength back as fast as I could.

The next day, they sent a servant to feed me. The poison was almost gone. I could sit up and hold down a little bread. When I could walk, I was going to walk from this room and hold a knife at Hannibal's throat and make him tell me where my baby was.

It was on that next, third day that Parisa sneaked into my room. My strength was returning; I could put my legs on the floor. I tried to stand, but the room spun. I sat on the edge of the couch, willing strength into my legs, fumbling with my fingers at the bindings across my chest, as Parisa entered.

She once had made me afraid, even shy. But I felt nothing for her now. I had only one thought.

She sat next to me, silent. I glanced over at her when several moments had passed this way.

"Why are you here?" I asked.

"To see if you are well. You are not the first one to lose a child here."

"Tell me where my daughter is."

Parisa cocked her head at this. She reached up and rested a hand on my shoulder. I pulled away. She had the eyes of a snake.

She put her hands in her lap, and I felt the couch shake. Her shoulders rose up and down. She was crying.

"I should not be here," she whimpered. "Tanis will be so angry with me."

I grabbed Parisa by the shoulder, turning her to look at me. "Tell me where my daughter is!"

She pressed her lips together, tears streaming down her face. I still saw nothing in those eyes. Not even tears brought them to life.

"Answer me!"

"Tanis does not want you to know. She warned everyone not to tell. But we all have babies there."

I stood, wobbling, grabbing her shoulders for balance. "Take me there. Now."

She opened her mouth to protest, to give some other excuse, but I dug my fingers into her shoulders, trying to drive strength all the way down my legs. If I had to crawl I would get there.

She stood, slipping an arm around my waist for support, whispering in my ear. "Do not make a sound. I will show you."

Something in her voice was cold, like her eyes. She had been waiting for me to gather my strength and stand; I did not know why.

We slipped from the room. She was as quiet as I. I did not know what life she had lived before this place, but I knew what sorts of things made girls learn to be silent when they walked.

Parisa led me from the room and into a hallway I did not recognize. We went up a stone staircase that had windows to the outside.

The breeze was cool and fresh, giving me much strength. I had not smelled fresh air in several days. The world smelled sweet and green. I did not smell death, but I should have.

At the top of the stairs, a small wooden door stood closed. Parisa put a finger to her lips for silence, but a smile flickered in her eyes. Bumps rose along my arms.

She opened the door, and it creaked as its hinges turned. I saw blue spring sky and a bright light from the sun. The heat hit me, but I did not feel warm. Summer was so close.

Parisa, standing behind me, pointed down. We were on the roof of the temple. If I looked to my right, I could see the Philistine empire stretching before me, and the great wide sea was to my left. The roof had a huge flat expanse, with stands along three sides so a crowd could gather with a view of the front of the temple.

After taking it in, I did look down, as Parisa wanted. I squinted, unsure of what I was seeing, and she pressed her palm against my back, urging me to bend deeper, to look closer into the gutters. She wanted me to be sure.

My daughter was dead. All the daughters, all the sons, were strewn, dead, in the gutter. How many there were, I could not say.

I will not describe it further. You, too, would go mad with grief, as I did. I fell to my knees, screaming, and Parisa fled. I screamed and tore at my tunic until servants came and dragged me back down to the windowless room. It would be days before they stopped drugging me, and weeks before I could open my eyes without seeing all the bodies, all those secrets of this temple. I thought Dagon was a god of life, of harvest and plenty. He was nothing but death, and no one seemed to care.

How could that be? I understood now that men and women did things here together, things I did not want to do, but were they not happy as they did them? Did not the babies they made in those rooms bring them joy?

I hated these questions as I hated the images in my mind. I would beat my head against the wall until I left a red mark on the stones and a servant came with the wet rag that stank, the rag he forced into my mouth, and my neck burned and grew stiff, and my eyes closed again.

I scratched at my chest with my nails, long ragged red marks down my chest, opening my chest to the cold air of my chamber, whimpering my thanks for the blindness of pain, until the servant came again, with a new drug, one he poured in my mouth, and I, foolish, thought I was drowning and blessed him in my heart. But I woke again, a day later, an hour later, I did not know. Where was I? And what were we worshipping? Why did it end in death? In agony I passed my hours, until the blood dried between my legs and I no longer screamed in my sleep.

And yet, the strangest part of my tale is yet to be told, for soon a man would seek me out. He would love me though I had nothing to live for, and it was this last great love that would change the course of my life.

Though I was forgotten by my gods and broken by a hard life, I would soon hold the fate of two gods in my hands, both Dagon and the Hebrew god Yahweh. That is how it would seem to me. Only now I know the truth: Only one God lived, and He held my fate in His hands.

Three thousand men went out to find Samson. Manoah was not with them. He had left the meeting pale and shaken, going home and staying inside.

"Go," he had whispered to me, his voice cracked and hoarse.

"I've never traveled anywhere without you!"

Manoah just shook his head, a tear rolling down his cheek.

The men walked for two days, and I rode my donkey behind them, keeping my distance. On the second night, we had arrived at the sharp, cold place of Etam, where rocks grew more than trees or anything green. It was a place you could not farm, could not build upon, and most of all, it was a place you did not want to fight in. The rocks that stacked one upon the other, higher and higher, leading into cold dark caves—these rocks had no soft places, no safe place to fall.

"Samson!" the village elder called out, raising his walking stick, as if he were Moses and doing some great thing. I spat behind my palm, so no one would see me.

From the dark mouth of a cave, my son emerged. He was thinner and looked tired. I ducked behind a rock to watch. I could not shame Samson. If he saw me, he would feel shame. But perhaps, if I was not here, he would rise up in his strength and become the man I wanted him to be.

"What do you want from me?" Samson called back, his hands on his hips. He was still a big man, an imposing bird of prey above us.

"What have you done to us? Are we not your brothers, your family, your tribe?"

Samson turned to go back in his cave. Good boy. These men were not brothers or family. Not to my son.

"Stop! You know the Philistines rule over us! Now you've stirred them up! A thousand of them march, even now, toward our people."

Samson shrugged, his back to them.

The elder slammed his stick against the ground. The echo ricocheted through the rocks.

Samson turned. "As they did to me, I did to them."

The men grumbled and shook their heads. His answer did not please them.

"My son," the elder began.

I made fists with my hands when he used those words. When Manoah recovered, he would be angry at this arrogance.

"My son, come down. Don't make this worse for your family, or for us. We have come here to bind you and deliver you to the Philistine army. As you can see, there is no escape. We are three thousand strong."

Samson watched them without fear. Then, slowly, he raised one finger, one small concession. "Swear to me you will not try to kill me."

"He is afraid." The men were talking.

"He should be."

The men murmured and snickered. How they had hungered for this moment all their lives, their chance to wound their healer, to crush their savior! But I saw the truth, even if they did not. Samson was going to spare them. He wanted an oath, so that he would not have to rise against his own people and spill their blood too. I loved my son. He gave me hope, and my heart revived.

The elder spoke. "We will not harm you. We vow only to tie you up and deliver you. Any man who dares to strike you will be cut off from our people."

The warning sent a chill through the men. I saw their backs stiffen and hands drop to their sides. Samson was not worth dying for.

All I wanted right then was to be gone, with Samson, to be back at home with Manoah and a full meal and stories and jokes. I wanted peace. I wanted a type of death, a hiding from all that we were called to do. I wanted my son and nothing else.

Ropes were passed up to the front, new ropes from a sparrow-wort shrub, a shrub that thrived in the desert, the one spot of life where there was little else. Samson hopped from stone ledge to ledge, descending with grace and speed like a gazelle. He smiled broadly as the men tied him under the watchful eye of the elder.

My son was a captive. They led him east to the hill country. We stopped in Lehi about two hours later. I stayed in the back, unwilling to be seen, covering my head, but not my face, with my shawl. He had not seen me.

My son, bound in ropes like an animal, was going to be delivered to the Philistines. They would surely kill him. Surrounded by three thousand Hebrew men and facing one thousand Philistines, what could I do but pray?

I prayed with such ferocity that I was sure would rend the heavens open. Every muscle, every bone, ached with the urgency of calling upon my God, my great and mighty God. This was the moment to act. This was the doom only He could save us from.

And do you know what God did? The mighty God who parted seas and sent plagues and struck down traitors where they stood?

Nothing.

Nothing at all.

As Tanis entered, I was sitting up on the couch, cleaned for the first time in two weeks. The room still stank. The servants could not mask the smell of this place. I made no move as she entered, gave no sign of what hid in my heart.

She watched me for a moment, pulling in her lower lip between her teeth, then sat beside me. She had dark circles under her eyes, as if the last few weeks had not been easy for her either.

The only living thought in my mind was the approaching moment of her death. And then I would work to destroy this place. I would pull down everything, as far as the eye could see. I saw my final death, a great flash that made me shudder and turn away. I saw stones falling as I, too, fell through the air.

Tanis threw her arms around me then, comforting me with little noises. I did not resist. I kept my eyes open, though, staring at the floor.

"What you saw—"

I bit at her, making her jump in fear. A servant grabbed me, forcing me face down onto the couch as I kicked. I thrashed and screamed, but she screamed louder until I heard what she said.

"Your child is not there!"

My lungs burned. I could not draw air through the blanket smothering my face. The servant, mistaking this for weakness, pressed my arms harder together, pinning them behind my back, allowing me to rise slightly for air.

I stared at Tanis, watching the vein in her neck pulse with life, the silent rhythm making me wet my lips. Her hand went to her neck, as if by instinct. I looked up at her face.

"Your child is not there. She is not dead, Delilah."

I laughed. I remembered that name. I had been a girl once, hadn't I? Before this room, before those awful, stupid ewes, I had been a girl once named Delilah, a girl nobody loved. She was gone now.

"How did you find that door, Delilah?"

I cocked my head. Why did she use that name again and again? Did she not see?

"Who showed you that gutter?"

"I found it myself."

Tanis slapped me. I gasped from the fresh sting, but the look of sorrow on her face was unnecessary. I was grateful for the shock of pain. I felt something. I had not felt anything in so long.

"I do not want to hurt you, Delilah. But you must tell me the truth. Who showed you that gutter?"

"I found it myself."

Tanis wiped her hands, disappointed. She knew I was lying. She stepped away from me, toward the door. "You have been in here too long. I miss you."

She paused, watching me for some sign. I gave her nothing.

"Tomorrow, you will appear before Hannibal. Parisa is not your friend. You must tell him the truth."

So she knew. She wanted me to betray Parisa, perhaps to get rid of her at last. Tanis wanted my loyalty, wanted me to take her side and tell the truth. But truth would save no one now.

MOTHER

The roar shook my feet as Samson was led into the Philistine camp at Lehi, the land of rolling hills and rocky soil. We had marched past wide clusters of dark green trees and polite rows of olive trees. The Philistines had probably picked them over for any remaining olives. We were past the harvest. Anything good that was going to come from the earth had already come. Only rains and winter remained for us.

We entered the camp, and men stood, cheering. They grabbed him roughly and shoved him, closing in around him, sealing him from me. The men of Judah fled, their work done. They pushed past me like little fish swimming fast in a group, blind and quick.

I hid myself. I would not let Samson's body remain in this camp. If I had to drag it home myself, I would do it. There was a little grove of olive trees not far, and I hid myself there.

No sooner had I stolen into the comfort of the trees and let my tears fall, then a strange hum filled the air, like the sound of thousands of wings. A shimmering rose from among the thousand Philistines soldiers, and I knew what was happening. The power had come upon Samson. I clutched my tunic to my neck, holding my breath.

I heard those noises again, the same wet thumps and screams I had tried to forget from Ashkelon. I refused to look away. I had to know if my son would live, if perhaps he might reach out his hand at the moment of death and I could run to him and be reconciled. Even if they slew me next, I would do it.

But I waited a long time. The chaos, the running, the confused commands made no sense to me. All the fighting was in one spot, and the Philistine army was getting smaller, until at last I saw, in the clearing, a pile of bodies tall enough to build an altar on.

My son stood swinging a strange curved club at the men as they attacked. Samson took one or five down with every blow, blood spraying in all directions like a red storm burst loose on Lehi. I covered my ears with my hands so I wouldn't hear the sounds of death. Yet I couldn't look away. I had to know what happened, in case he needed me.

Even the strongest man might sometimes need his mother.

Samson worked for the entire day, eight hours perhaps. It took him that long, and he was fast. Finally, he threw down his club and shouted, "With the jawbone of an ass, I have slain one thousand Philistines!"

No one was alive to hear. I looked intently at the club. It was indeed a jawbone.

He was covered, dripping in blood. His hair dripped red, his arms and chest were red, his face was red. Even his teeth were red. If he had cut himself or tasted their blood, I did not know, but there was blood coming from his mouth. Only his eyes were white. And I was afraid, sorely afraid. My legs trembled, and I held onto a tree to remain standing. I did not know what he might do next.

I was looking at a wild animal made angry by his kill and restless for more.

Then Samson collapsed. I hid deeper in the trees, and I heard him cry out.

"Lord, you gave me this deliverance! And now what? Should I die of thirst and let the uncircumcised people carry me away?"

The ground nearest me, the only clean place, began to sink. I watched in horror as the ground sank lower and a shadow passed over it. I looked down at my own feet, the ground beneath me, but it did not move. Still, I clung to a tree to be safe.

Water, clear and bubbling, rose up from the pit near Samson. He lifted his head, perhaps scenting the water on the wind. He crawled to the spot, over bodies, through red pools, kneeling at the water's edge, lapping at it like a dog.

He looked up suddenly, those white eyes against that red face, looking straight into the trees, but he did not see me.

I breathed softly, praying that God would have mercy on my son and deliver our people some other way. All I could do now was pray. Silently, I unwrapped my arms from around the tree and took a careful step backward. I had to get home before my son knew I had witnessed this, too. I did not want to help him rob the bodies. I had seen enough death to last a lifetime.

I was led from my room the next morning, after a servant had combed my hair and changed my robes. I gave him no fight. He never reached for the dagger at his side. These eunuchs, though, are so weak. I could have taken it from him without much effort. The men here underestimate the power of a woman.

In the main hall, Hannibal sat on his chair, his face impassive. His own eunuchs stood behind him on either side. At his feet, assembled before him like an audience, were the women of the temple. Though I was one of them and served the same god, they all seemed to me to be strange, unblinking creatures of the night. Why would they destroy the work of a god if they pledged to honor him?

As I entered, the women parted, making room for me to approach Hannibal. I looked them in the eye, one by one—Tanis, Parisa, Rose, and the others. The others looked shocked by my appearance. I had lost all the fat around my hips and stomach, and I knew my hair was thinning out. Clumps of it came out with every brushing.

Before Hannibal, I bowed, then squared my shoulders, waiting for him to speak.

"When Delilah was in great grief, someone took her to the roof of the temple and showed her what was hidden in the gutter. Who among us would do that?"

No one moved.

"I will not tolerate cruelty." He extended his hand, and the eunuch to his right placed in it a whip. "One of you will have to remain robed tonight."

I heard the women behind me exhale in fear. Lashes were reserved for slaves. The marks might not fade, no matter how long the robe was worn.

Tanis stepped forward, coming to my side. She bowed before Hannibal. "I did it."

I reacted sharply, my body jerking away from her, unwilling to even touch her by accident.

"Liar!" Parisa shouted.

"If you must punish someone, punish me. I am guilty." Tanis acted as if she had not heard Parisa.

Parisa pushed me aside and grabbed Tanis by the shoulders. "What are you doing?"

"You couldn't have meant to hurt her," Tanis answered. "It must have been an accident. Punish me, Hannibal."

Hannibal stood. "I will neither punish Tanis nor banish you, Parisa. That is what you wanted?"

Parisa let go of Tanis but did not step back. Instead, she drew a breath and spat in Tanis's face before walking out. As she turned, our eyes met, and I saw a flash of something odd, a feeling I did not think she was capable of. Parisa looked sad. Defeated, perhaps.

But as fast as it surfaced, it left, and she winked at me, a cold smile in place once more.

Hannibal dismissed the women, encouraging them to return to their preparations for the evening services. He then motioned for me to remain, and Tanis as well. Tanis raised her arm as if to put it around me, but I stepped away, glaring at her.

"Why did you defend her?" I did not sound angry, but Tanis frowned, worried. I wanted the truth. Was this what worried her?

"Parisa would love to be banished, Delilah. She thinks Lord Marcos would divorce his wife, and he would be hers."

"If she doesn't want to be here, let her go."

"I can't. She has no future outside of this temple. Lord Marcos doesn't want to buy her as a wife. Even if she were to get her freedom, she would die on the streets, in disgrace."

"So you're going to keep her here, no matter what she does to anyone else."

"Until she realizes that we only want what's best, yes."

"When Tanis brought you in, you had suffered so much already," Hannibal interrupted. "I thought you understood the ways of men. I did not know you would cause such trouble."

"Me?" I couldn't help my voice sounding shrill.

"You know at least how women should please men, that this is how Dagon is honored. What did you think we did with the fruit of these celebrations? No one wants to care for another man's child. Life is good, but when life is unwanted, we have every right, a duty even, to end it. It's the only way to prevent suffering. Are you so blind?"

Tanis stepped in front of me, shielding me from his impatience.

"No!" He insisted. "How much time have we wasted already, waiting on her? You asked me to wait for the birth, and I did. You asked me to wait until she recovered, and I did. How long must I wait now, for her to understand?"

"She will understand, and she will serve." Tanis used a soothing, reasonable tone, as if she was not speaking words of madness.

"She will never serve like the others. I've held my patience for your sake. But you saw how she reacted to the birth, and how that stirred all the women. What if everyone reacted this way? The temple would have to shut its doors!"

Tanis looked at me, dipping her chin as if to implore me to speak in my own defense. I shook my head.

She held a hand up at Hannibal, requesting his silence, before addressing me.

"You have nowhere else to go. You know that."

I watched her and moved not a muscle, not a bone. She stepped closer to me, still holding her hand up at Hannibal.

"If I tell you where your daughter is, will you do as I say?"

My heart beat faster, but I did nothing to show it. "What is your request?"

"Stop feeling everything so deeply, as if everything that happens to you is a great tragedy. We all suffer here. But we can pass our years in peace, if you will promise to trust me."

I thought of the scales at the markets, of how some were weighted to cheat the buyer. A hungry buyer had no way to test them, and he had no choice but to eat. His mind saw the trap, but his hunger pushed him on.

I had to know. That was my hunger.

"I promise."

Tanis gently rested her hands on my shoulders. "Your daughter is not dead."

"Where is she?"

Tanis frowned; I watched the lines along her forehead gather and bunch into a knot. She glanced back at Hannibal.

"I will not cause anymore trouble. I just want to know."

"An important man in our city has a wife who is barren. She has sought the help of the temple, sent sacrifices, paid for healings, begged us for a way to open her womb," Tanis said softly.

"And you could not."

"Dagon chose not to." Hannibal's voice as sharp as if he had been insulted.

Tanis shook her head. "Your daughter is in the home of a very wealthy man and his wife. She will be loved and well cared for. But you will never see her again, and she will never know of your existence."

My knees went out, and Tanis caught me. I tried to stand quickly; Hannibal was rolling his eyes at me. I was causing too much trouble. I had come here a frightened, grateful girl, but the birth had changed me. He did not like who I had become.

I pushed her back and stood straight. "I should eat something. I have work to do." I looked up and stared hard, right into Hannibal's eyes. He nodded his approval.

A servant brought me food. I ate without tasting it. I forced it down my throat. I would not let Hannibal know the deep wound ripped open in my belly again, the incurable sadness of the condemned. My daughter would be loved, but not by me.

She was better off without me. Everyone was.

I returned from Lehi by night—not a safe thing to do for anyone, especially a woman. My heart beat wildly, and I often had to stop and press my hand against it, willing it to slow down. I heard footsteps behind me many times, and the coarse breathing of a beast.

Samson was following me. I had done this to him, brought this curse upon him, his destiny to hunt and kill. He was angry with me. He stalked me like I was the animal. I fled, faster and faster, frightened of his wrath.

I slid into my home with an anguished cry of relief and found Manoah sleeping on his pallet downstairs. This was good. It was normal for us, and how I needed normal again! I was never so grateful to remove my tunic and lie down beside him, covering myself with his blanket. He was warm and I was so tired from my journey, from my life and my son.

In the darkness, I noticed that his breathing was labored. I should have left him with bitter herbs or made an offering for healing before I left.

I rested my head on his chest. "I should not have gone. I should have stayed with you."

He reached for me and rested a warm, strong hand on my side. "The Lord is good."

I had not known he was awake. "How is that an answer?" I chided him gently. He needed to sleep.

"How is it not?"

With that, he went back to his sleeping. I laid awake for the remainder of the hours, daring myself to believe this again. Daring myself to believe in a God that watched His chosen one slaughter so many—slaughter until his beard ran red—a God that offered no comfort to a weary, confused mother, or to a wife terrified that her husband was dying.

When I proved I would eat everything set before me and would not harm myself again, I was brought back to the main sleeping room. I was given the couch closest to Tanis's and encouraged to fix my hair after the evening meal.

The temple women would begin serving soon.

"When a man speaks to me, what must I do?"

Tanis stopped combing her hair and pressed her lips together in thought. "You are not ready. Just serve the women tonight and watch."

"I know why you brought me here. It was not to carry platters and cups."

She made a clucking sound, a gentle reprimand. "I do not like it when you talk this way. I think you know very little of why I brought you here."

I walked to her and picked up her comb, setting to work on her hair. She sat straight up, her back to me, as my hands worked so close to her neck. I wondered what she thought of me now, now that she had seen me go mad, seen me look at her with my animal eyes.

I braided a section of hair along the sides, wrapping the braid to the back, securing it in place with a pin. I did another braid along the side, saying nothing to her, securing it with another pin.

Rose stopped her own preparations and admired Tanis.

I walked around Tanis to face her, checking my work from the front. Grasping a thin reed in the kohl pot, I swept a long line of black across her eyes. She looked stunning.

I sat beside her and held the reed out to her. "Now do mine."

"No."

I put the reed in her hand and closed my hand around hers. "I have to do this."

"What if you didn't? I want you to wait for a little while longer before joining us."

"Tanis, you knew this moment would come. You knew it when you bought me from my father."

"He was going to stone you."

"Better off here than dead." I forced a serene smile that meant nothing to me.

"I didn't want you to suffer."

I did not know if she meant at the hands of my father, or for the loss of my child. I had no desire to know.

"The kohl," I urged her, shutting my eyes.

I felt the cold wet reed slide across my eyelids, and her hand resting on my cheek for balance. She set to work on my hair next, and Rose set in my lap a jeweled pin from her own hair. The other women in the room took notice as I was groomed. Some nodded in approval. Others stared down at their hands, running fingers over thickening veins and brown spots, choosing then to spend more time on their own hair. As if we would compete for the same man. As if all men were not the same.

No touch would ever make me flinch again or feel pain or fear. I had stopped feeling everything in that birthing room weeks ago. But one desire had not left me. One burned hotter as the others faded to gray ash and floated away. One desire kept me alive.

I would find a way to punish Parisa for what she had shown me. If I had never seen that, perhaps I could have believed in the power of offerings made to stone gods. I could have lived with hope. Hope was all I had ever had, and Parisa had taken it from me. She had betrayed me once. I wanted her to regret that as much as I did. I wanted her to feel what I did now, and weep. My pain had focused on one small goal, and that felt so good.

At last, I had grown strong enough to hurt her, just as I had been hurt.

Perhaps that, too, was hope.

Parisa leaned on Lord Marcos's arm, turning her body into his, leaning forward as she spoke in soft tones. He held a bowl in his opposite hand and laughed loudly at her story. I smiled at him from across the room and saw the catch in his breath when our eyes met. I bowed my head so our eyes would not meet again.

Like a cat, I slid one foot in front of the other, moving across the floor in complete silence, rolling my hips with each step, gliding past him, pausing only when I was safely behind Parisa to look back again.

He was watching. I lowered my head in modesty and moved on, gliding to another man standing alone. That man straightened at once, sucking in his stomach, talking fast. He was telling me his name and his desire of great blessings from Dagon and was I a new priestess at this temple because he had not seen me before and he was a devout man.

I nodded and replied only, "Yes."

He stammered on, then stopped as if hit over the head with a stone. He seemed frozen, unable to say anything else. I had to help him.

"You want to go upstairs with me, yes?" I whispered.

He nodded and wiped his glistening face.

I turned my head, curving my body around as I did, to catch sight of Lord Marcos. He glanced in my direction, then glanced again when he saw me looking at him. Parisa stopped talking and was turning to look in my direction when I turned back to my victim. I took him by the arm and led him up the stairs to our right, not minding the cold, dark stairwell or the animal noises that greeted us when I opened the door.

The more noise the better.

We walked to a room where the curtain stood half-open. I held the curtain back and motioned him to step inside. He did, and at once removed his belt. It hit the ground with a loud thump, and I knew his money bag was heavy. But after all, I had not chosen him for his looks.

I crossed my arms. "What do you want Dagon to do for you?"

He became bold, now that we were alone and the curtain was drawn for privacy. I had chosen well.

"Why don't we show Dagon the blessing of life and celebrate his goodness to us?" He was moving closer to me, his fingers already fumbling at the pin on his shoulder, holding his robe in place.

I stepped back. "Who is stupid, you or your god?"

He stopped, jerking his chin to his neck, as if he had not comprehended my words.

"What kind of god must be shown how to bless his followers?"

His face, clouded with confusion, suddenly brightened. "Is this a game?" He frowned again. "Do I pay extra for it?"

I took a step toward him, glaring at him with my animal eyes. "How can you ask Dagon to bless you with a harvest if you curse the fruit? You are a stupid fool."

He was trembling, his mouth open. I did not think he was a regular. He would have had words.

Bending down, I took hold of his bag, satisfied with its weight in my hand. With the other, I opened the curtain and nodded for him to leave.

He gasped in indignation, but seeing I had his money and his reputation, too, he left. As he stepped past me, I leaned toward him and whispered a little encouragement with the sweetest of smiles.

"Come back next week."

He did everything I could have asked for, and well. Stomping through the portico, a shocked look on his face, he caught the attention of Lord Marcos and several of the others. I stood at the bottom of the stairs and watched him go. Without looking at anyone, I turned and slid away, my keep earned for the night, my suspicions confirmed. The lifeless body of Dagon stood over them all in the portico, his blind eyes seeing nothing they did.

Dagon was everything I suspected him to be, which was nothing at all. And his followers were ignorant, no better than a foolish young girl with two ewes.

How easily disaster could find the foolish.

I dropped the bag at the feet of Hannibal and walked away, ready for sleep, pretending I did not hear the murmurings of the women—the hushed, frightened whispers. I had seen their faces when I had dressed for the evening. I was no longer the young fool, the pregnant child they could be tender to. I was a woman now myself. And I had earned more money in my first night than some of them earned in a week.

"Delilah. Explain this." Hannibal had picked up the bag and was weighing it in his hand as I turned. He frowned, displeasure evident.

"What must I say?"

Hannibal and Tanis spoke in each other's ear. She looked unhappy as well. Tanis addressed me next.

"Who gave this to you?"

"Was I supposed to ask his name?"

The demure among the women cleared their throats. Those less refined just giggled.

"I will do that next time. And he didn't give it to me. I earned it."

"Everyone, go to your chambers. Delilah, you stay here."

From his red face, the women judged that I was in much trouble, guilty of some secret crime. They filed out without another word, Rose giving me a pitiful look, her lips pressed together and eyes wide with worry. I nodded to her to go on. Parisa lingered at the edge of the group as they disappeared into the sleeping chambers, watching me with narrowed eyes.

Hannibal clapped his hands at her, hurrying her along.

When I returned to the sleeping chambers within the hour, no one was asleep. Although no one spoke when I pushed open the doors and entered the room, I felt their piercing gaze. Was I crying? Had I been punished? And for what crime?

At my couch, I began getting ready for bed, removing my outer tunic, sitting on the bed in my linen shift and bringing a foot up to my knees to massage it. My ankles were still swollen at day's end, from the birth. I had no energy to tell them anything, to answer their questions or endure their wrath. Hannibal had been well pleased with me. He was going to reward me.

Tanis had remained in the other room with Hannibal, discussing how his plan would begin in the morning. I pressed my lips together to keep from smiling. The women thought I had been scolded and shamed, as if I was not supposed to work alongside them.

I imagine some even felt superior. I was a child to them, and how could I do the work of a woman?

Parisa came and sat beside me on the bed. I looked at her with such innocence.

"Are you mad at me, too?" I asked her.

"No." Parisa couldn't hide her complete lack of interest in anyone else.

"Did you have a good night with Lord Marcos? I've seen the way he looks at you. He is in love."

She did not acknowledge my words. "Why did you not betray me to Hannibal?"

I looked down at my lap, keeping my voice low, like hers. "You are the only one who told me the truth."

Neither of us knew if I was sincere.

MOTHER

I did not see Samson again, not for weeks. Some nights I would bolt upright in bed, in the darkest hours, imagining that he had called my name. Trimming a lamp, I would go to the roof and look out into the night, craning my old neck for a sign of him. The wind would moan his name to me, and I would let down my hair and close my eyes as the sound of his name rushed past me. Only there, alone and cold, arms outstretched into darkness, could I weep for him.

Months had passed, and I no longer spoke to anyone in the village or from our tribe. Those men tied my son up, delivered him to be killed, and now he was their hero. They recounted his victories, they sang of the numbers of his dead. These selfish men cared only that the Philistines feared Samson and gave his tribe special respect. The men of my village never asked what the cost to Samson would be, or me. My name was certainly never on their lips.

And I had other sons to raise now, for Syvah's sons came to live with us. They were almost young men now and worshipped Samson, which I discouraged. They, too, did not understand the price of deliverance.

Kaleb ran and fetched me from this poisonous stew I was swilling as I pressed raisins into cakes for storage.

"It's Samson," he said, trying to catch his breath. "He's drunk, and he's calling for you."

I picked up my tunic in one hand so I would not trip and followed Kaleb out our door, hobbling. My knees were stiff from sitting, and I could not spring up like young people did. Kaleb led me down a dirt path between houses, toward the edge of our village. Samson was sitting, his back against a wall, his head on his knees. His hair splayed all around him in the dirt, thorns and briars caught up in gnarled mats. I saw his shoulders moving.

My son wept.

I stood before him, watching. My chest grew tighter from the pain of seeing him this way. Even if he had made mistakes, if he had misinterpreted the Lord's will for his life, he was still my son. But I could not be tender with him, not until I knew he had seen his mistake.

"It's the middle of the day, Samson. And you're drunk?" I kicked at him with my toes.

"Do you know what they did to her?" He looked up at me as he said it. He had lost more weight. His eyes were bloodshot and sunken, his cheeks gaunt. His lips were red and cracked, as if he often slept in the sun.

I shook my head, more from the sight of him than his question. I did not want to talk about Amara. Not again. His grief over her betrayal was endless.

"They burned her alive. With her whole family, even her little sister. The Philistines murdered my wife because of me," Samson moaned.

I stepped back. I could not help it. Kaleb caught me by the arm, but I jerked away from him. Samson was not thinking of me, but I saw what he did not. I was his mother. They might kill me next. Or Kaleb and Liam. He had to see the error he had made, or we would all be in danger.

"She told them the answer to the riddle. She did not love you."

Despite myself, I softened. My beautiful, broken boy, weeping in the dirt for the one death he did not cause, the great price she paid for loving him. I fell to my knees, wrapping my arms around him, and together, we wept.

When we rose the next day, the other women attended to their daily business—caring for their tunics, and the temple, and fulfilling all the work women everywhere must do: to keep up their looks and their worlds, which are both always in danger of decay.

Tanis led me to Hannibal, who sat on his chair in the main room, going over accounts with his servants. He smiled and rose when he saw me.

Tanis whispered in my ear as we closed the distance to him.

"Do not try to befriend Parisa. She will hurt you, worse than before."

"Are you saying there are more terrible sights in this temple?"

"Stop that."

"I won't befriend her. You have to trust me."

Tanis and I bowed before Hannibal, who came down the steps to greet us with a kiss on our cheeks.

"Are you ready to begin?" he asked.

I smiled, my cheeks pulling apart all the way to my ears. I was not lying when I said yes. Hannibal had offered me everything I could have ever wanted. I was going to be educated. I would learn what men learned and understand the ways of this world. There would be no more secrets.

Hannibal and Tanis led me to the portico. I had not been there in the bold light of the afternoon sun. It was very warm, with the summer months being upon us, and although we had trees planted, the plantings were made more for privacy and mood than for comfort.

An old man with a clay tablet sat on a bench, his head wrapped in a turban, his face darkened by the sun. His eyebrows were bushy and white, and his eyes were yellowed and watering. He grinned and tried to stand as he saw us approach. I noticed that his front teeth were missing.

"Delilah, this is Akbar. He is the finest tutor in the city. He will be here every day at the first hour after rising. You are to be on time. You are to be ready to work, ready to listen, and ready to do whatever he asks."

I glanced at the tutor as he nodded along eagerly with Hannibal's instructions. "Very good, very good," he muttered. I did not think he would ask me to do anything I was afraid of. I took a deep breath and bowed my head.

"I am ready."

"Walk around the edge of the garden. Walk and do not stop." He spoke in sharp, brittle bursts.

I looked at Tanis, thinking I had not heard right. She motioned for me to begin. Like a fool, I obeyed, walking around the edge of the garden, as the tutor called it. I wondered if he had ever been young enough to worship here. Surely now at this age he just sent money along with one of his sons. I walked in circles, one lap, two laps, then three before I stopped and addressed Hannibal, who stood watching.

"This is not education. You are making a fool of me."

The tutor advanced, shuffling along, pulling a reed from his robes, lashing me on the legs. I jumped back, the surprise greater than the pain.

"Walk!" he screeched.

I walked. One more lap, two more, then on the third, again, I found my voice.

"No."

"What?" the tutor shrieked.

"Explain to me the benefit. Show me why this must be done, and I will do it."

He grinned and faced Hannibal. "Six laps! Not so bad. Tanis stopped at four, but then, Tanis was always my favorite."

He sat back on the bench and patted the seat beside him. Tanis and Hannibal bowed and departed, Tanis grinning at me as she left.

I sat, my heart returning to a slower rhythm.

"My child, education must never be one man telling another what to do. Education is a great struggle between two minds. Both teacher and student must make demands on each other. Do you understand?"

"But I stopped the first time and you whipped me."

"You were whining. When you asked a proper question, I did not whip you, did I?"

"No."

"Then this is your second lesson: Beware of teachers who whip their students for asking the right questions. Beware of teachers who are afraid of the struggle."

"Yes."

"Now, fetch me some lunch, and we will talk more. The temple always has such good food."

And this is how it began. Akbar struggled with me many hours through the lessons of the Greek minds, and the Egyptians. I learned of the Philistines around me, of the five cities that comprised the heart of the Philistine empire. I learned that there were five Philistine lords but no king. And I heard tales of the enemy of the Philistines, a Hebrew religious zealot who was prone to savagery.

I was not allowed to serve men at night alone in the upper chambers anymore, but Tanis did allow me to serve wine and circulate among the couples, as long as I said nothing and kept my eyes on the ground.

I almost obeyed her. When Lord Marcos was sitting with Parisa, I looked at him. Sometimes I would lean against the stone pillars and watch him, and he knew that I watched. He was not displeased. I was careful not to draw attention to myself, though, and careful never to look at him when Parisa could see me.

Tanis waited for me one night, after I refilled the bowl of Marcos while Parisa had excused herself to attend to her needs. Parisa had drunk a lot of wine, and it showed in her heavy, awkward steps and slurred speech. I had not stopped pouring, and I had offered her my arm to lead her back into the sleeping chambers where she could relieve herself.

She fell asleep on the stone toilet in the corner.

I returned and was making my way to Marcos. He sat up straighter, his mouth pursed in a smile. He was much older than I was. He smelled as men do, of salt and sweat and heavy spices. He rose, taking a step toward me, extending his hand. His palm was smooth, his fingers straight. He had never worked in a field or worked for his bread. Not with his hands. How did he eat, then? Did he steal?

Right then, I saw another man in the moonlight instead—the one who had changed the course of my life. I saw that awful night again, but Tanis appeared suddenly, saving me for the second time from him, wrapping an arm around my waist and leading me away. I glanced back, returning to my senses.

Lord Marcos was still standing, waiting for me, but a strange new look was in his eyes, one that made my stomach roll.

He looked upon me with compassion. I saw it in his eyes, the way his eyes narrowed without anger, and in the way his face softened when he looked at me. He wanted me, the way men do, but I did not know why he also offered me compassion. I had to run.

"What are you doing?" Tanis whispered to me, pulling against me. She led me to the edge of the portico, closer to the main doors of the temple, where we had the privacy afforded by many people coming in and out.

"Serving wine."

"Liar. Whatever you're doing with Lord Marcos, stop. Nothing good can come from provoking Parisa."

"What is it to you? She is not your friend."

"But you are. Nothing good will come from this."

"I don't understand why you are loyal to someone who hates you."

"I am trying to protect you, not her. Do you know what you have become?"

I hesitated. What did she see in me? I had hidden everything as best I could. I turned my face away. I didn't want her to see what I had become. I was an open, screaming wound.

"You have become beautiful, Delilah. The most beautiful among us, and younger, too. Someday you will have any patron you desire.

But now is not the time to test your beauty on other men, especially Lord Marcos. What will Parisa do if she catches you?"

"She will know that stealing someone's innocence always has a price."

Lord Marcos approached us. I held my breath, having no plan for this moment. He was a big man, standing this close to me. He stood at three hands' length over me. He had tiny wrinkles at the corners of his eyes, and they softened his sharp gaze. I did not know how to manipulate him, not with this softness he had.

Tanis slid her hand out, and he took it in his, embracing it with both hands.

"Must you leave?" Tanis asked. Her voice was smooth and passionless.

"Parisa is not feeling well. I do not know if she will return, and I have business to attend to very early tomorrow."

"I am sorry. May we make an offering to Dagon on your behalf?"

He shook his head no. "Good night, Delilah."

I raised my eyes and looked at him. I did not see the phantom from my memory. I saw a kind face, which made me feel a hundred times more afraid, because I did not know it. I knew evil. I knew harshness and anger and violence. But I did not know this kindness, and it seemed an unpredictable force, one that broke open deep wounds with its careless attention.

I did not say anything to Lord Marcos. He reached out and touched my cheek, one finger resting lightly on it, then turned and left.

"Delilah?"

I shook myself back to attention. Tanis was stroking my arm.

"Why are you crying?"

I fled to the sleeping chambers. I could not serve any more wine tonight or overhear flattering words or watch couples go up those stone stairs. Tanis came for Parisa and together with eunuchs got her in bed, where she snored loudly and moaned in her dreams. I drew my knees up to my chest and pulled the little blade I kept hidden under the bedding. I was careful, always, to wait for everyone to be asleep, but tonight it was just Parisa snoring loudly, and myself, alone in this room. I slid the blade's edge along the bottom of one foot, feeling the skin break, gasping from the pain. Sweat beaded along my upper lip. All the pain became real, and in one spot that I could feel and touch and see. I closed my eyes, knowing I would not sleep. But at least I knew the pain was all in one spot, one spot that did not spread.

I had wanted to provoke Parisa, to hurt her even, but trying to lure Marcos away, if only for one night, was too much for me. I hurt deep inside, where I was not beautiful or alluring, but hungry and unloved, sneaking through the darkness alone.

The knife let that girl out, just for a little while.

Kaleb helped me bring Samson home. Liam saw us from a distance and joined, each boy under one of Samson's arms, supporting him. I was grateful for their strength, that they could use it to carry a weak brother.

One evening, many weeks later, Samson took Kaleb and Liam out spider hunting. This made my heart glad. I did not know how to comfort them. They refused to call me Mother, and I was awkward with them, still.

It was early enough in the winter; a few spiders should have been out. Samson promised to teach them how to dig a pit and trap them in the fields. I made Samson promise not to kill any.

He gave me an odd look.

"Because spiders eat the insects that damage our crops," I reminded him. "We need spiders." It was not a snub. We had been getting along so much better as long as I did not mention death, dying, slaying, slaughtering, blood, jawbones, or anything else related to the things he had done. We stepped back to a happier time in our lives, before he came of age, before he killed his first man. Before I became his enemy, and not the Philistines. Before he realized he would never be able to marry, or love, or have children. His strange gift, this strength, left anyone who loved him exposed and weak, like rabbits under the shadow of the hawk.

He helped more around the house and insisted Manoah sit at night and rest. Samson hunted for us, saying he preferred that to the market. He dressed our meat and roasted it, and we ate with greasy fingers, laughing at each other's remarks. Kaleb and Liam had been silent at night for so long. Samson taught them how to begin again, how to try to live without making sense of it all. He had a gift for that, a very good gift, and it served Syvah's sons well. Samson, too, seemed to heal, and though he called out for his wife in his nightmares, he sometimes slept through the night without weeping.

Tonight, I had to announce it was time for bed, because the boys and Samson showed no signs of exhaustion yet, and Manoah was not feeling strong. Samson and the boys wanted to go up on the roof to tell stories. Samson promised that he had the best of all imaginable stories to tell them tonight. I shooed them all upstairs so Manoah at least could get to sleep early. He had been so pale today, stopping sometimes to try and catch his breath. I had held his arm, rubbing his back, standing there until his pride return and he ordered me back to my dishes. I liked that very much. When we were young, we had fought. I missed it now.

I did not mean to eavesdrop. But what I heard, this fantastical story that Samson told, was so dreadful and so wonderful I did not know whether to celebrate or kick him out.

"Come closer," Samson said quietly to the boys. "So Mother won't hear."

I was only at the bottom of the stairs. And it was night. I could hear everything if I just eased myself across the floor to the bottom step. It was not difficult.

"How strong do you think I am?"

The boys made thinking noises and then took their guesses. "Strong enough to tear a tree from the ground!" "Strong enough to push this house over!"

Samson laughed. "Would you believe I am strong enough to tear the gates of Gaza off the hinges and carry the gates all the way to the top of Mount Hebron?"

The boys gasped. This was unbelievable. Truly. The gates took twenty horses each to pull to the wall when they were built, and the horses used wheeled carts, too. The hinges were each thicker than my body. No man, no army, could wrench them off.

"No, I did! I will tell you why. I was spending the night with a lovely young girl...."

My heart stopped. I thought he decided never to marry, never to love?

"Wait!" Kaleb interrupted. "Was this girl the kind of girl you had to pay?"

"What do you know of that?" Samson asked, unhappy.

"I'm old enough to know that if a woman isn't married by a certain age, and she likes to entertain, chances are good she'll entertain me if I have money." It sounded like Kaleb's voice.

"Ow!" It was definitely Kaleb. I knew his howl. Samson must have smacked him on the head. Good.

"That's none of your concern, anyway. I was spending the night with a lovely girl in Gaza when I heard noises outside her window. I wrapped myself in her veil and crept to the window, peering out, and what do you think I saw?"

"Her husband?" Kaleb spoke again.

"Ow!" And Samson corrected the boy again. Kaleb had a man's imagination already.

"No, I saw many men gathering around the house. They gave me a sign, and that's when I knew: This harlot had set a trap for me. The Philistines of Gaza were lying in wait, growing in number as I waited inside. So I waited and watched. They made no move to attack, and I began to see that they were going to wait for dawn. They needed the light if they were going to face the strongest, fiercest warrior in history. And so, at midnight, still wearing the veil, I sneaked out of her house and made it all the way to the gates. Then I threw off the veil and, right there, wrenched the gates off their hinges and carried them away. If you could have seen the look on the guards' faces, the guards in the towers that flank either side of the gates! They saw those gates pop right off and walk away!"

Kaleb and Liam howled in laughter, and Samson joined them.

My head was spinning. Which was more outrageous to me? That he tore gates off a city wall, or that he was sleeping with harlots in Gaza?

"Then what did you do?"

"Took them up to Mount Hebron and left them there. They'll have a hard time getting them back to the city, never mind getting them hung again." Samson sounded so proud.

"But Samson?"

"Yes?"

"Why did you do it?"

Samson was silent for a long while then said, "Go to bed."

"Why don't you just find another wife? Your mother said it was your own fault, what happened to Amara."

"Go to bed!"

The boys stomped down the stairs, and I caught them before they woke Manoah, shushing them, patting them on their backs, steering them in the dark toward their pallet. They did not know our house in the darkness, not as well as we did.

Samson never came down that night.

The next morning, he was gone.

I had betrayed him, too.

Parisa shook me, knocking me onto the floor.

"You tried to tempt Marcos?"

I landed on my bottom, startled awake. She kicked at me. "You think you can steal him? Because you're younger? Or do you think you're more beautiful?"

"Parisa!" Tanis had her by the arm, dragging her off me.

"Because you are neither one, Delilah! You're dirty and used. Your face will catch up soon enough."

No woman moved. Each had been dressing for the prayers and first meal. They stared at me with varying degrees of interest. Interest or satisfaction. I was too shocked to absorb it all yet. I stood and raised my hands out to Tanis, who was still holding Parisa, threatening her if she moved against me again.

"It is all right, Tanis. It is my fault," I said.

Tanis pursed her lips as one eyebrow lifted, questioning me.

"I am guilty," I said.

Tanis released Parisa, who crossed her arms, waiting for my confession. I began to dress for the meal, having nothing else to say.

Education was a struggle between student and teacher, and Parisa was going to learn her lesson.

I was sweet to Parisa during the next week, doting even, and each time, she reacted with anger, as expected. Her anger slowly burned down, revealing her fear. I could see the shadows under her eyes when she woke, and the way she clutched at Marcos with white knuckles, her eyes darting around, looking for me, while he spoke of his concerns. I wanted her to hurt. I did not want to be the only one who suffered.

She did not see Marcos sigh in vexation or tap his foot as she complained yet again about her life within these walls. She brought up his wife, and her own desire for children, and how she would love to do more for him, in every way. She grew bold in her words. Their sweetness had an edge.

I stayed hidden, moving between the stone columns only when I knew she would not see me, careful to let Marcos catch only a glimpse of my flowing tunic, or an arm reaching for more wine. He knew I was there. He knew I watched him. And yet I did not allow him to look on me again, not fully. It was as much for his temptation as my relief. I did not want to look into the eyes of the one I tried to entrap.

No matter, though. By the end of the second week, I knew I had failed. Marcos had done nothing. He did not pursue me or make a spectacle of Parisa, seeking me out over her. If I wanted to hurt Parisa, I needed to find another way. But with such a cold woman, it was hard to know where she felt pain. It wasn't fair that I was the only one who suffered here.

On the first morning of the following week, I laid awake in bed while the other women began to rise. There was no point in getting up. Defeat had nauseated me; I could not imagine eating anything. Parisa, too, stayed in her bed. She had slept well.

Marcos had not come for Parisa last night, but she had been elated. Rumor had come to the temple that Lord Marcos had given his wife a certificate of divorce. Parisa had waited for me to return to the sleeping chambers after serving the wine. When I climbed on to the couch at last, she came over and spat at my feet, then laughed.

"When I am his wife, perhaps I will send along a nice offering to you, and you won't have to take many men upstairs."

In the darkness, sweat dotted my forehead. It was hard to breathe, and my stomach began to tingle. I pressed my palm against my mouth to silence the whimpers that rose up, thinking on her words again.

Every day in these courts brought me closer to the day I had to serve as a real priestess. I would have no control. Any man might reach for me, his hand extended in the evening shadows, and where would I run? Who would save me? I knew this one truth: No one saved a girl except herself. But I had no power to save myself. I never had. I had no power at all, not even to cause someone else the slightest pain.

My hand slid under the bedding, searching for the cold blade. I didn't want to. A force inside me wanted it, would not rest until I let it free. I ran the blade along the sole of my foot, wincing without sound, relieved for the piercing pain, the cold shiver of relief. The pain had a spot I could touch, a place I could name. My pain, all the pain of the world, was reduced to this small red line that bled in the dark.

⁂

Akbar placed five smooth stones in my palm. We sat together in the courtyard, just under the roof. The sun was dotted all around with white clouds. The rains had begun for the season, but this afternoon was dry. I was grateful to be outside; the rains could keep us inside for days at a time.

"Show me." He placed a clay tablet in my lap, and I squirmed to settle it into a steady position with one hand.

I swept the dust from the tablet and put down the stones, one by one, in their order, just as they lie along the sea.

"Now name them."

"Gaza, Gath, Ekron, Ashkelon, Ashdod."

"And who governs the Philistines?"

"Lord Marcos governs the city of Ashdod, Lord Karan the city of Gaza, Lord Adon the city of Gath, Lord Baltsar the city of Ashkelon, Lord Kanat the city of Ekron."

"Interesting that you put Lord Marcos first."

I kept my face impassive, so he would know nothing.

"Even an old man hears rumors. He has sent his wife away," Akbar said.

He made his face impassive, so I learned nothing more. He swept the stones into a pile at the edge of the tablet with one hand, then clapped his hands together, freeing them of dust.

"Tutor, I have a question."

He cocked his head to the side. It was how he waited for my questions.

"Once, a girl was brought into this temple, and Hannibal cut a lock of her hair off. Why did he do this?"

"You have other things to learn." He lifted his chin, looking away.

"I want to learn this."

"No."

"Please. Please." I laid a hand on his cold thigh. His hollow old bone was just under the surface of his skin. I tried not to shudder.

It worked. The corner of his mouth twitched and he scowled, removing my hand and placing it back on my own leg. I scooted closer to him. He did need the warmth. I was not tricking him now.

"Please."

"All right. But only because I am tired. I don't want to fight with you about it."

"You said education was a struggle to be fought."

"When I said that, I had just had breakfast. I was feeling quite strong. Now, the hour is late and I am tired."

Though it was not late and the sun had only now begun to grow warm, I smiled wide and brought my hands together.

He cleared his throat, a terrible sound for an old man to make and a young girl to hear. "Hair is the essence of a person. Hair holds all their secrets, all their powers, all their history. If you take a lock of hair from someone, you can cast much magic on them. You can change their fate. Or even your own."

"How? How could I change my fate?"

He recoiled, shocked.

"You are to become a priestess of Dagon. Your power will come from Dagon. Not magic."

I knew very well the power of Dagon, that god with blind stone eyes. Ask the dead ones lying in the gutter about the power of this god. I had no hope in him.

"'All greatness comes from learning.' You said this yourself."

He groaned, vexed at my nagging. But he told.

And I began to see what I could try next. A new plan began to form, though it had only a small sting. Parisa had won Marcos and would leave us. She would be the most honored woman in the city. She would want to bear many children for him. Children, sons especially, those would be her security. Even if Marcos divorced her, too, someday, a son would take care of her. A son would be the one man who could never send her away. Sons were security.

Though she would be leaving us, I could still find a way to make her feel pain, just as she had done to me.

All I needed was a little magic, which could be made from a lock of her hair.

I had to wait for Tanis to be alone. She was always busy, attending the women, helping them prepare for the next night's work, or consulting with Hannibal, reviewing money and discussing patrons. Once the temple doors were closed, worship became a business. Tanis made sure her wares, the women, were ready for the services, and Hannibal made sure the services were profitable. I watched them from behind the pillar as they sat in the main hall. Hannibal sat in his chair, Tanis leaned over, standing at his side, observing as he counted coins from a bag. A servant sat on the steps below them both, holding a clay jar in his lap.

As Hannibal counted off the coins, he dropped them one by one into the jar. Tanis commented in his ear. I heard only the rough edges of whispers, but they looked comfortable with each other. I wondered if Tanis had ever loved Hannibal. The way she rested her hand on his shoulder made me uncomfortable.

Hannibal dropped the bag next to the servant and rose. Tanis bowed her head and departed. Hannibal and the servant now stood, talking together, Hannibal gesturing, making clear his plans for the temple and the money. As Tanis passed me, I stepped out from behind the column, taking her arm in mine.

I glanced back at Hannibal and smiled.

"What is it, Delilah?" She drew her head back as if alarmed by my sudden appearance.

"I wanted to ask a favor. Will you walk with me?"

"Is the sun out?"

I paused and listened. I heard the hiss of rain against the stone roof. Tanis smiled and nodded toward the main door at the end of the hall. "We'll sit on the steps outside, under the roof. We can talk there."

I would be glad when the rains were done. Those who depended on crops did not mind huddling under roofs all day and all night, because the rains brought them wealth. For me, rains were a soft, cold prison that made me sleepy just when I needed to be alert.

Outside, the steps were cold. I tucked my tunic between my legs and my hands under each arm.

"Cold?" Tanis asked.

"No." I smiled and shook my head.

She frowned at me and turned her face to look out over the city. Ashdod was beautiful in the rain. The temple stood higher than the city, and we looked out at the buildings in muted shades of sand and shell. The heavy white mist of earliest day had evaporated by this hour, leaving only a soft veil over the city. In the center of the city was the market, with a few customers moving between stalls. The largest building was there, the home of Lord Marcos. From here he made his ruling and heard cases. To the west was the great sea. Today, the rains had left it shrouded in white and gray clouds. If I closed my eyes, though, I could hear it, the sounds of the waves carried here on the wind.

"I have wanted to talk to you, too, Delilah." Tanis stared ahead, looking down on the city. She drew a long breath, then looked down at her hands before releasing it.

Marcos would come soon, tonight even, for Parisa. I shook my head to stop her.

"Tanis, I need your help."

"Is something wrong?" Her body tensed as she looked at me, leaning toward me.

"Where does Hannibal keep the locks of hair?"

She pulled back, her brow knotting. "Who have you been listening to? Surely not Akbar."

"It does not matter—"

"Yes! Yes, it does matter. If you do not understand our plans for you by now, then let me be clear. You are becoming a priestess, not a witch. You have no need of magic."

"Please—"

"No!"

She stood, her face red and mouth set in a hard, straight line.

"I am afraid!" I sounded shrill. I could still find the voice of a child inside, even if I did not remember her.

Tanis did not move but judged me, her head tilted, her face open.

I spoke slowly, as if every word came from a painful place. "When I first came here, Hannibal took a lock of my hair. When he raised the knife, I thought he was going to kill me." I smiled, looking up at her through my lashes. "But he took a lock of hair, and I always wondered why, but I did not ask anyone. I trusted, in you especially."

Tanis's face drained of color. "You do not trust me now?"

"I do! It's Parisa I do not trust. She said she was going to steal my lock of hair and burn it. She said when she did, pains would come upon me, and I would die. I would never have a chance to serve in the temple." I lowered my voice and looked out in the distance. "I would never become like you."

Tanis hesitated, putting her arm around me, drawing me in. I held my breath so I would not smell her perfume, so I would not weaken and cling to her.

"Parisa is lying. Only Hannibal and I know where the locks are kept. And even if she found them, burning your lock would not cause you pains."

"What would it do?"

"Nothing. Only a witch could use it to cast a spell. Not even I know the incantations."

"But there is no witch here. Where do you find a witch?"

Tanis pressed her lips together, then ran her teeth over her lower lip, pulling it in, pushing it out. She wanted to say something to me, so I waited.

"Delilah, I want to talk to you about your baby."

I lurched up, catching the hem of my tunic under my heel. Struggling for balance, I backed away, tearing my tunic to get free.

"Thank you, Tanis." I ran from the steps, back into the cold darkness of the main hall.

But I couldn't run far. Though my heart was stung, and I fought to hold back any thoughts of that day, of that room of birth and death, I hid behind a column once more, and waited. I waited until my feet turned cold, and the cold rose through my legs and into my belly. I trembled, pulling my tunic tighter in around me.

The door opened to the main hall, and Tanis entered, her face red and blotched. I covered my mouth with my hand so that not even the sound of my breath would betray me. I knew Tanis had been crying for me. I held out the thoughts, far from me, not letting them hurt me. Tanis loved me too much.

She wiped at her nose delicately and walked to Hannibal's chair. The main hall was silent, except for her footsteps. Looking around, she seemed satisfied that she was alone and then lifted the gold seat from the chair. My eyebrows raised in surprise. I had not known his chair had a secret too. Inside the flat square chamber, she ran her hand back and forth, then picked up a lock of hair and held it closer to her face. She returned it, and as she set the lid back into place, Hannibal opened the main doors. A cold wind snaked round my ankles. I could only see him in profile, and the robes of a man standing behind him. If I moved for a better view, Tanis might see me.

Hannibal called to her, and she turned, unafraid. "Tanis, Lord Marcos has arrived."

"I am ready."

She came down the steps, smiling at the men. Whatever they would be discussing, it was clearly not the first time. Tanis moved with ease, perhaps even joy. She took Lord Marcos's arm, and the three went out the main doors. Lord Marcos's home was in that direction, the seat of the city government, and the empty bed. A cattish laugh caught my ear; Parisa was awake too, dressing for her evening, perhaps her last one among us.

I had no choice. I had to do it now, before the services began, before Parisa collected her things and left.

I crept from my hiding place and ran across the cold floor to Hannibal's chair. Lifting the lid, I saw dozens of locks of hair, all tied with cords that were looped in the center, each marked with a clay seal. I did not read the language of Ashdod. Turning the locks over, I looked closely at each in frustration. One had an image that I knew at once: a young girl with a swollen belly. I held the lock up to my own hair. It was mine. Placing it inside my belt, pulling it tight against my waist, I again turned over the locks, one by one. Each seal had an image of the girl or woman. They must have been images of the woman as she was when she first came here, as mine was. I turned them over, frantic now. The women in the next room did not need much more time to be ready.

Then I found it. An image of a thin woman, ragged hair, in chains. It had to be Parisa. Her expression, even in a clay seal, was one of defiance. She would wear another expression after today, one of bewilderment, wondering why she could not conceive, why she could never have the one thing she needed when her beauty faded and Marcos had moved on: a son.

"What are you doing?"

A hand caught me by the back of the neck. I jumped, frightened, trying to turn and see who had caught me. As if I didn't know. Parisa's grip grew tighter, her fingernails digging into my neck.

"I asked you a question."

"I'm sorry! I was only trying to help!"

"By stealing my hair?"

"I have heard rumors! Someone is going to put a curse on you, so you can never bear Marcos a son!"

Parisa dropped her grip on my neck and wrenched my arm toward her, prying the lock of hair from my hand.

"You're nothing but a liar. And a thief." She smiled, her lips pressed together, gloating. "Now, if you want to keep your hands, give me your own lock of hair. Perhaps I will keep your secret."

I removed it from my belt and handed it to her. Thieves get their hands cut off.

She grinned. "Or perhaps I won't. Girls like you deserve everything they get."

She turned to take a step down from the chair, and I threw myself on her. We fell down the steps, and I landed on top of her as she screamed and tried to throw me off.

She was fierce, much stronger than I had expected. I fell to the side, and as I scrambled to get up, she lunged at me, knocking me back down, pinning me flat to the ground. She sat on me as her hands went round my neck, shaking my head up and down as she choked me. I did not want to die this way.

I tried to scream, but everything stopped under her hands—my screams, my voice, my breath. My face was swelling with trapped air as black spots swam in my vision. Through this swirling haze, I did not see clearly what happened next.

Parisa was knocked off of me. There were grunts and a dull, wet drumbeat.

I tried to raise my head but fell back into darkness as I heard shouting and running footsteps. I do not know how much time passed before I was on my bottom with my legs spread out before me, as I retched into my lap, coughing, trying to breathe again as a woman stroked my hair.

"Did she hurt you? Are you all right?"

Blinking, forcing myself to see and to think, I looked up. Tanis lay on the ground, her expressionless face turned to me, her eyes open wide. A dark pool spread out from under her head, moving toward me. Above me, Hannibal stood with Parisa, who was in chains. Two guards from the city flanked her.

Lord Marcos parted the women clustered all around, searching for someone. When he saw me, his expression changed to one of relief, and he rushed to me, helping me to stand, one hand around my waist.

"Get her a chair!" he commanded. A chair was brought, and he helped me sit, then kneeled before me, reaching up to stroke my hair. His hand came away clean. My skull had not split as I thought, though that was a miracle.

"Better now?"

I nodded, trying to peer around him. My head hurt too much to move it far, but he moved to block my view of Tanis.

"I should have come sooner," he said. "This is not your fault, Delilah."

"What happened?" I did not know how Tanis had died. What had I done?

"Hannibal said you caught Parisa stealing your hair and she attacked you. Tanis tried to stop her, and Parisa killed her. Hit her head on the floor. Tanis died to protect you. She must have truly loved you."

"She brought me here." I meant it as an argument, but he only nodded in agreement.

"She saved you twice, then. I have heard stories of your family."

My mind cleared more with every passing moment. I looked around, my breathing coming fast. I tried to stand, but Marcos caught me by the shoulders. "Shh," he whispered. "Wait until she is gone."

Parisa was glaring at me, one cheek red and inflamed, the mark of a handprint visible. She spat on the floor, leaving a red spot. The guards dragged her backward, and she went limp, her mouth set in a snarl, her eyes never leaving mine.

"But what is happening? Where are they taking her?"

Marcos watched her go, disgust evident on his face. "All that beauty wasted."

I heard a guard giving directions to the others. Parisa was to be jailed. A former priestess, imprisoned with men awaiting punishment or execution … condemned men would relish the distraction. Marcos saw her fate as well as I, but he did not see the truth, not all of it. She had acted for herself, always. She loved no one more than herself. All people were like this, I knew. Just as there were no real gods, there was no real love.

Hannibal turned his attention to me. I shrunk in my chair, drawing my shoulders up, cringing away from certain punishment. Marcos stood and faced Hannibal, nodding. Hannibal held something out to me in his hand. I glanced at it.

It was my own lock of hair. I stood.

"I requested it be given to you," Marcos said. "I do not want you to serve me in fear."

"What?"

Hannibal tried to force a smile. But something was broken inside of his spirit. I could see that in his eyes. I looked down at his hands. They were shaking. "Lord Marcos came here today to request that you be made his permanent consort. You will serve no other man."

I froze, aware that Marcos was watching, that everyone was watching. No one laughed. It was not a joke. The irony made my blood cold. If I had known the truth, Tanis would still be alive. I had been made a fool, again. My hope was in one man now, one man I did not want or love. He had only been a means to hurt Parisa. And now, he was all mine.

I smiled weakly and felt his arms slip around my body as my knees went soft and I fell.

Two days later, my hands trembled. I could not tie the sash around my waist. Rose rushed to my side, crooning my name, helping me sit back on the couch.

"I know how you are grieving. We all miss Tanis."

I clutched her hand to my chest, nodding. I wasn't grieving. I had no time, no will for that. I was terrified.

Tonight, Marcos would come for me.

"You look beautiful, Delilah. Do not be afraid."

I looked at Rose as if she spoke a new language. What hope did beauty offer anyone, especially me? Anyone who thought me beautiful had hurt me or hated me. Beauty was no blessing.

Because of this curse, I would attend Marcos, and when he desired, he would take me to one of those curtained rooms upstairs. I did not want to go. I did not want this man! I had two long nights to consider what I had done. I thought hurting Parisa would sate my thirst, that justice would give me peace, but it did nothing. Justice was a dead thing, perhaps, and no use to the living. And vengeance was not a perfect art.

Now I had a dead friend, a man I did not want, and a night ahead of me that made me sick to think about. My tutor had taught me of governments and gods, not of all the necessary deceptions that had to take place when the curtains were drawn. No woman could want to do those things with a man. I did not know how I would disguise my feelings when he reached for me.

None of the other women would even look at me, and certainly they would not welcome me into their secrets. Whatever tricks they used to hold down their meals when a man touched them, they would keep those secrets from me for one more night at least.

I was alone in my ironic little disaster.

I tilted my head, letting my hair fall to one side. Running my hands through it, my fingers remembered what to do, braiding it into one long, strong rope. I remembered the wool I had hoped to weave, to make something beautiful and earn my place. I had been unhappy, but in those days I had understood what must be done.

I knew the cold was there but did not feel it. I had already exhausted myself in my preparations, which never seemed enough. How could I have allowed this to sneak up on me?

By the fourth hour of the afternoon, the sun had begun to fade and night encroached, with purple shadows and cold winds from the sea. I had just released my braid and was preparing to redo it when Hannibal entered our sleeping chambers.

"Lord Marcos has arrived."

Everyone stopped their grooming and watched me as I stood, bowing slightly to Hannibal. As my eyes swept downward, I saw my tunic shaking violently over my knees. I had to open my mouth and draw the deepest breath I could before I straightened up. It didn't work.

"Are you all right?" Rose asked.

"I will do what I have to do."

Hannibal helped me walk to the door leading to the portico, and with one hand on the door to push it open, he leaned to my ear.

"Please Marcos, or do not return to these chambers." He pulled away and smiled, nodding for me to smile as well.

I did, drawing one last breath before I entered Marcos's life and became his consort.

Marcos stood when I entered, pleasure in his eyes, as if he did not know what this night had cost me. Perhaps he didn't. I did not yet know him. Hannibal presented me with a silent flourish and then backed away, leaving me alone with my lord.

He sat and motioned for me to join him. I clasped my hands together in my lap so he would not see them shaking.

The temple was going to be busy tonight; I knew beyond these walls that the wheat had been planted and the barley was coming near to harvest. Men would be coming from nearby villages to plead their case to Dagon, to make love—and life—with a priestess.

I flinched as I thought of the couples soon to drift up the stairs. Lord Marcos noticed and put an arm around me. Perhaps he thought I was cold.

The high winter rains had made the air cold, that was true. A fire burned in the center of the portico, and a few couples stood over it for warmth. Men pleaded in soft tones for blessing and wealth. My womb was empty. I knew what it was to be given blessing and wealth. I knew what it was to lose it all.

Marcos seemed to be content to sit and watch the flames with me. I considered things to say, gracious or learned things. I knew I should entertain him, or impress him. I edged my body at an angle to look at him, removing his arm and setting it in his lap as I cleared my throat.

"I have conditions."

"Conditions?" He seemed amused. I bit my cheek to keep from crying.

"First, no one may serve you wine but me. I don't want to be surprised by another woman taking my place someday. And I will not go upstairs like the others. You must take me from here when you want to do those things."

"I did not agree to these conditions when I asked for you."

"I did not ask for you."

He laughed, not taking his eyes off me.

"I will agree to your conditions if you will agree to mine."

I narrowed my eyes, searching his face for a clue to what he wanted.

"First, no more conditions."

I nodded. "Agreed."

He leaned over and grabbed my leg. I squealed without meaning to, and turned my face down when another woman glared at me, as if I was delighting in my stolen fortune.

He ran his hands down my calf and then kneeled at my feet. My heart began thundering, fast and loud. I froze, praying for some quick clue as to what I must do in response. He paid me no attention and removed my sandal, running his hands over my feet. His fingers rested on the cuts and scars, tracing them as he looked up into my eyes.

He replaced my sandals and tied them before sitting again.

My whole body began to recoil. There was no way to conceal my shock. He held me there with one heavy palm now resting on my thigh.

"That is my second condition. Do not harm yourself anymore. Whatever troubles you, come to me with it."

I stared at the fire. "How did you know?"

"You flinch when you walk. But not every night. And I know that you have suffered."

I did the strangest thing, without meaning to. I lifted one arm and placed my hand on his. He smiled, putting his other hand on top of mine. He was warm and strong. Relief flooded my body, making my knees weak.

"As long as I live, I promise, Delilah, you will be loved."

Lord Marcos kept his word. He did not take me upstairs on that night, or any night after. He visited nightly, after his business had finished for the day. He told me of the cases he had tried, of the decisions rendered, of the fortunes won and lost in the city. He told me stories from his childhood and legends from the people.

These were the tender years of my life, when stories were told for amusement and instruction and their lessons learned at a distance. Suffering was no longer my teacher.

When the night came that he took me outside the walls of the temple, I cannot say I was ready. That would be a lie. But I had less fear. He placed one arm around my waist and led me out of the portico, down the steps into the city street.

"Welcome to Ashdod, Delilah."

He led me through flame-lit streets, and above us, the sun had descended in pink and yellow bands across the deep purple horizon. We walked without speaking, spying on families eating around low tables with flickering oil lamps, past quiet shops with tools resting on tables and mice scampering through straw on the floor and great fat cats leaping after them. Dogs trotted through the streets, whining when they saw us, hoping for a treat. A boy leaned out of a window, whistling, and his dog bounded past us. The boy's mother stood at the door to let the dog in, then shut the door behind him, closing her home for the night.

These were wonders I had never seen.

"It is a peaceful city," I said, sighing. Lord Marcos kissed me on the top of my head, and we walked on.

"This is my home."

I had seen it from a great distance; now I stood in its shadow, dwarfed by its size, sand-brown bricks rising up before me, windows set in the walls higher up than three men stacked head to feet. Above the door, nothing. For almost two years now I had lived in a temple, where the main door bore an inscription that welcomed all men in. "Enter and enjoy," it read, or that is what the other women told me, but I had hoped they were wrong. That would have made us harlots, not priestesses.

His door had no inscription. He was a free man.

He pushed open the double wooden doors and bade me to enter.

Crossing the threshold, I saw a mosaic tile floor of blue and white, images of women and gazelles, and three whitewashed columns along each side of the home. On the back wall was a staircase to the upper chambers, and low tables stood behind the columns.

"Citizens wait here for me to attend them," Marcos said.

"Where is your throne?"

He laughed at me.

I frowned. "You are the ruler of the city."

"The five lords rule with intellect, not force or fear." He walked to the stairs. I hesitated. "Come."

I had never been allowed upstairs as a girl, and at the temple, I had never wanted to go up the stairs. Everyone else lived above me, and things happened above me that I did not like or could not be a part of. I was not a girl who climbed stairs with men, even men like Marcos.

"Delilah. It's all right. Come and join me."

I took a step forward.

At the bottom of the stairs, he held one hand out to me.

He was a gentle man.

❧

Always, he held out his hand for me. I climbed those stairs many times. My life settled into a comfortable routine—a life without fear, a strange delight. I returned to the temple before dawn and returned to Marcos's home before the sun drifted away completely. Hannibal did not mind that I no longer entertained Marcos at the temple. Marcos made generous offerings to Dagon every week, even better offerings than in the past. Hannibal was pleased enough to say nothing.

Marcos was busy with men who had urgent business. Tonight he saw to it that I was comfortable in his chambers, then went below to attend them. I looked around me, a foreigner in this room without him. His bed was empty, the pallet resting on the floor, draperies around it to keep the pests out in the summer. The windows brought in the strong salty summer breezes from the sea.

A dressing table stood against the wall, with a stool, and a table by the bed with lion heads on each corner, for trays of refreshment. A lovely, perfect room that no woman could find fault with. Marcos had even purchased a jar of exquisite perfume for me. It was a luxury I had never known. With Marcos, life itself had become a wonderful luxury.

When Marcos returned, I had a question. I had always had this question, but until tonight, I did not have the courage to ask. His love was making me bold.

"Why do men divorce their wives?"

Marcos shrugged and began removing his sash. "Do you mean, 'Why did you divorce your wife?'"

"Was she no longer attractive?"

He draped his sash across the foot of the bed. "She was one of the most beautiful women I've ever known."

His answer did not make me feel good.

"Was she barren?"

He was removing his robe. I should have stood to help him, but I was afraid he would stop talking if I came near.

"I don't know. I stopped lying with her years before the divorce."

"But you said she was beautiful!"

"Delilah, whatever you may think of men, we are a bit more complex than you realize. A beautiful woman is just as likely to displease a man as an ugly woman. Maybe even more so."

"I don't understand."

"No, you don't. Whatever has happened to you in the past, whatever behavior in themselves men have excused on account of your beauty, they were wrong. If a man claims he was compelled to hurt you, he is either lying or no man at all."

He was in his linen robe now and nothing else. I stood to help him remove it. He shook his head no and got into bed with a sigh.

I wanted to say many things to him just then. I did not want him to be mad at me, but I was not sure this was anger.

Without deceit, I had nothing to say, so I disrobed and lay beside him. An hour or more passed as I waited for him to touch me. When he did, I turned my body into his and did not resist him. That was all the truth I was capable of.

We passed most all our evenings in this chamber or on the beach, watching the waves break and little crabs scurrying for their dinner. In the distance, birds flew straight at the water, diving below, then surfacing to float effortlessly. There were dancers, acrobats even, in the market on warm nights, but these birds were the performers I preferred. Marcos, too, I think, was glad to be away from the city, away from the problems and accusations and pleadings of the citizens.

Tonight was such a night. We sat on the sand, the day's heat keeping it warm though the sun was setting in a blaze of yellow and orange. Brilliant white clouds reflected the last of its rays. I had served as Marcos's consort for a full year now.

He watched the birds at the horizon. "Do you ever wonder if all of this"—and here he gestured to the world around him—"is all there is?"

"But my love, you have everything! Wealth. Passion. Even power. How could that not be enough? How could you wonder if there is anything else? What else could there be?" I was breathing rapidly, my nostrils stinging from the effort. I wanted to know what he would say.

"Is it enough for you?" he asked, with a steady gaze that made me doubt myself. This must be how he ruled the citizens.

"Nothing is truly my own. I cannot say it is enough, because nothing is mine. I was made your consort, not your wife."

I stood without grace, my chest still rising and falling.

"It will not always be like this, Delilah."

I turned to him with a shudder. "Please do not send me away for speaking like that. I am sorry. I don't deserve you."

"You deserve much more."

That summer passed without any more frightening words. We drank of love, and I grew to know his body, and his heart, so much better than my own. Slowly, this man I had once claimed no desire for, now claimed all my desire. In him, I knew my place, my home, my purpose. I did not fail him. Even when I was weak, he showed me how to be strong. When I was sad and could not explain why, he comforted me with walks, and love, and tenderness that left me breathless. He kissed me on the forehead when I was unlovely and angry.

That is why I did it.

I opened myself to a great pain, thinking I was stronger now. But always, always, life has its surprises. Unguarded hearts always lead to disaster.

I was such a fool.

We lay in his bed, and he told me of the day's business. A man and his wife had found a child in the fields and made claim to it. He had blessed them and given them a silver coin for luck. I asked their names, but I did not recognize them. I had met most everyone of any importance in the city, and even the other four Philistine lords, but none seemed to see anything unusual in my face. No one saw their daughter's features in mine.

"Do you know of anyone who adopted a baby from the temple?" I did not want to reclaim her. I would not even know her in the streets. I just wanted to know if they were good people. I wanted to think she was as happy as I, that the gods had been just as kind to her.

"Of course not."

"No one?" I felt cold. His tone was not right.

"Who would take a baby that had been birthed at the temple? That would be like stealing from the gods. A curse would follow the baby."

"But I do know of a child that was given to a nobleman's family."

In the darkness, I heard him catch his breath. He understood why I asked and what lies had been told to me.

I tried very hard to make no noise, but he held me as I cried.

That is, truly, where my story ends at the temple. I knew Tanis as she had truly been, a tender liar who served only herself. Or her god, not knowing that they were one and the same. Perhaps she had wanted to tell me the truth the night she was killed, but whether she wanted that for herself or for my own sake, I would never know.

I lay awake, thinking of who else might hurt me, who else might hide. I must have fallen into a deep asleep, because I awoke alone, shivering, though the room was not cold.

And here was the greatest irony of all: One last secret was being played out upon me as I slept. One last secret, one that would change my fate forever.

Stretching, lazy in the late afternoon sun, I was the last to rise. The other women were already dressed and at work on their hair. I sat up, crossing my legs on the bed, waiting for sleep to clear from my eyes. Spring was here. We all felt it, even locked away in this room. I smiled to myself, thinking of the flowers already in bloom and all the treasures of freedom Marcos would show me.

Hannibal entered the room, a dark look on his face.

"I would like to be alone with Delilah. Everyone, please go and eat now."

A few glanced at me. Rose did, a fearful look on her face. I smiled at her. I had nothing to fear from Hannibal.

When the room cleared, Hannibal did not move. He stood at the door and did not look at me. I rose, my stomach beginning to tighten into a cold knot.

"Have I done something?"

He did not reply. He was pressing his lips together, rubbing them back and forth. Hannibal was always sure of himself. Nothing had ever made him nervous in my presence.

"What is it?" I rested a hand on his arm, hoping he would look at me.

"Marcos died this morning. He was listening to cases at his home, and he slumped over at a table. No one could wake him," Hannibal said.

I fell to the floor. My breathing sounded clotted, rasping. I willed myself to die too, before the heartbreak took me. I think I was moaning. I do not remember much after this.

What is there to say of such grief? My heart was torn from my body, and I was weak, and pale, and grew thin. For months, I had no appetite, no desire for food or wine or words. I lay on my couch, my body aching from a grief that numbed every sensation except crushing black sorrow.

Rose tried to sit on my bed once in the early morning when she returned from her service, to comfort me. I smelled men on her and turned away. She did not try again. Hannibal gave up reasoning with me and ordered servants to hold my head back as he poured a thin soup into my mouth, shutting it after each pour, blowing in my face, tricking my body into swallowing.

One morning he lost his patience. He had something to tell me that would not wait any longer.

"Delilah, you must listen to me. Lord Marcos loved you."

I moaned and thrashed against Hannibal. I couldn't bear to hear the name. I couldn't bear to lie here anymore, cold and alone. I had had everything, and everything I had lost. It had been enough, I wanted to scream in sorrow. It had been so much more than enough, a wealth beyond imagining, and I had lost it all again. I wanted to die, and I did not even have the strength to find my blade and lift it. If only I had known I would need this last strength, maybe I would have saved it.

"Lord Marcos bought your freedom. Before he died, he came to me early one morning. It was the middle of the night, really." Hannibal was smiling softly as he told it, remembering. "I could not imagine what had gotten him out of bed at that hour, especially when you were in it with him. He banged on the main doors, refusing to enter through the portico, demanding to see me. He said he would buy your freedom at any price. I asked him if he was going to marry you, if that is why he demanded your freedom, and do you know what that man did? He hit me. In the face. He said he would buy your freedom for your sake, not his. What you chose to do with it was your own business, or it was not really freedom."

Hannibal placed his hand on my cheek. "Your color is better. You need to eat again. Lord Marcos bought your freedom, Delilah. It is a thing that is unheard of. But he did it, for you. Regain your strength, and you can go."

A new lord lived in Marcos's house now, a man chosen by the people, who voted with stones dropped into clay pots. I knew Galenos to be a moderate man, moderate in drink and food, which would have pleased Marcos, and moderate in judgments. He did not move too fast to punish, or sweep away offenses as if they meant nothing to him.

I wanted to get away from this city and this temple. I took the money Lord Marcos had set aside for my freedom and bought a little home in the Valley of Sorek. I could walk to a market in Ashdod if I chose to, but on the streets near my home, I was granted the blessing of indifference.

I was nothing more here than an oddity, an unmarried woman who controlled her own fate. I had a past that gave them a little meat for their gossip, and a former love that still afforded me respect among the noblemen. Even if, in their hearts, they honored Marcos and not me. It did not matter. They could talk as they pleased. They did not care about me, and I found great relief in this.

I could not bear to remain indoors. I had never lived alone, and I had never known how terrible silence could be, how it suffocated and made the mind race, desperate for escape. I had chosen a small brick home in the center of the city, safe within her walls, where the noise and cries of the streets would reach me at all hours. Hannibal had been of great assistance in securing it and had even introduced me to the new lord, Galenos. Galenos was married with no interest in me, which was a relief. I had heard his wife was quite lovely. I wished them many children and much happiness, everything I had been denied.

Wandering in the market became my favorite pastime. If a dead heart can claim to be amused by anything, it was looking at the wares, watching the shoppers bargain and argue and rejoice over little victories. The market was life, and I walked through it, remembering.

A loom stood in one of the stalls, its wood beams clean and polished. The loom was old, the merchant had said. One eye wandered without control as he spoke, and gaps in his brown teeth showed themselves as he smiled without mercy on me. He clutched my hand in his, pushing his face closer.

"Why do you want an old loom? You should have the best. Go to Cornelius. He sells new ones."

"No, but I thank you. This one will do."

He dropped my hand with a sigh. "I will not argue with a woman."

I tried a smile, though I felt nothing. "You don't have the heart for it?"

He grunted. "I don't have the strength. Take it. One piece of copper."

I paid him and took up the loom in my arms, cradling it like a child. The thought struck me coldly, and I shifted it at once, carrying it in front of me. It was an older loom, true, but one that rested easily in my lap. One I would have wanted many years ago. So much had been abandoned in the years since.

Weeks passed, and I stared at the loom, setting by my bed. Another woman should have bought it, not me. I once knew how to weave, once had dreams of the fine things I could create. Maybe I had hoped the loom would stir something in me.

It didn't. One night I poured myself a bowl of wine filled to the brim, determined to numb the pain for an hour, and climbed the steps to my roof, where I could sit and look at the stars. In the far distance stood the temple. I sat with my back to it.

The horizon was black, as was the sky above me. This was my life, the temple behind me, nothing before me. Just darkness.

I drank, emptying the bowl in one long draught, and waited to feel the warmth spread into my cold, dead limbs.

I didn't know what to do with my freedom any more than I knew what to do with my past. Everything hurt.

The orange sun was setting in the west, leaving the sky a turquoise blue. White clouds dotted the sky above, rolling on to some distant adventure. I wished them gone. I was eager for the relief of night and of darkness, when the heat would soften and shadows covered my home.

Moving through the market, I needed to buy one last thing before returning home. Pits along the street hissed, with white smoke rising from them, dry bones scattered at their edges. The smoke stung my nose. I held out my coin, and the cook rose from his stool, pulling a skewer from the fire pot of blackened pork. He scraped it into a straw basket and handed it to me with his familiar nod of thanks.

I had never learned to cook. I appreciated his lack of interest in my problem.

A young girl stood watching me in the shadow of a doorway. One bare foot lifted to rub the top of the other. She tucked her chin down but still watched me, her foot rubbing faster.

Turning back to the cook, I held out another coin. He stood and filled a basket, with the same solemn expression that he had worn for me not even a minute ago. Taking the steaming meat from him, I turned and held it out to the girl.

She did not move, but her nostrils flared. I held the basket farther out to her. She glanced in either direction and scurried across the lane, scooping out the pork with one hand, eating like an animal, unaware of anything but the food and her hunger. With one hand I stroked her head as she ate. My chest tightened with the memory of this hunger, of any hunger. I envied her that she felt anything at all, and I said a silent word of thanks, that money could make someone happy.

I knew no one would hear the words spoken in my heart. There was no one left for that now, and no god, either. All had proven so fragile.

A man charged from the doorway of a wine shop, bursting upon the two of us, slapping the basket from my hands. Bits of meat scattered on the ground at my feet and the girl jumped behind me, hiding behind my tunic.

"What are you doing?" he screamed at me. "If I wanted her fed, wouldn't I do it myself?"

He raised a hand to strike me in the face, and it was the last movement he made that night of his own free will. Another man, a strange and powerful creature, turned down our lane and attacked the man while his hand was still lifting through the air. The stranger leaped with the power of a lion, felling the man and toppling down after him. I turned, pushing the girl's face into my tunic so she would not see. The stranger beat the man, screaming profanities, showering him with curses and fists.

When the noise stopped, I tilted my head to look at the stranger. He stood over the body, his chest heaving, his fists bloody.

"Did you kill him?" I whispered. I did not want the girl to hear.

"Should I?" He had the voice of an innocent. I looked in his eyes to be sure he didn't mock me, but his eyes were pure and questioning.

"No. She needs him. Perhaps he will be kinder in the future."

He craned his neck, spying the girl hidden in my tunic. Squatting down, he held out a hand to her. "Did he hurt you?"

Her body stiffened. I stroked her hair. "It's all right, my pet. Go home and tell your mother what has happened."

She crept to the edge of my body and stole a glance at the stranger, who still squatted, one hand extended. He did not see the blood on his hand, did not understand what it meant to her.

She broke free and ran.

He stood, wiping his hands on his own tunic with a shrug. "I thought she was your daughter."

"No. I have no daughter." I wasn't sure if that was a lie. I wasn't sure it mattered, not anymore.

He held out his hand to me.

"I'm Samson."

If only Marcos could have seen it! The troubler of the Philistines, making peace in our streets, saving a young Philistine girl from her father.

"Don't you have some crops to burn?"

He did not react. "What is your name? Why was he going to beat you?"

I picked up my tunic, moving quickly through the market.

He followed me through the narrow stalls, weaving his way around people who stopped and stared, struck stupid by his appearance. He looked like a monster from a tale of the Greeks, with that bushy brown hair hanging past his hips, and that beard, and his size. Gath had the giants, but we had a few in Ashdod, too, and Samson almost came up to their height.

Marcos would have driven him from the city.

I realized, too late, my error. At my door, I turned to face him.

"If you do not leave, I will have you chained and beaten."

"By your own hand? I might stay for that."

I spat on the ground and went inside, shutting the door hard in his face.

Tomorrow I would find Lord Galenos. Samson did not belong in our valley. He would be forced to leave.

But that plan, like so many of mine, failed. Samson, indeed, did not return.

He never left.

When I rose the next day, I knew I must first open my door to look out into the street, to make sure he did not watch for me. Like a fool, I had run straight here yesterday. He knew where I lived, and perhaps, if he was an observant man, he knew I lived alone.

I did not know what a Hebrew man would think of such a woman. They had once been slaves, Marcos said, who had revolted against their masters. They were not to be trusted. How could such a man like that Hebrew understand a woman with freedom?

I rested my hand on the door handle and pulled gently to open it.

The door flew toward me, and Samson landed on his back, opening his eyes, staring up at me. He stank of drink.

"Good morning."

"Get up, or I will have you stripped and beaten." Immediately, I wished I hadn't said that. He giggled like a boy. He was still drunk, a mischievous gleam in his eyes, as if he was being bad.

No one here cared.

"You're filthy." I pushed him with my foot, holding my nose with my fingers. "If you go and wash, I will wait for you at the market."

"You will?"

"Yes. Now go wash."

He lifted his torso up, swaying even as he sat. I helped him stand and gave him a push out the door, pointing him in the direction of the gates. He held out one hand, bracing himself against the wall of my home.

I motioned for the neighbor's boy to come near. He was watching from his own doorway, fascinated by the Hebrew.

"Go and find Lord Galenos. Tell him Samson of the Hebrews is in the valley and drunk. He will know what to do."

I stepped back inside my house and closed the door, wishing for a way to brace it, to make it stronger, so I would be assured the Hebrew could do no harm if he came back.

For two days I remained in my house, not going to market even when I ran out of food and wine. But I could not last like this forever. The more life returned to my heart, the more life my body wanted. Hunger was again my enemy.

Samson was not outside my door. He was not in the streets and not in the market. Lord Galenos had expelled him. My thoughts turned to the day ahead, the expanse of empty hours I would have to fill before night came again. In the market, I bought a salted fish, its dead white eyes staring at nothing; and a loaf of bread, flat and brown; and a skin of wine. All this I carried in my arms, trying to hold it away from my body, at my sides.

I turned for home, and there he was again, his face unwashed and sunburned from living outside for three days. He was a madman. His eyes shone with a fat, fine pleasure when he saw me.

I turned away in disgust.

He trotted to my side, walking alongside me. I turned abruptly, changing directions, walking toward the sea.

"Your house is not in this direction."

I walked.

"What have you heard of me?" He was eager to talk.

I stopped, setting down my dinner carefully, then dusting off my hands. I shoved him with both hands against his chest.

"What do you want from me? What is it?"

He would later say that he had already fallen in love, but I had no such feelings. My dead heart had not stirred, until I saw his expression when I asked that question.

His face went blank. He had no answer. He could think of nothing he wanted from me.

He just wanted me.

It was then, at that moment, that I remembered how often the living feel afraid. The cold sinking weights in my stomach, the numbness of my fingers and toes, the pinch of my lips pressed together. I wanted nothing to do with this man.

❦

We sat under the stars on my roof, drinking the last of the wine. My face was flushed and warm; the wine had no obvious effect on him. The sky glowed lavender at the horizon, and the dusty brown stone buildings looked beautiful for just that one hour, when twilight softened the day.

"Your hair is beautiful in the light."

I raised my eyes from my bowl to look at him. How odd that any man could find beauty in me. But I had my reason for bringing him up here, a reason that would only sound reasonable to a woman as exhausted and broken as I.

"Hebrews hate the Philistines," I answered.

"I've attended the festivals at harvest. I've even been to the temple of Dagon."

"In Ekron?" I had never seen him there.

"In Gaza."

"You like to wander far from home."

"Not much to keep me there."

I smiled to myself. I understood the sentiment. Pouring out the last of the wine into his bowl, I settled back on the cushions, yawning.

Samson looked uncomfortable, glancing about as if he would find a reason to make more conversation. He frowned, as I shook the skin to make the point. It was empty. Our agreement was met. One skin, one hour, and then he would leave me in peace. I had a talent for negotiating with him. This pleased me, his acceptance of my offer.

But he had something new to say, some desperate, deep topic that was ready to surface. At last. He assumed I would care.

"No one wants to be delivered. Except children. And they're all afraid of me."

"Cut your hair."

He recoiled. I leaned forward. He needed to leave.

"You look like an animal."

"And your people live like one."

I laughed. He pouted like a child when hurt. His lower lip trembled in anger.

"Then why are you here, Samson? We do not want to be delivered either. No one wants you here."

He stood, knocking over the little table that separated us. I did not flinch. "Go home, Samson. Go home to your family."

He stomped down the stairs, making the roof shake like thunder had struck close by. The door opened and slammed shut, and his footsteps faded into the night.

I lifted my bowl, letting one last drop roll across the lip and into my mouth, a last burst of sweetness before the dreams came.

I was not surprised by the knock at my door the following morning. Only the hour seemed unreasonable.

I rubbed my eyes as I moved across the cool earth floor. Opening the door, I saw Lord Galenos nodding in greeting. I knew he would be calling for me. I had made no attempt to hide Samson's visit from my neighbors. And Lord Galenos had a family, and families did not sit up half the night drinking wine. He had, no doubt, slept for hours.

"Good morning, Delilah. May I enter?"

"No." I grabbed a sash from the dressing table nearest the bed, then returned to the door. "We will walk in the market. I need to buy my food for today."

Lord Galenos made no protest, and so we walked. I did not want him in my home, although Marcos had spoken well of him. Lord Galenos was a man of power. I did not want to be swept into that world again.

"So the Hebrew, Samson." Lord Galenos sampled a bit of roasted grain proffered by a woman with young children grabbing her legs as she worked. He raised his eyebrows in praise and held up two fingers to buy us two loaves of her bread. The wheat harvest had just finished coming in all over the valley. Already, I could see dusty clouds billowing up from rooftops above us. The time had come for threshing. Those with smaller fields threshed on their roofs, letting the wind carry the chaff away.

"I do not know why he visited me. And he is not what I expected."

"Go on." Galenos handed me a small round loaf, no bigger than my palm, dotted with raisins. I held it to my nose out of habit, inhaling before the first bite that would crack the brown crust and send crumbs all down my tunic.

"He talks a lot."

"About what?" Galenos tensed, nodding for me to continue. I had something of value to offer him. I saw it in his eyes.

I was slipping, just a little. When a woman has known powerful men, she is forever changed. She knows that power is always there; just a little push and it can be hers, too. She thinks she can fix what is so deeply wrong in her life. Until she discovers that power will only make her wounds worse. Power without goodness is an infection.

I wanted none of it. I was not good. When I had power, I used it to hurt others.

"Nothing at all. He just talks. If he said anything at all of importance, I would tell you."

Galenos pointed to the sun overhead. "I have to go to Ekron today. The lords are meeting to discuss this problem."

"All five lords?"

"Have you not heard what he did in Gaza? He tore the city gates off their hinges, carried them all the way to Mount Hebron."

"I still do not believe it." I was not a man, but I was educated.

He grasped my arm, frowning in earnest. "It happened. I saw the gates myself."

"It's impossible!" My stomach was cold and tight. Fear brought my body to life. I pressed a hand to my stomach to soothe it. "It would take twenty men or more just to set them on their hinges."

"Took forty to bring them down from the mountain, and on carts at that. Samson is a dangerous man. Do not entertain him again. Have nothing to do with him. For my sake."

I did not understand. He patted my arm with a sigh. "Marcos was my friend."

I bit my lip to stop any sign of grief. I had not heard his name spoken in months. Had it been months? I did not know time anymore. I knew only emptiness. Inside there was absence, a lack, a dreary day where there is no movement in the clouds, no sun and no storm, just a low and heavy gray sky.

Lord Galenos kissed my hand and departed. I stared at the baker's oven, the orange flames rising around the blackened base of the stones, the white ashes floating up and away. The wind was carrying all of it off, the ash and the chaff, all the evidence that we were alive on this day. I looked down at my own hands, trembling in the warming sun. They were cold, so cold. One hand moved toward the flame, stretching out toward the warmth, as if I did not control it. I wanted to burn my hand. I pushed it closer. I wanted to feel something again, something real, a pain I could see with my own eyes. I needed to see my pain, so I pushed my hand toward the flames, my tunic singeing at the edges where it touched the stones.

Samson was upon me, grabbing me, one arm sweeping under my ribs along my waist, pulling me along the lane.

"Why would you do that?" He forced me to walk fast, anger in his voice.

"How much did you hear?" I thought he was talking about Galenos.

"If you want to hurt me, then do. But I never want to see you do that again." He stopped, grabbing me by the arm, forcing me around to look at him. "Whatever it is, I can help you."

He picked up my hand, inspecting it. It was not truly burned, but it was red from the heat.

"You are said to be a dangerous man," I said.

"Not to you. Never to you, Delilah."

"Then leave me alone. Just talking to you brings trouble to me."

"I cannot do that."

"Why? Have we made slaves of the Hebrews now?"

"Because I'm going to marry you."

I laughed until I bent over, until he turned red in the face and crossed his arms. He sounded angry, not petulant, as he spoke. "I've watched you in the streets. You have no one."

"That does not mean I need you."

"No. But, in time, you will desire me, just as I desire you. And you will want my God to be your God, and my people to be your people."

Did he not understand the way of the world? Expectations were always met, and never with goodness. Anger rose in my heart, stiffening my arms as I looked into his face. His face with the soft brown eyes, and a mouth that was soft and red under that hair. He was an appealing man, if one looked closely. I took a step back.

I had no pity for the poor wounded Hebrew. He needed none. What he needed was a man strong as himself, one who would throttle him until he stopped whining and started seeing the world as it was, a world indifferent to him and his god and his destiny.

But there was no such man. There was only me, and I knew that sometimes in this life, only a woman would dare to do what a man should.

"I have conditions." Tension rushed from my shoulders, loosening my arms as I took a deep, satisfying breath.

Samson offered his arm, and together we walked toward my home. If he wanted to marry me, first he had to save me. No man could do that.

~

Again, we were drunk in the moonlight. Samson had bought me a beeswax candle in the market, a luxury I would not buy for myself. I went without light. It suited me. Samson, however, preferred light. I suspected that what he preferred was fire, the flame, but this I would not say. Not yet. I would wait to provoke him but was glad the thought had come to me.

"Will you let me kiss you?"

He leaned too close to my face. I pulled away, fanning at him with one hand, deciding to refill my bowl with the wine.

"What? Do I stink? Or is it because I am a Hebrew?"

"I don't want to kiss you. That is a reason in itself."

"How can I please you when you won't talk to me?"

"Don't bother trying to please me." I felt no pleasure.

He grunted as he stood, and he walked to the edge of my roof.

"I should leave." He sounded hurt, drawing a deep sigh, releasing it with great effort.

I said nothing.

"I stopped that man from hurting you because it was the right thing to do, the right way to use my strength. And when I looked at you, after he was lying on the ground, I thought you were the most beautiful woman I had ever seen. I had not known I could feel that again."

He said those last words with great emphasis. I knew I was supposed to ask him to tell me his tale.

I drank more wine, letting it sit on my tongue, breathing through my mouth, trying in vain to taste it, truly. It burned and gave me no satisfaction.

"I won't come anymore. If you really want me to leave, I will." He turned to face me as he said it, crossing his arms. He was testing me. He wanted to know what was in my heart.

I decided to show him.

I stood and walked to the edge of the roof, sweeping my arm out across the view. "In the distance, you can see the temple from here. And if you look across the valley, you will see tiny dots of light, little houses near the fields." At this hour, the homes with light and the temple with its yellow orbs were like stars resting on the black earth. "They will be harvesting the grapes this month, and the figs, and the olives. There will be much rejoicing if the fields are fertile."

"We will hope for a good harvest, then." Samson looked hopeful. He was not thinking of a harvest. He was thinking I would soften if the news was good.

"But if there are worries, if the fields are bare and trees wither, they will return to the temple and teach Dagon what he must do. There will be lovemaking. And sacrifices. And next spring, babies thrown in gutters."

Samson said nothing, made no response, no expression. I shoved him toward the roof's edge. He caught himself, cursing.

I knew I was smiling. I didn't care. "You're afraid."

"Afraid to die, yes!"

"There are worse things."

I walked to the edge, resting my toes at the tip of the roof. The temple lay straight ahead. Its yellow light teased me. It was beautiful, from a distance. Everything was, until you knew the truth. Glancing at Samson, I took one last step off the roof, into the night air.

He caught me, strength coming upon him, pulling me to his chest. He pressed me close, my face just under his, warm against his neck.

Only one man had ever held me like this. And he had not saved me. He had only betrayed me, giving me my freedom before he made sure I wanted to live.

Samson's heart beat fast, pounding through his tunic. Tears came to my eyes, running in cool rivers down my cheeks. Samson was afraid—and not just for himself. He was afraid for me. He was afraid I would die, as if that would mean something to him. I closed my eyes, letting him hold me like this. I fought with the sweet softness of memory before I composed myself and shoved him off of me, furious.

He grabbed my arm. "I'm not leaving you alone."

"I am already alone!"

"Not anymore. Not if you will just talk to me."

I paused, waiting for the tears to dry up, willing my heart to turn cold again.

"Do you want to stay the night?" I asked.

"With you?"

I laughed. He was so suspicious now.

"Yes, with me."

"Then I do, yes."

"Be quiet, and you can stay." I don't know why I did it, only that the memories were so near, so sweet, that I could not bear to be alone with them tonight.

He pressed one finger to his lips, in mockery of my command. I pulled two blankets from a basket near the wine table and laid them out on the roof. It was too hot to sleep below, and I planned to do nothing but sleep.

He was not pleased, I think, with the arrangement, but he said nothing. He should not have agreed to my conditions without knowing what they all were.

He breathed heavily at night, not like Marcos, who slept peacefully. Samson thrashed and snorted, like an ox with a blanket thrown over his face.

Poor Samson. Not even in sleep did he find peace. If he spoke the truth to me, then he was born to save others, and others did not want to be saved. If they had allowed him to fulfill his destiny, perhaps he would not have been keeping me awake, pestering me even while asleep. But I understood. His people didn't want their freedom.

I didn't want mine either.

"Are you awake?" Samson was sitting up, watching me. I wiped my cheeks in the darkness, angry. I had not realized he was watching me, and I had been crying.

He crossed his legs and settled back.

"I will tell you a story," he said.

I said nothing. Stories were better than questions, I supposed, and this man was determined to talk.

"Many generations ago, a young boy had a great destiny but not much sense. His brothers hated him, and one day they betrayed him and sold him into slavery. The boy was taken to a foreign land, where he suffered again, until he found a kind master who gave him freedom and honor, but the boy, who was now a man, was sad, broken. He had everything he ever could desire, but he was dead in his heart. Then a famine came upon the land, and all suffered a great hunger. Now this man had been given a job, a job of counting grain and storing grain and rationing grain, and so during the famine he became the most powerful man in the world. All who hungered came to him for grain. One day, he saw his brothers in the line for grain. What did he do?"

"He had them killed."

"He fed them."

"What? They were his enemies, the beginning of all his pains!"

"But that was what he had been born for, why he had been given his power and strength, to feed those who had hurt him, to save many, even those who did not deserve it."

I sat up, hoping he saw my eyes blazing in the dark. My teeth were on edge. "Why do you tell me this story?"

"My God uses the cruelty of others to push us into a position to save them. To save many. Whatever has been done to you, perhaps my God was at work in it, too."

My heart was beating faster. How could he have known this story was for me? As if a god was speaking to me through him.

"I do not know your god. I know Dagon."

"Dagon is no god. He has given you nothing. He will never be at work in your sorrow."

"You have power, Samson. Why must you talk of gods? Surely you see that power is the only true god in this world. Yet here you are, on the roof with a Philistine woman, half drunk and a nuisance." I wanted him gone.

"I have strength. Not power. I cannot heal. I cannot change a heart. I cannot even win your trust."

"I feel such pity for you. Now go home."

He was mad with god-talk. As if I would feed my brothers or father and mother, as if I would bless the man in shadows or any of the men who used their worship to serve themselves. Not that a woman, even in Philistine lands, could have such power over others. But should that moment come to me, I knew what I would choose.

"Delilah?"

"Yes?"

"Do I have to go home? I promise not to say anything else."

I hid under the blanket, pressing my hand over my mouth so he wouldn't hear me laughing.

Every winter, just before spring arrives, the almond trees bloom. They are a promise from God, each of those white blossoms, that He is watching and His words will be fulfilled in their appointed time. Sometimes, this appointed time comes before we are ready. Sometimes, it seems to come too late. We cannot understand His timing, any more than we can understand our children, when the children we love break our hearts again and again.

This was not the season of blooms.

I waited by our grinding stone for Kaleb and Liam to bring me some grain from our storage jars in the corner. I could have done it myself, but boys need to be kept busy.

Manoah spoke. "I miss our son."

I whipped my head around to peer at him. I thought he had been sleeping. He needed so much sleep these days.

I tried to make my voice gentle. "Kaleb and Liam are our sons now too."

"Where is my son?" His voice faltered.

"I know where he is." We turned to stare at Kaleb, who was standing still, listening to us.

He cleared his throat, addressing Manoah instead of me. "He has fallen in love with another Philistine woman. Her name is Delilah. He spends all his nights with her. He says she is soft and doesn't have to work for her meals like the Hebrew girls."

"Every woman works for her meals. Trust me," I said, with narrowed eyes and a lowered voice. "You are too young to understand."

"So you have seen him?" Manoah tried to sit up on his pallet.

"Liam and I saw him when we were helping the servants plant the wheat. He said he knows how Mother feels about Philistine women. He does not think he can come home now."

Manoah's face brightened as he rubbed his hands together. "Give him a message for me, if you see him again. Tell him to come home. I want to see him."

"And you?" Kaleb was waiting for me to say something, a sweet message of my own to bring my wandering boy back.

I came to him, embracing him warmly but whispering in his ear, so Manoah would not see.

"Remind him of what it will cost her. She'll be dead before spring."

The creek glittered in the noon sun. I watched as children ran through it, screaming with delight as the cool water ran past their ankles. I did not mind watching older children. I had never had one. I picked up my tunic, walking back toward my home now. It had been less than a day's walk to Ashdod, but I could have gone faster if I had wanted to.

I hadn't.

Lord Galenos had called me to his home. He sent word that he had something of importance to discuss with me. He had welcomed me from his perch in the center of the room.

"Lord Marcos preferred to sit on a bench, with the others," I told him.

Galenos shrugged. "Did he? I always liked Marcos. He was a good man. But we have a matter of official business, Delilah. Sit down."

My throat was swelling, closing. I clenched my jaws together, shaking my head, refusing his offer. I did not want to sit in this house. I wanted to run. How could he not understand? I had lived here once, one brief happy window into another way of life.

"The five lords are prepared to make you an offer."

"For what?"

He smiled. "Don't you want to profit from what is inevitable?"

"In my experience, Lord Galenos, the inevitable is death. And the dead do not profit."

He stood, offering me his arm, as if we should walk like friends through my former home. I had no wish to see it, so I refused again, shaking my head. Color flushed to his cheeks.

"Each lord is prepared to pay you eleven hundred pieces of silver. That's five thousand, five hundred pieces of silver, my dear. A man's life is worth only twelve, maybe twenty if he has some special merit," Lord Galenos said.

The money he spoke of, the sum, was immense. Silver was power. Much silver was much power. My father had worked a year for five pieces. With the sum Galenos offered, I wouldn't just have freedom. I would have freedom and power. That might make life worth living, if only to see that others suffered as I had.

"What could I do to earn such a fee?"

"One small favor. We know of your affair with the Hebrew, Samson."

I remained still. I would not have called it an affair, but there was no reason to share that secret.

"All you must do is ask Samson about the source of his great strength. Our magicians have been of no help, but after all, he is a Hebrew, and we do not understand his gods."

"His god."

"What?"

"His god. They only have one." I suddenly did not like Galenos. I did not like him standing in Marcos's house, or speaking to me as a friend, or offering me such sums.

"Strange people, aren't they? Not at all like us."

I pressed my lips together as my stomach rose. Perhaps it had happened—his strange god had been at work in my sorrow. All had led me to Samson, had it not? But for what purpose? To make me rich?

I bowed before Galenos and walked home, taking a slow pace, letting others pass me, unwilling to return home before nightfall.

I did not want Samson to read my face. I did not know what it would reveal.

Children watched me from their windows, giggling as I walked by; terse whispers from mothers corrected them, dragging them down. Word was spreading. Samson, the enemy of the Philistines, had been tamed by a temple priestess. I don't know what made me more of a curiosity to them—that I lived alone in freedom after service in the temple, or that I had won the heart of the strongest, strangest enemy our people had ever known.

Samson was waiting for me. He had retreated into the quiet of the home below. He had a side of lamb on the table for me, raw and wet. I flinched, my eyebrows rising in question.

"I was hungry," he said.

"I don't know how to cook."

"You're a woman."

"Yes, I've heard that. But still, I don't know how to cook. You'll have to take it to the market. Someone there will cook it for you."

"What other secrets are you hiding from me?" He was moving toward me, a smile on his lips. He did not know I had made my choice. Or perhaps he did; who can say how his god moved in this world?

I stepped back and raised a finger. "I am not the one with secrets."

"What? If you heard about the brothels, that happened in the past."

"You told me so much, didn't you? But not the whole truth. That, I am sure, is reserved for the woman you love."

"Stop."

"It's all right. I know you cannot love me. I am your sworn enemy." I narrowed my eyes so, if his god was willing, he would not fall into my trap. I could be merciful, too. If anything he had told me was true, it was this: The Hebrews hated the Philistines. We were his enemies. He should not be here.

Not if he had told me the truth.

"What will you give me?" he asked. "If I tell you the whole truth, whatever you want to know?"

"What do you want?" The words hung in the air between us, like the first chill air of a building storm.

He pulled me into his arms, and I kissed him, hard, on the mouth, fighting him in my way, my back rigid as he removed my tunic, my neck stiff as he bent it back to press his mouth to mine again. He leaned back then, pressing his hands on either side of my face, forcing me to look up into his eyes. He did not blink. I saw myself in him, my hard face with smeared lips, my cold dead eyes. I didn't want to be that woman. I didn't want to choose that path.

I softened under his control, and we did not have need to roast that lamb until much later in the night.

❧

I kicked him with one foot. The sun was already high, and he was sweating on my blankets.

"Tell me."

He sat up, rubbing his eyes. "You woke me up for this?"

"I woke you up to see what kind of man you are on the morning after."

He groaned but did not lie back down. He yawned and shook his head side to side, the heavy braids flinging with dull flapping sounds in all directions.

"Seven fresh bowstrings," he said. "If you tie me with seven fresh bowstrings, I'm powerless. That's the secret of my strength."

I frowned. The answer had come too easily to him. I could not tell if he was lying or telling the truth.

"Our magicians don't use bowstrings."

"Your magicians are worthless."

I went below and fetched a child, who was to fetch a lord, who was to fetch the seven fresh bowstrings. By the fourth hour after the morning meal, I had them. I laid them on the table below, where the bones of the lamb were piled in a gnawed heap. Samson came below to see who had knocked at my door. He saw the bowstrings on the table and smiled at me, the smile of an innocent. I smiled in return, a silent promise of treachery. Or truth. Maybe they were the same.

He lay down on my pallet, crossing his feet, watching me as he tucked his arms behind his head.

"What are you going to do with those?"

"Tie you up."

"I'd like to see you try."

"I'm going to find out if you are a liar."

"You don't need to know the secret of my strength. Unless there is something you are not telling me."

"There's not!" I shouted it, provoked. It was foolish of me.

Samson grinned. He had won the exchange. "Maybe you are the liar."

I grabbed the bowstrings from the table. They stank of animal and felt like dried gristle in my hands.

I dumped them at his feet and knelt, struggling to slide a rope under his feet. He offered no assistance, but just lay there, still and amused. I tied his feet together and moved to his head, yanking each heavy arm free, laying it on his belly. I was sweating by now, and he seemed to find it all great entertainment. I hoped that the bowstrings would burn his bare flesh if I ripped them fast enough. Laying each wrist on top of the other, I pulled a bowstring around them, tying it down to the wrists in a knot, then tying a knot over my knot, yanking up as hard as I could to tighten it beyond endurance.

Still, he grinned.

I had one bowstring left, and I had seen how butchers tied their animals. I pulled the bowstring under his neck, tying it in a knot at his throat, then pulling the ends down and securing them at his wrists. I stood, bracing against him with one foot, and yanked, so that his head was forced down as I shortened the length between his neck and his wrists.

The great enemy of the Philistines was bound like an animal before me, and still he laughed, a high-pitched giggle, as if he was playing a game. I was not going to release him. If he had told me the truth, he was going to die in this position.

"Now, what do you say?" I poked him with one toe. "Were you lying? Or do you love me?"

He struggled to raise his head. "That's not funny."

I opened my door, looking out in the street. The boy who had fetched the bowstrings was standing not far from my door, eager for my sign. I nodded, and he whistled, calling his two friends out from their hiding places under a blanket in the corner of the room.

I turned back to Samson. "There are men here, Samson! The Philistines are upon you!"

He pushed against the bowstrings, one small pulse, and they fell from his ankles, wrists and neck. Standing without effort, his mouth was set in a hard line. The boys cowered when they saw his size in such close quarters. He did not even glance at them.

"I don't care if you test my strength. But don't test me. Don't make me try to prove what I feel."

"I don't need to! I know what you feel for me." I spat the words at his feet. He was a fool to think I would want him after he lied to me.

The boys crept like kittens toward the door, and ran.

"I don't think you do. I don't think any man has ever loved you like I do."

I crossed the distance to him and raised one hand to slap him into silence, but he caught my hand and then caught me around the waist, lifting me off the ground so that my toes grazed the earth and nothing else.

But of what happened then, I will say nothing except this: I did not need to feel the ground anymore. I knew only Samson and thought nothing else of this earth.

Samson had returned. The men were shouting, and the children running about squealing, and the women talking behind their hands. Only Samson could inspire such simultaneous delight and scorn.

Samson had returned to us in the spring, just before Passover. He looked terrible, my beautiful son, with dark circles under his eyes, and fat covering his ribs where once only muscle had been. That woman had been cruel to him, I could tell, and what she was feeding him was an injustice. She had no idea how to care for a man.

He did not knock on our front door but opened it and strode in. I tried to conceal my hard breathing, so he would not know I had been at the window, watching.

He entered our home as if it were still his and, coming to me first, gave me a kiss on the cheek. I was sitting next to Manoah, who was eating at our table. Manoah tried to stand, and I saw his legs shaking. Samson rested a hand on his shoulder, pushing him gently to remain seated.

"When do we roast the lamb?" Samson smiled, as if today was a cheerful day.

I replied. "It is not a celebration. It is a memorial. That we were spared the wrath of God."

Samson nodded, not listening. He sat beside Manoah to tell him news from the territories.

I stepped back, tears stinging, as I pressed my lips together, unwilling to display any emotion. He was home, my son. He was still a judge among our people and still chosen by God to deliver us. It was enough, for today, to dwell on these truths. Truths, and not circumstances, because the two did not match at all.

I was already losing Manoah, a little bit more every week. All my strength as a woman, as a mother, was gone. I could not bear another moment of loss.

I forced a smile and set two bowls on the table.

"I will fix you both some curds. And I will roast the lamb. It is good to have you home, Samson."

The game continued. Samson did not find it fun. But I had caught a scent, like a lioness stranded and hungry. I couldn't help what I wanted. If he didn't understand that, his god would. Maybe his god even knew which I desired more: a life with Samson, or life through Samson's death. A life of immense power. I had no thoughts for what I would do with it. Only the certainty that it might protect me from pain. Immense wealth, immense power, might be enough.

I wrinkled my nose, considering the choices. Samson had been talking. I blinked my eyes and tried to pay attention to him. He was leaning against my legs as I sat working my loom. I did not know what I was making.

"I can protect you without telling you my secret. I can overpower any enemy of yours."

Songs of the harvest girls made me lift my head and pause to listen. The women had a hard life here. Maybe everywhere. I did not know. Their hands would be calloused and dry when I saw them in the market, and they would hold their backs in their soreness. And when they finally stopped the harvest, it was time to process all their bounty. Pickling, pressing, fermenting, spicing, stewing, roasting.

"If we didn't have to eat, life would be easier," I said to Samson.

"Without food, there is no energy for love."

"Again, life would be easier."

He turned around to face me, ready for another argument.

"Don't worry, Samson. I know what you want. That, at least, is no secret."

He stood, not even looking at me now. He walked toward the door. I picked up an empty spindle and threw it at him, hitting him right in the back between his shoulder blades.

"You have made a fool of me! You lied to me!" I screamed.

He didn't turn back. A red welt was already showing itself. "I'm trying to protect you, Delilah, from yourself."

"Don't come back!" I screamed again. He opened the door, and I saw neighbors outside, peering in with interest.

He paused, his back to me. "If anyone ties me securely with new ropes that have never been used, I'll become as weak as any other man. Think about what you will do with this knowledge."

He did not return that night. I sat alone on the roof, watching the fires in the village as families cooked their meat, mothers laughing as children chased each other under the stars. The harvest was almost over. Soon there would be a feast, and after that, for all of them, even the women after their work was done, a rest. A long, quiet rest. Like death. Or sleep without faces that disturbed the dreamer.

Samson returned the next morning, stinking of new wine but not women. That surprised me. He collapsed onto my pallet below and was soon snoring, his face to the wall. He did not take off his sandals.

He might have told me the truth. He might expect to be taken away, or murdered right there, and a man would want to die with dignity. A man of any culture would want to die with his sandals and tunic.

The ropes rested in a woven basket by the door. I had sent for them last night. I slid silently to them, lifting them up in the cool, soft air. They did not scratch like old ropes; they still smelled of the fields and were green as meadow snakes, coiling around my arms, fresh and alive.

This time was different. This time, Lord Galenos had sent his own guards to be hidden on my roof. Even Lord Galenos knew Samson would lie to me the first time, that he should not waste real men on my first attempt. I had not been sure. I still did not understand the ways of men and their secrets.

I tied him up. He was drunk and asleep, and that made my task harder, not easier.

When his feet were bound, I moved to his wrists, and when his wrists were bound, I leaned down and kissed him on the cheek.

He murmured my name.

I sat back on my haunches, looking at him.

Deliverance was always offered to the wrong people.

"Samson, the Philistines are upon you!"

At my cue, Lord Galenos's men stormed down the ladder from the roof. I counted four of them before Samson burst up from behind me, shaking off the ropes. He ripped the sword from the first man and drove an elbow into his throat. The second man was already swinging his sword, and Samson brought the first man's sword around, plunging it into the second man's abdomen. Philistine swords were made for cutting on both sides; now I understood why they were esteemed.

What happened to the other two men I cannot say. I hid behind my tunic while men fell dead in my quiet, cool home. Blood pooled and ran toward me, circling me, my toes growing sticky and hot.

Samson said nothing. He dragged the bodies into the street and returned with straw, laying it across the red stains.

"I'm hungry."

I stood there, unmoving. I was not even breathing.

I pointed to his face. A smear of blood, rested on his cheek, the same cheek I had kissed, the same cheek that had made me reconsider what I was doing.

He frowned, not understanding.

"You have … something … there." I pointed again.

He smiled, happy to know the answer, and wiped his face with his tunic. It was stained red, too, but he did not seem to see it. He did not see blood. He did not see death. What he saw, when he moved against the Philistines, I did not know. It was a mystery—a holy mystery perhaps—known only to him and his god.

He extended a hand to me. "Let's go to the market."

Liam was screaming, tears popping from his eyes as he squinted and howled. Poor thing had cut himself while harvesting the grapes. I cradled him, though by now he was taller than me, and clucked my teeth while I waited for him to calm.

It was good to see him cry at last.

"I wish I had died instead of her." His body convulsed as he said it. I rubbed his arms and back and said nothing. He was learning so young this lesson that I had only now begun to understand. We love, but we cannot save. God does as He wills, and sometimes, His will is unbearable.

Liam settled after a while, and when I felt his back straighten, his breathing slow, I released him, lest he be overwhelmed by embarrassment and turn cold to me again. Better to let go before they realize they need you.

Better to let go before they realize how very much you need them.

"When will Samson be back?" he asked, choosing to stand and stretch.

I shrugged as if unconcerned. "I do not know."

"He wants to marry her someday."

I forgot that the boys were old enough to have heard of his first disastrous marriage. If he expected to see a reaction from me at this, I disappointed him.

"He might. We will wait and see."

Liam inhaled to say something, but then twisted his mouth. I did not sound like the woman he knew.

"Can I ask you a question?"

I smiled at him, hoping he would sit next to me. He did not.

"The Philistines think Samson is a sort of god. Or that he uses magic to become strong."

"You know this is not true."

"I don't." Liam was earnest now, stepping closer. "I don't know how he does it."

I stood, dusting off my lap. Liam had carried in leaves and dirt from the harvest fields.

"Get back to work."

"I just—"

"Out!"

He scooted out the door at once. I could not understand why everyone devoted themselves to understanding the secret of his strength. Why did it matter? Why did no one care what his strength was for, why it had been given to him? Why did no one seek that answer?

No one wanted to know. They preferred the excitement of miracles to the hard work of change, the hard work of breaking away from a culture that enslaved them all so comfortably.

They were the real mystery.

DELILAH

We walked through the dusty streets as the orange sun set in the west, beyond the scrabble of little stone homes that stood in the center of the village. The air was thick with smoke from burning wood and metal. The blacksmith's home sat away from all others, and his orange fire rose high above him as he worked. Philistines should have had a god of cleanliness, for all their worship of it. Homes were allowed in the center of a village or city, but never industry. Industry stank; industry made raging fire and sparks and blood that ran in fast red rivers. Industry attracted flies, the lords said. It was not a clean way of life, no matter what the job.

But all the men walked about at night when their wives were done scolding, always finding their way to the blacksmith's to watch him work. He made swords that were one piece, from handle to stem and blade—swords that cut in both directions—and he saved his copper for decoration. Other peoples still used copper for their blades, or bronze, and in battle it was said they often stopped to brace one foot against a bent sword and straighten it. More men died straightening their swords than swinging them.

Samson had no interest in our weapons and technology, how we planned for war and trained for it and, some would say, hoped for it.

We had no worthy opponents near us. We had to travel to Egypt for a good fight, and we had made our peace with the Egyptians long ago.

Samson whistled a tune I did not know and ran a hand through my hair as we walked. He let the soft strands flow between his fingers, stretching his hand open wide to claim as much of me as he could.

His own hair was a mess. I kept my hands at my sides, with no interest in his lover's game.

"What should we eat?" he asked.

I shrugged. Of course I would pay for it. I had money, and Samson had his strength.

"Figs." I liked them. They did not weigh me down like meat, did not make me feel heavy and clumsy and slow. I could eat my weight in figs and still glide across a floor like a spirit. I liked feeling weightless, insubstantial, as if I weren't here at all.

Samson grunted. He wanted meat.

"Figs and meat."

He nodded, and I pulled my bag from my sash as we approached a little stall set up outside a home. We did have a market during the day, but at night, if one was lazy or delayed and had not gone to the market during those hours, one could knock on a door and buy what was needed. A merchant was always glad to see money, whether he was at home or the market.

We bought our dinner and walked to the stream to eat it. A large cypress grove grew along one side of the stream. On early mornings you could see a lion or deer emerging from the trees to drink. For us, tonight, it would provide cooling shade. I did not like to sweat as I ate.

Samson sweat like a beast all the time.

My stomach was sour. I didn't want to eat, not really, and everything Samson did irritated me. Odd that a man so devoted to me could be such a source of frustration. If I had ever thought I loved him, even suspected I might, surely this aggravation was proof that I did not.

We sat, and he held out a fig to me. I brushed it away and turned to watch the sun's last descent.

"Do I smell?"

"When do you not?"

"Why are you angry with me?"

He started eating. Whatever upset me was of no concern to him. He must have thought he could overpower anything, even my objections.

"I wish it would rain. I should make an offering to the gods. Maybe it will rain early this year," I said.

"There is no 'gods.' There is only God."

I exhaled in a loud rasp, my annoyance too big to hide. He didn't even look up. I wanted to tear the pork rib from his hands and hit him with it. I had to stand up and walk away.

He finished eating, humming to himself as he did, content with ribs and figs and dirty fingers. I did not even want to think what his beard would smell like tonight when he tried to kiss me.

And he would. That was why I was inconsolable tonight. I realized this only when I had walked a good distance away, when I stood still and listened to the night encroaching, sneaking up on us, loud and dark. Insects began to shriek and in the trees, a flutter of wings. The heavy, fast panting of a big cat warned me to be careful, not to get too far from Samson.

I needed him.

No. I wanted him. That was worse.

And I was a liar, a filthy, cruel liar who would ruin everything for a chance at relief. I didn't want justice or revenge. I wanted relief. I would hurt anyone I had to, even myself. I did not know why that sum had changed my heart about money. Maybe I had never had a chance to have so much. But theories about wealth fell apart when wealth became real.

But it was not too late. Nothing had been done, not really. I could pretend it had been a lover's game. Samson was fond of those. He would not know how wretched I could be, how I had tried to use him. We could still go on.

His hands on my shoulders made me jump. The cat ran through the forest, alarmed by the sight of Samson, I am sure.

"Will you talk?" he asked.

I turned to look at him.

"The bowstrings, and the new ropes? It was a silly game for me to play," I said.

He shrugged me off with a laugh. "Doesn't matter. I didn't tell you the truth anyway."

My stomach tightened. Everything tightened and hardened and flushed red with anger. Whatever his powers were, he had the power to make me furious without trying.

"You lied to me? There really is a secret?"

"If you knew the truth, people might try to hurt you. I have enemies. You saw that for yourself."

"I would never reveal your secret!"

"Of course you would."

My mouth opened for a scream of fury before he finished his thought. "Under torture, anyone will reveal a secret. And then, once they killed me, what would they do to you?"

I couldn't even hear what he was saying. I made fists from my hands and trembled, holding them up at my chest, so furious I could not even decide where to hit him first. He had lied to me. He had kept a secret from me. I hated secrets.

"Why are you so angry?"

I swear on the feet of the gods, he was trying not to laugh.

"Delilah, I was only protecting you."

"You lied to me! You betrayed me!" I grabbed my head with both hands just trying to clear the rage from my vision. I did not know where we were or how to get home. I just wanted to hurt him.

So he kissed me. He grabbed me around the small of my back, his arms drawing me in, pressing down against my arms so that I was trapped. He kissed me, and I bit him. His eyes lit with anger and surprise, and I tried to step back, thinking I had won my release, but he drew me in tighter.

And what can I say? He was a very strong man. He got what he wanted, until I wanted it too.

"I love you," he whispered in my ear. No man had ever said that to me. I wasn't sure what I should feel.

When he had finished, I made my voice small and sweet as I rested my head on his chest, moving his beard aside and breathing through my mouth so I would not smell it.

"Please."

He wanted sleep. He was a man of big appetites. He wanted to sleep, and I saw how that could be a useful appetite. All his appetites could be useful. He had no restraint, no discipline. He lived like a very bad donkey, his reins loose and untended. All he needed was someone to take the reins, and his strength could be used at last.

So I made my small, sweet voice in his ear, stalling his hunger for sleep, and he told me. He told me because he wanted sleep, more than he wanted to protect me, more than he loved me.

That is how I made my last choice. I knew his real secret long before he knew mine.

He did not love me, not really. No man ever would again.

After the first sleep, when others stirred at midnight and put out lamps and checked on the animals, we went home. Samson slept on the pallet below, simply because that was where I led him. He made no resistance, offered no criticism that the roof was surely cooler. He just wanted to sleep.

I let him.

I let him sleep while I carried the loom over to his sleeping form and rested it on my lap, settling down on my rear end near his head. One by one I lifted his fat rough braids and wove them into my loom.

His brown hair wove into my red pattern.

Slowly, I tightened the loom with its pin. His braids were secure but did not pull on his scalp. It was lovely work, my finest yet, and Samson would bring me more income than any fleece I had ever dreamed to make.

I arched my back, sore from bending over my work. Without disturbing him, I set the loom beside him. Gliding across the floor one last time with him sleeping in my bed, I opened my door to the night and did what I had to do.

When I returned, I had three Philistine guards with me. They waited outside the door. No matter what I said, they would not enter, not until they were sure he was weak.

"Samson, the Philistines are upon you!"

Samson awoke from his sleep and jumped up, his braids ripping the fabric from the loom, a sharp crack echoing from the stone walls as the loom exploded.

The guards ran away, their swords slapping against their sides as they ran.

Samson was busy picking the splinters of wood from his hair.

I crossed the floor, not bothering to be silent, and struck him on the chest. "How can you say, 'I love you,' when you won't confide in me? This is the third time you have made a fool of me and haven't told me the secret of your great strength."

"Delilah—"

"Get out!"

"No."

"This is my home!"

"Not anymore."

He sat down on my pallet and tucked his arms behind his stinking foolish head. "When you calm down, you can come back. I won't even punish you. Unless you ask me to." He wriggled his eyebrows at me, which made his beard wriggle, which let a few fat splinters fall free into his lap.

I stomped out the door and slammed it, making as much noise as possible.

"No razor has ever been used on my head, because I have been a Nazarite dedicated to God from my mother's womb. If my head were shaved, my strength would leave me, and I would become as weak as any other man."

That was his secret. And I did not win it by seduction, by promise or threats, but by persistence. When Samson let me return in the morning, I was neither shocked by the experience nor shaken. Worse had been done to me.

What Samson wanted from me, I thought, was a rare kindness. He wanted someone who knew his destiny and did not judge him by it. I did not care about him, and he mistook that for the acceptance he craved. But what if I did accept him without judgment? What if I pretended to love, and because I loved, wanted to know everything?

I returned in the morning with a plan. I would love him. I would love him, and because I loved, I would nag. I would ask, and inquire, and prod, and hope. I would love him as no other woman had, until he was ready to die from so much devotion.

He lasted less than a week.

Even neighbors noticed the change in me, and old women gave me such frowns. Sleeping with an enemy is one thing, but loving him? That was poor character, especially for a Philistine.

So when I called for the lords and their men this time, they all came, silver in hand. I bid them wait outside until the first sleep had begun. My little friend, my boy who ran and fetched these men for me on the other occasions, stood alone at the door, a knife in his hand.

I spoke kindly to Samson that night, running my hands along his hair, stroking his cheek, letting my fingers graze his skin with tender attention. He rested his head in my lap as we sat on my pallet together and spoke of the future.

"How many children do you want?" he murmured, sleep coming to him already.

The question was a cold one. But he could not have known.

"None. I had one, once."

"What?" he murmured, the end of the word falling off like the speech of a drunk.

He was asleep.

What happened next has been repeated in the streets many times. Often I was asked to tell it myself. I never did, not once. The lords did not pay me to tell it. My work was done.

I felt nothing, not for days. When the feelings came, they were so frightening, so unlike what I had thought possible, that even now, this story is like sand in my mouth.

I put him to sleep in my lap and whistled low for the boy. He cut off the braids, one by one. They fell like severed ropes at my side in a tangled pile.

Samson changed. We both did, actually, but I would not know that for days.

He seemed smaller, softer.

Then I called to him, "Samson, the Philistines are upon you!"

He awoke and stumbled as he stood, like a newborn doe.

Then the Philistine guards seized him, and with those fine smelted daggers they gouged out his eyes right there, in my home, as I watched. He looked right at me as they did it. I was the last thing he saw on this earth.

I could not turn away, as if some unseen hand grabbed the back of my neck, forcing me to watch.

With that, he screamed like an animal, like a small, wounded animal. And they dragged him outside, through the streets, where people threw stones at him and emptied pots on him until the lords begged them to stop, if only for the guards.

They took him down to Gaza. It was a journey of a week's time, and I have heard tell how they stopped in every village so the people could see their enemy shamed and bleeding and blind. How he survived the walk, I do not know. Perhaps some strength remained, strength I knew nothing of, the strength of a very mortal man who knows a very real god.

I was free at last to live long and in luxury. I could buy anything my heart desired, but no one had told me this: My heart still desired nothing. Money left me cold, colder than the dead.

I could not forget how his hand reached for me, after he was blinded and struck with many blows, how he reached for me still, even knowing I had betrayed him.

He had still been calling my name as they dragged him away.

Manoah was wringing his hands like a woman. I had never seen him like this, frantic with worry, pale and sweating. Kaleb and Liam had sneaked away to a Philistine festival. Our neighbors had told us, with a certain amount of pious satisfaction.

"Get a stick. I'm going to beat them when they return." Manoah gestured to the door. It was late summer, and there would be dead wood about. "I will not allow the same mistakes to be made."

He was not strong enough anymore to lead the family, but what could I say? I took him by the arm and led him to our table.

"Sit. Let me worry about the boys."

"I will not allow my brother's name to be dishonored. Not like ours. I blame myself for this. I blame myself for it all."

"Shh. Sit. I will make you something to eat. What would you like?"

The boys stumbled through the door, making me jump from fright. Manoah's mouth opened in shock as we saw them, stripped and bruised, red with shame.

"What have you done?" I shouted. I grabbed them by their ears and drew their faces to mine. "You almost killed us with worry! And look at you both!"

"It's Samson!" Kaleb said.

I dropped my hands from their ears, grabbing them by the elbow to lead them outside. I didn't want Manoah to hear this. My heart was ice.

Manoah tried to stand, keeping one hand braced on the table for strength. "Tell us."

The boys went to him, and I stood, helpless. The world was a man's affair, not mine.

"The Philistines captured him and are taking him to Gaza." Kaleb's face was white with fright. He must have been near when it happened, but why had Samson not saved him? Probably wanted Kaleb and Liam to learn a lesson about sneaking away from home.

I clapped my hands together and laughed, too loud. "Then there is no worry, my boys! Samson has defeated many, many Philistines, even all at once! I've seen it myself. He is only playing a trick on them. You wait. This will be his greatest act yet!"

I wanted to believe myself, that this was the moment God had been leading us all to.

Liam shook his head. "No. They gouged out his eyes. They beat him until …"

Manoah collapsed onto the table, a groan breaking open from deep in his heart.

"And they shaved his head," Kaleb added.

I fell to my knees in shock. That is why, when Manoah died, I was not holding his hand.

DELILAH

My feet bled, cracked and dry. The road to Gaza was punishing. I once had willed this pain, found it sweet, but I could not remember that girl now, the girl who wanted to control her pain. I was a woman, and a woman knows that there is too much pain in the world, too much pain that hobbles us all.

I entered the gates of Gaza, a huge stone arch flanked on either side by two towers. Inside the archway, shadows fell upon me, feasting, and I shuddered.

I followed the rejoicing crowd to the temple, though I could have found it without them. I knew it by its scent, the incense and perfume heavy, not just for worship, but to cover the stench of their works. The people were assembling to offer a great sacrifice to Dagon, to celebrate Samson's capture. "Our god has delivered Samson, our enemy, into our hands." This was the cry in the streets that brought all good Philistines to Gaza on this day.

Dagon had not given Samson over to us. I had.

I looked at my people and saw that they had blinded themselves, too. They would never see the truth. They did not want to.

I understood why Samson had been born. Not everyone could be saved. I had to find Samson, though, and ask him one question. I hoped he would still speak to me. I hoped he would still do that.

I approached the temple and pushed past the crowds gathering at the entrance, some seeing it for the first time, like me. I was not impressed. A temple is only as good as its god.

But I did see at once that the temple in Gaza was nothing like the one in Ashdod. In Gaza, the temple was like a box with one side missing, and this was the entrance. The roof was long and wide, supported by the three walls and two massive columns in front, smoothed and polished and shining in the summer heat.

Grain offerings were being burned on a horned altar in the center of this temple as onlookers peered over the roof, already crowded with hundreds—perhaps a thousand or more—hungry Philistines.

I did not recognize Samson. I had to ask a temple servant where he was being kept, and the young boy laughed and pointed to the back of the temple. I found Samson walking in slow, labored circles, the yoke of an ox resting on his shoulders as he moved around and around, threshing wheat. He did the job reserved for donkeys.

Bronze shackles were on his ankles and hands, with bronze links running between them. Bronze! The metal that was too weak for battle was strong enough to control Samson. He looked old to me. Blood had dried on his face from his eyes and wounds, and the blood had settled into the wrinkles and lines, flaking off and peeling away, making him look older than his years, with his shaved hair only now growing back. His hair grew in wild patches, like river weeds.

He lifted his head as I came near, a grimace on his face. It might have been a smile.

"Delilah?" He stopped walking. "I recognize your perfume."

"Why did your god not save you?"

"Maybe I was saved from myself."

"You are sure he is real?"

"Yes."

"Could he save me? Even now?"

Samson groaned under weight of yoke. I saw that his shoulders had open sores. They must have stunk. I did not notice. I reached out with my fingers to touch them, gently.

"I am sorry," I said, my voice small from shame. "I did this."

"You did what you had to do."

"I loved you."

"I know. I am glad you came."

"I don't know who I have become."

"I have a question for you," he said.

"Yes."

"What did you really want? What would have made you happy?"

I sighed and swallowed, my stomach stinging with the agony of the moment. "I just wanted … relief. From this world. From what happened to me, to my daughter."

He nodded, letting my words affect him before replying. "I must become who I was born be. But my eyes are gone. Help me."

I could not help him, this strange and beautiful man. I had nothing to offer.

"Tell me what you see," he whispered.

I did not understand what he wanted, but I told him everything. There were no lover's games, or spiteful words, or cold silences. I just told him all I saw at the temple.

"Delilah, will you make me a promise?" His breath was ragged. I suspected they had not given him water, perhaps even for days. His life was fading, that part of him that was wholly human, wholly his.

"Yes." I meant it as a vow, the only vow I would ever make to him.

"Leave."

A guard came and dragged me away. I wept as I went, and he did not see it. I was grateful for that. I would spare him that pain.

The twisting pain rose from my belly, not the pain of hunger or disease, but the pain of sorrow. So many sorrows I had known. The pain was too big for me. I had no strength from a god to face it.

I broke my vow.

It was time to release the dream and die.

MOTHER

I did not know how to live without Manoah. I did not know how to live without Samson, either. In all my grief, only one name was on my lips. God.

Kaleb and Liam were good to me, like sons. They watched over me and fed me broth and covered me with a blanket, though it was the end of summer and the house was not cold. Even when I sweated from the heat, I accepted the blanket from their hands as if in a trance. The world had ended, but I was still alive. How could that be?

I sat up from my pallet one night. Kaleb sat up right away beside me.

"Mother? What do you need?"

He had never called me that before.

"I have to see him with my own eyes," I whispered. I bit my lip and waited for his answer.

He lay back down and said nothing. Liam spoke instead, with authority. How death had changed us all.

"We will leave in the morning."

The guards were not satisfied with the money I palmed them. They sneered at each other, then crossed their arms.

"I will go in alone, without my sons." Perhaps they were worried that Kaleb and Liam were here to cause trouble.

"No."

"And you're not going to give me back my money, either, are you?"

One guard snickered.

"What money?" the other asked.

I grabbed them both by the ears and yanked them hard to face me. "I tell you I am Samson's mother, and if you want to see where he got his strength, then you just cross me one more time."

They let me through, but without Kaleb and Liam.

Prisoners at the temple were slaves. They were made to work day and night until they died of exhaustion. There was no time, no energy for escape. And so no one was worried that an old woman would bring anything that might aid his escape. I could not bring him strength.

But they were wrong. I brought words from the Lord, the words spoken over him before he was born. That is what I prayed under my breath, the last prayer I would ever make for the son I loved: "God, raise him up, as You promised. Raise him up to be the man You meant for him to be!"

Samson was sitting in the dirt, a large millstone between his legs, his hand wrapped around a smaller stone. I could see a huge circle dug into the earth all around him, and a yoke off to one side. He was grinding grain. His shoulders and back were raw and red.

Dagon was the god of grain, and Samson was serving him now. I moaned in anguish.

"Mother?" He lifted his head. Dark, crusted holes sat in his face in place of eyes. I covered my mouth with my hands to keep from screaming. It was true. His hair had been shaved. That was true too, even his beard, but his hair was growing back. I recognized that soft fuzz on top of his head. He had looked like that as a baby.

I knelt before him and took his face in my hands, kissing him on his cheeks. He grabbed me, groaning, burying his face in my neck.

"I am so sorry." We both said that, whispering our apologies for everything, for everything that we had never said and never done.

"Where is Father?" Samson pulled back and sniffed the air.

I rested my hand on his shoulder, my mouth sealed. I was so grateful to God that Samson could not see my face.

He pulled back, understanding, his face tilted down, away from me.

"I saw the gates as I entered. I could see the marks where they repaired them. You really did tear them off, didn't you? I wish I could have been there to see it," I said.

"You should go."

"But—"

He reached for me, fumbling, and managed to find my arms. "Listen to me. You must go. Promise me that you will leave the city, right now, and do not turn back. Please."

I heard trumpets blow, and a shiver went down my spine.

"I love you," he whispered to me, then yelled, "Guards! Get her out of here!"

Guards pushed me back. Samson stood, holding out his wrists into the air, to be shackled and led away.

All around me Philistines climbed to the roof of the temple. Our enemies were here to watch my son's humiliation. They sat above in triumph.

They did not know my God, or my son.

I took my place on the roof, my steps slow and heavy, all my effort required to move my legs one at a time up the stone steps. I seated myself at a distance from the lords. I did not want my name spoken aloud, for fear Samson would hear and know I had betrayed him one last time. I could not leave him alone in his shame. I could do nothing for him now, but I would not leave him again.

Lord Galenos stood and addressed the crowd, many of whom were still trying to be seated. The roof was overflowing with lords and noblemen and families. "Our god has delivered our enemy into our hands, the one who laid waste our land and multiplied our slain."

A great cheer went up.

Samson was brought to the front of the temple, and guards teased him cruelly, lashing him and stoning him and setting wild dogs on him. I could not watch. This was my fault. How Samson had suffered because of me! I was no better than those people who had hurt me.

As I turned my head away from the spectacle of Samson in shame, I lost my breath from shock. My family had all come to the festival, even my brothers. They had come with people from my village. The man of shadows was there. I did not know which one he was, but a breeze caught his scent and sent it to me. I remembered it, though I had tried never to think of it again. He smelled like a beast. Revulsion, and the hot stinging tears of a girl, welled in my body.

I hated my people. Not just for what they had done to me, but for all they did for their stone god. All the pleasures in the world, without a living god, brought only suffering and death.

No one recognized me. I ducked my head down and away, shaking like the child I had been. At last, the guards stood Samson between the pillars. Samson needed to rest before the final act, they said. A lion roared in fury somewhere beneath us, caged and starved for days, I was sure. He would rip Samson to shreds. I had to help Samson somehow; I had to free him from his shackles.

I stood, the hairs on my arms rising, as I pushed through the crowd. "Let me pass! Let me pass!" I fled down the steps, taking them two at a time, landing so hard I jarred my teeth with each new step.

I heard Samson shout, one last scream in this world. "Let me die with the Philistines!"

I screamed his name, but it was too late. Flinging myself down the stairs all the way to the bottom, stone smashed all around me. I raised my hands over my head to shield myself as Dagon's stone head crashed to the ground, its severed head with those dead stone eyes rolling at me. I turned away, running for an exit.

The ground under my feet shook violently, and I heard the screams of the dying. I ran as stone fell from the sky.

I was barren. Did you know that? I could not conceive. My husband had the right to take other wives, but he did not. He was tender with me and never scolded me for my barrenness. He said the Lord was good. No matter what.

God intervened in my story to give me a son. My barrenness was part of God's plan. My barrenness made Samson's life clear to all: This child was here by the will and miracle of God.

The miracle, I think now, is not that a barren woman gave birth, or that one man began a great deliverance, but that God intervenes in our stories. We are the miracles.

I screamed in agony as the ground shook under my feet, but I kept a firm hand on Kaleb and Liam. I kept them moving. We approached the city gates, and I saw them shaking too; and I remembered seeing Samson silhouetted under a gate, arms outstretched, alone—my brilliant, blinded hero.

A woman stood from a distance, facing the temple as it fell. She looked broken, a grief I recognized well etched on her face. She was losing someone she loved. I ran to her.

"Do not watch. Come with me."

She turned and looked at me, not comprehending. She was a

breathtaking young girl, no more than twenty. And she was alone. I understood.

"Come!" I commanded, and she blinked, seeing me suddenly instead of the temple.

She grabbed her tunic with one hand, and together we passed into the darkness of the gates.

DELILAH

Standing there, the dust swirling around me, I wondered who had truly saved me: Samson, or his god? When a man acts with a god's love, is there a difference? I would never know, perhaps.

And so it was, at the end of His servant's life, and the beginning of mine, this great living God wept. Rain spilled in warm, salty drops. I tasted one on my lips and looked to the sky. The God of ice had shown me that nothing is as it seems, especially not our gods. Especially not Him. I lifted my face to Him, and loved Him back, at last.

I stood, unsure of what to do, feeling a strange new peace enter my body, a balm I had hungered for all my life but never found. Yet here, as the Philistine empire fell down around my ears, it found me.

An old woman with two young men fled toward the gates. She stopped when she saw me, her eyes both kind and sad, the eyes of a good mother.

The four of us stumbled toward the light at the end of the gate. And as we did, each of us lost, each of us in agony, we lifted our eyes and saw a man standing in blinding light. Rays flashed from His robes and face, as if He were suspended in lightning. We fell to our knees, Kaleb and Liam pressing their faces into my tunic from fear. The woman with us fell to her knees too.

"Well done, my good and faithful servant. Your name will be repeated for every generation to come." The man's voice echoed through the gate, but the noise that returned to me was not His voice alone. I would have said that I heard the stones crying out, too, a murmuring of joy, but how could that have been? I glanced at the woman, but she did not seem to hear these same words. Tears ran down her face, as she opened her arms to Him. He must have spoken in another language to her, a secret language written in the words of her own heart.

I knew this man of lightning. He was my God.

I shook my head. "Not my name, Lord. Not mine."

Samson came into the light and stood with my God, whole and strong, his glorious mane of hair restored. Manoah came into the light and held his son, and then the burning image of my Lord embraced them both, and they were gone.

There, as I knelt in the dust of the fallen Philistine empire, covered in the dust of my failures and sorrows and greatest fears, I found the strength to lift my hands.

May His name be praised, forever and ever, the God who works through weakness and delivers us from ourselves.

May He intervene in each of our stories, for we are His miracles.

... a little more ...

When a delightful concert comes to an end,

the orchestra might offer an encore.

When a fine meal comes to an end,

it's always nice to savor a bit of dessert.

When a great story comes to an end,

we think you may want to linger.

And so, we offer ...

AfterWords—just a little something more after you

have finished a David C Cook novel.

We invite you to stay awhile in the story.

Thanks for reading!

Turn the page for ...

- **Discussion Questions**
- **A Note from the Author**
- **Acknowledgments**

DISCUSSION QUESTIONS

1. Samson's mother is given a great promise for his life. What were her expectations, and how did reality differ? Were her expectations a product of her imagination, based on the angel's words, or both?

2. Does God's favor equal a life free of adversity and failings?

3. How can mothers completely trust in a God that allows their children to suffer rejection, humiliation, and all the mistakes of youth?

4. When you consider any of the great figures of the Bible (Moses, Esther, John the Baptist, etc.), did God's intention to use them spare them from heartache or increase it?

5. Many great biblical heroes made terrible personal choices. Did this prevent God from using them to accomplish His purposes?

6. Delilah suffered many times because of her lack of understanding and knowledge. How did this set her up to betray Samson's secret?

7. Why could she not accept Samson's love, if love was all she needed?

8. The biblical account of Samson and Delilah never reveals what happened to Delilah after Samson's death. What do you think she did? We know she was a very wealthy woman after betraying Samson.

9. If God offered you a superpower, like the one He gave Samson, which one would you request, and why?

NOTE FROM THE AUTHOR

The *British Journal of Sports Medicine* conducted a study in 2009 on the "Samson effect." The Samson effect refers to the impact of shaving prior to athletic competitions. Shaving one's beard, in particular, is commonly believed to impair athletic performance, but the good scientists across the pond reassure us that this is indeed a myth.[1]

I wanted to clear that up immediately.

Myth and Samson are two words that seem to always pop up together. Because the Samson saga resembles the legend of Hercules, some scholars accuse the biblical writers of plagiarizing the Greek myth to create the Samson character. I disagree. If you read the biblical account you'll notice that the story mentions specific towns, families, and political events. The biblical writers wrote about Samson for an audience that lived in these towns, knew these families, and had witnessed these political events. The scribe who recorded Samson's story had no intention of creating a myth.

But he did record a legendary account, which we still repeat today. Samson's story impacts us all, whether we worry about shaving before an athletic competition or refer to some annoying slob as a Philistine.

And yet, I must confess, Samson has always baffled me. He has a cool story, but was his a life worth celebrating? Why is he even

---

1 Karim Khan, "Athletes may shave without ending like Samson," BMJ Group Blogs, December 11, 2009, http://blogs.bmj.com/bjsm/2009/12/11/athletes-may-shave-without-ending-like-samson.

mentioned in the Hebrews' "faith hall of fame"? Why was such a self-indulgent guy mentioned alongside the great King David and Samuel?

> *And what more shall I say? I do not have time to tell about Gideon, Barak, Samson, Jephthah, David, Samuel and the prophets, who through faith conquered kingdoms, administered justice, and gained what was promised; who shut the mouths of lions, quenched the fury of the flames, and escaped the edge of the sword; whose weakness was turned to strength; and who became powerful in battle and routed foreign armies. (Heb. 11:32–34 NIV)*

The above phrase, *weakness was turned to strength,* is my only explanation. I believe Samson was an illustration to us of what would happen if we were given a completely human savior. Samson was born to begin the deliverance of his people. He was given supernatural strength to conquer any enemy. And yet, Samson, being completely human and not God, used this strength to serve himself. Samson proves to us that we cannot save ourselves and we cannot save each other, no matter how powerful we may be in our flesh. We may have the power to conquer anything and anyone, but we cannot conquer the sin within our hearts.

Jesus Christ, however, was both completely human and completely God. He understands our weakness because He has experienced it. He has walked with bare feet over hot sands; He has suffered loneliness and betrayal and hunger and embarrassment. Jesus did what Samson could not: Jesus conquered sin. Jesus taught us that strength is not enough. Although Jesus had access to the same supernatural strength Samson possessed, He saw that this strength is ultimately useless in this world.

Our true enemy is sin, and sin is never overcome by our own strength. Sin is overcome by grace, the grace of a Savior who gave Himself for us. Jesus' deliberate embracing of human weakness unleashed an eternal flood of grace and mercy for anyone who cries out for help.

I think Samson made it into the faith hall of fame because Samson is us, in so many ways. If we were given strength to overcome all our enemies, our lives would not look so different from Samson's. I doubt most of us would use this strength to feed the poor or rescue the homeless. We'd be amassing fortunes and buying trinkets and sleeping around. (Or at least enjoying the constant flirtations.)

Samson's supernatural strength did not lead him to a life of greatness. His supernatural strength was overcome by ordinary human sin, and Samson stumbled along in a life of profound humiliation, disappointment, and grief. I grieved for his mother, whose name is never referenced in the biblical account. She was barren, and an angel appeared to her, giving her the promise of a son and the promise that this son would begin a great work for God. How she must have dreamed of the honor and pride he would bring the family! And how she must have suffered as he made all his foolish mistakes. I can only imagine that she was forced to live a life of radical trust, trust against all odds. How lonely her journey must have been. She, too, was a foreshadowing of the Christ story. Like Mary, she suffered as she watched her son betrayed and humiliated, and she suffered the unimaginable pain of losing her son to a brutal death. Through her story, I am reminded that God may allow adversity, and even sin, to bring about His ultimate will in my children's lives. A life of great purpose is not a life of great ease.

Which leaves me with one more major character to examine: Delilah. Often portrayed as a seductive vixen who used her feminine wiles to betray Samson, the biblical account is quite different. Delilah is not a cardboard character used as a plot device. If you read the actual account, she gets what she wants from Samson by being persistent, not seductive. The danger she posed to Samson was not that she was seductive and able to overwhelm his manly senses, but that he had given his heart over to her. He loved her. And she was not interested in his destiny, his God, or his people. She was, however, interested in the 5,500 pieces of silver the Philistine lords offered her. Considering that Judas only got thirty pieces for Jesus, you can begin to understand that Delilah became an instant billionaire by our standards. And she didn't hurt Samson. She just shared information, like WikiLeaks.

But whatever the story means to you, whether it's a tale of redemption despite personal failures, or an encouragement to trust God with your prodigal children, I hope that it has encouraged you to reread the biblical account as found in the book of Judges in the Bible. Read it, and let the Lord draw new conclusions for you.

And I'd love to hear them, anytime.

Until we meet,
Ginger Garrett

ACKNOWLEDGMENTS

I am so eternally grateful to those who made this book possible and those who made this book better. My friend and fellow novelist, India Edghill, offered encouragement and a few important corrections at just the right moment. My editor, Nicci Jordan Hubert, was just brilliant in her criticisms and coaching. I just cannot express my thanks to you, Nic, heartily enough. I also am grateful for the entire team at David C Cook, including Don Pape, Terry Behimer, Marilyn Largent, Ingrid Beck, Karen Stoller, Caitlyn York, Amy Konyndyk, and everyone who helps my books shine. Caitlyn in particular put the spit-shine on the project, challenging my pronouns and attributions. I owe her nothing but thanks. Kirk DouPonce of DogEared Designs designed the cover. Isn't it gorgeous? Thank you, Kirk! And of course my agent, Chip MacGregor, who listened to my endless worries about meeting my deadlines despite another ankle surgery and the holidays.

As always, I relied on the love and support of a few other writers who understand this business so well: Siri Mitchell, Cecil Murphey, Nancy McGuirk, Sandra Byrd, Shelley Hendrix, Kimberly Stuart, Johnna Stein, and my Silver Arrow friends. I am so blessed to know each of you. My friends offered a lot of support and love as well, especially Louise Reinoehl, Gidget Johnson, Susie Hale, Lisa Marzullo, Tinsley Spessard, Shannon Holthaus, and Sherrill McCracken.

And of course, my family. My dad gave me my storytelling DNA, although his stories are generally true, except the ones about aliens.

(I think.) My mom is a painter who creates such gorgeous work that I can only try and write as well as she paints. God even saw fit to give me a great husband and three amazing kids, all who know that "deadline" means "take-out." My in-laws, including Priss Waldie, Elaine Arias, Andi Arias, and Meghan Arias: I love you. Sorry you are stuck with me.

But lastly, I want to acknowledge you, my readers. I am so honored and humbled when I hear your stories. May every one of you find your own happy ending.

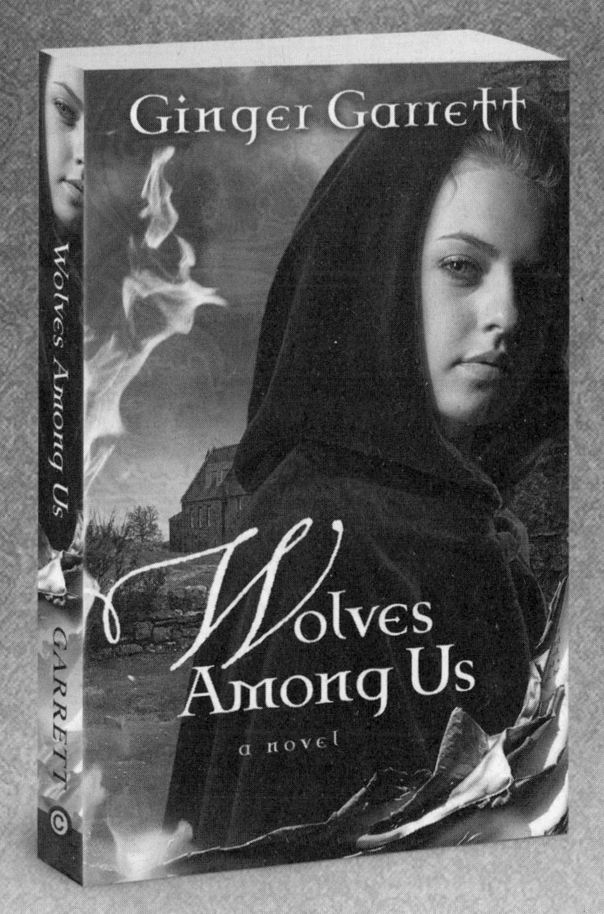
Ginger Garrett
Wolves Among Us
a novel
Wolves Among Us
GARRETT

David C Cook
transforming lives together